D1809198

OBSESSION

MYTHOS BOOK 2

JONNY CAPPS

INTRODUCTION

I will be honest—this book wasn't supposed to be written. In the first story, Cupid was walking around on Olympus, talking to Nemesis via cell phone (I wonder what kind of reception he would get there? I am sure Hephaestus set up some sort of cell tower or whatever; I'll figure it out later). He was explaining to her why he could not meet her for a night out, and the conversation was cut short when he saw Jason and Hercules. That was, originally, all that was supposed to happen. Later, as I was thinking over the scene, I began to wonder why the "no nonsense" Nemesis (that's a little alliteration for you, I hope you appreciate it) would call cool, casual Cupid. The story kind of grew from there. It started as a short story, then developed into what you're holding. In terms of time frame, it occurs during the events of "The Time after Oblivion", after Jason and Hercules leave Oblivion, wrapping up a little after that. You probably could have figured that out on your own, but I felt like explaining it anyway, and you have to read it, since I'm the author.

What I am trying to say is that, since I did not intend for this book to exist, I have no idea what I should write as an introduction. I could just act as though I had planned this all along, like the creative genius that I pretend to be, but you guys are smart (I assume, I mean, you're reading my book, so that lends credence to your literary taste at least), and you'd see right through that. I could go without an introduction, since many of you will likely skip this anyway, but something in my mind would always be setting off flares of INCOMPLETE, like a gigantic, neon, billboard. Therefore, I had to think of something to put here.

When I created these characters, I tried to steer away from the stereotypes typically associated with the characters. It worked for some of them, but not so much for others.

Zeus: I designed him around Monty Python's John Cleese. Zeus needed to be simultaneously both charming and bumbling, and no one embodies that better than John Cleese, with his dry wit and British sigh (I guess everything about him is British, but his sigh and eyeroll are what I think of). It just worked for my image of Zeus.

Cupid: Cupid was a tricky one to figure out. I knew that I wanted to get away from the swaddling baby image, and I knew he would smoke cigars. I went with a dark-haired David Anders. I've enjoyed David Anders in every role that I've seen him play and, in my mind, nobody embodies the "precocious scamp/punk rock god" quite like him. That made him perfect for Cupid.

Thanatos: Young Dakota Fanning. This one was easy. I wanted an eight-year-old girl in a tea party dress that everyone was terrified of. I'm not saying that every time I watch *I Am Sam* I think about death (although, after seeing it a couple times, that might be where my mind goes now; the sound track is nice, though). It's just an inspiration.

Ares: Ares is an asshole. No matter what story, which mythological recount, or iteration of the character—he's an asshole. Honestly, I didn't mess with that too much, because I needed Ares to be an asshole. I just messed with the character design. Typically, he's a big dude with a heavy beard. I drafted him to look more like early 2000's John Cena. It didn't take much effort, honestly; John Cena is already a polarizing figure. The only difference is that, with Cena, you either love him or you hate him. Nobody is going to love Ares.

Nemesis: With Nemesis, it was less about her image, and more about her fighting techniques and attitude. I chose Rhonda Rousey in her design. I've always respected Rousey, and I wanted to put a little bit of her into my character. Since Nemesis fights with a sword, I obviously didn't do that too heavily. Still, if you look closely at Nemesis, you'll see bits of Rousey popping out.

Hephaestus: This one, I had some fun with. Hephaestus is typically the ugly god, the one that Hera rejected. I wanted to play on the idea that different cultures find attraction in different things. Since he's the god of the kiln, it made sense that Hephaestus would be a muscular guy. Since I'm using him as the god of technology in the modern setting, I set him up with technological replacements for all of his physical deficiencies. I designed him after Jason Momoa; a big, muscular dude, riddled with cybernetics. He's awesome. Hephaestus is one of my favorite designs, and I wish I had a story to write about just him. So far, I don't, but it's coming.

All right, I think I'm satisfied with that as an introduction. Yeah, there are a lot of other inspirations for the characters, but those are the only ones that I want to talk about right now. You're probably already bored with me and wanting to head into the story (which was never supposed to exist). Think about that for a moment. This is a story that I had never planned to write, but here it is, and you're anxious to dig into it. Give me just a moment to breathe it all in.

Okay, moment's passed. Enjoy the story.

Jonny Capps

To the goddess who lives in the dark corners of my mind, where she redefines both beauty and sanity.

PROLOGUE
A LONG, LONG, TIME AGO...

HECATE WAS SITTING IN HER GARDEN, MEDITATING, WHEN SHE first heard that the world was in danger of ending. It was a distraction that she could have done without.

As she walked into the garden, before the information reached her, she had been feeling that something was out of sorts in the world around her. That had actually been the precipitating reason behind the meditation session. Something was wrong, and she needed to know what it was. It wasn't as if she was obsessive or that she had an unhealthy desire for control. Hecate simply hated feeling as if there was something important going on that she didn't know about. The Olympians tended to leave her out of the information circuit, since most of them did not understand her methods and, therefore, they did not think that she could be of much help. She resented that slightly, but not enough to do anything about it. She had her own ways of gathering information.

Placing herself beside a grape tree, she crossed her ankles and lowered herself to the ground, daintily. Lowering her head, she allowed her soft, sun-kissed hair to fall over her face, obstructing her view and minimizing distractions. Her eyes fluttered, shifting in color from blue to amber to dark and back again, as she entered her meditative trance. Her perception of the world changed as she grasped at the ties that bound reality.

Hecate was not an oracle in that she could not see the future. Her powers were more natural, driven by the Earth, and her knowledge was restricted to the things that occurred therein. Hecate was not Demeter; she could not feel and understand things that grow in the ground the same way. Her gifts were more mystical, seeing the hidden properties and potential in many sources, be they plant or mineral. Hecate understood that words had power, but she would never say that she was equal to the Titan Mnemosyne, who was said to be the developer of languages (although Zeus would likely deny that, since he never liked attributing any lasting progress to Titans). She simply knew how to use words in order to manipulate reality. Many called what she did sorcery, since her powers resembled magic. Hecate didn't argue with them. It would have been too complicated to make them understand how wrong they were, on the most precise level. It was not her responsibility to make sure that others were right. Her job was only to actually be right, or as right as possible, in as many instances as she could.

Reaching into the aether, Hecate asked the Wind to share answers with her. The Wind whispered its lies, mixed with slight truths, and told her secrets that she should not know and facts that she was familiar with already. She rarely gained any knowledge from the Wind, only rumors, gossip, and deception. Still, it was a good place to start. Wind saw many things and, sometimes, it sang about things that other forces didn't understand.

She asked the Earth to open to her, and Hecate found herself drowning as the flood of information poured over her. She swam against the tides, drinking in the forgotten and overlooked symbols that represent love, lust, hunger, growth, and an infinite collage of contradicting ideas. Taking a moment, breathing in what little serenity could be found, Hecate floated with the current, allowing her mind to absorb the influx. She found what she was searching for, something out of place, but she could not grasp it. There was something that did not belong, but it eluded her. The image remained a mystery.

Lastly, she begged the Moon to illuminate secrets for her. The light was blinding, forcing its image into her mind. The primordial images which it supplied, bathed in iridescence, held chaos and frustration, a madness so pure that it nearly redefined sanity. It wanted to show her something. There was something that needed to be known. Hecate opened her mind to receive it, to know the answers that she sought. As she stretched her mind to touch it, she found that it was no longer there. The shadow of the truth was there, she could see it, but it was fleeting, retreating from her, as her meditation was interrupted. She found herself torn out of the moment, painfully thrust back into her body, denied the object that she was seeking.

"Madam," a voice was speaking to her, a familiar one, one that she had affectionate feelings for. "Madam, I regret invading your sanctum. I would not have done so, my beauty, my queen, but the urgency of the situation was impressed upon me. Fair madam of the Moon, you have a guest."

The voice belonged to Horace. Hecate was quite fond of Horace, a eunuch in her court. He worshiped her, as all in her court did, but she treasured Horace above the others. The love that he had for her was pure and willing; she could see that through his eyes when he gazed upon her. He did not follow her because he wanted to earn her favor or to spare himself from punishment; he followed her because he loved her. It was the authenticity in his motives that endeared him to her. She treasured him, savoring his love as though it were fine wine.

It was that affection which made her feelings of frustration at being torn from her meditative state so difficult to justify. Horace would never have come to her had it not been an emergency. Allowing her eyes to refocus to the light of her garden, Hecate attempted to conceal her bitterness as she looked upon her servant with a gentle smile.

"You are forgiven, Horace," she said gently, as she rose from the ground. Reaching to the tree next to her, she pulled a succulent green grape from a bundle and tossed it casually into her mouth. Biting into it, she felt the outer skin burst, spraying the sweet juices against her cheeks and down her throat. Swallowing the grape, she was reminded of where she was. She was no longer in the aether, she was on Earth. Sweet fruit always made that disappointing reality easier to grasp.

"I know that you would never disturb me unless it was important," Hecate continued to comfort Horace.

Horace's gray eyes sank, and his bald head dropped in shame. "I would never, beautiful mistress," he replied earnestly. "It wouldn't enter my most fevered nightmares. I would never have dared, were it not for your guest and the urgency with which she demanded an audience with you."

"Demanded, did she?" Hecate frowned. "Who has caused you to be so distraught?"

Horace did not answer, for he did not need to. Hecate's eyes fell on the third occupant of the garden, a figure clothed in night, with thin lips that looked as though they had never smiled and dark eyes which held the chill of a thousand winters. She advanced on Hecate with a confident stride, striding through the environment with her slender form as a sharpened dagger advances through soft cheese. Hecate held her spot, unyielding, as the figure approached her. Once before her, the figure dropped to one knee, as if in supplication.

"Nemesis," Hecate breathed. "Why are you kneeling? You would not even bow before Zeus when he defeated the Titans!"

"I am in your home," Nemesis replied, the sound of her voice sending setting sparks aflame beneath Hecate's skin. "You are owed honor within your own home."

Hecate felt a soft burning in her cheeks, realized quickly that she was blushing, and resolved her will to stop it. Nemesis rarely came into the presence of any of the other gods, since she typically had other priorities. The cold sword of divine retribution, Nemesis was a legend amongst legendary creatures. Now, with Nemesis kneeling

4

before her, Hecate had to remember not to be flattered and to keep her head.

"Rise, sister," Hecate gasped eventually, after a moment of breathless shock, and offered her hand. "You are welcome in my home."

"Thank you," Nemesis replied, rising from her knees fluidly, accepting Hecate's hand in the process. "I've come to you with an issue that has arisen. It could lead to a greater problem, and I would like to have your assistance in dealing with it. Nature has never been a specialty of mine, particularly in regards to the darker properties, but it is yours. As such, I've come to you. The situation is not dire at the present, but it could be dire in the near future so, therefore, it deserves to be treated as dire now."

Hecate frowned as she digested the information which Nemesis had given her. She also resisted the urge to be entertained by the cold, serious, mechanical tone with which Nemesis spoke. It would have been inappropriate to laugh, after all, at the extreme intensity of another's tone, especially when that "other" was Nemesis.

"I've felt an irregularity," Hecate confirmed. "I was searching for it through my meditation, actually. What can you tell me about the situation?"

As Nemesis spoke, a cloud passed over her already dark features. Hecate fought against the urge to be intimidated, holding her poise as well as she could. Nemesis had come to see her, which means that the situation was dire. Nemesis did not like asking for help.

Actually, Hecate didn't know whether or not Nemesis liked asking for help. To her knowledge, this was the first time that Nemesis had ever needed to.

"There has been some unorthodox activity in the Quaesturas region of Maeotian swamp," Nemesis informed her seriously. "Many of the naiads there have been functioning in an uncharacteristic manner."

Hecate shook her head. "They're not naiads," she corrected Nemesis. "If they're native to the swamps, they're potamoi. The two are relatively the same in nature, except that potamoi have an unquestioning loyalty to their king, Achelous, while naiads serve only the spirit of flowing water. A lot of observers have suggested that a potamide doesn't actually have a mind of their own, but that Achelous thinks for them. If that's true, they wouldn't be able to function in an uncharacteristic manner, but only in accordance with what he desired for them."

Hecate hung her head, embarrassed. "I'm sure that you already thought of all that," she submitted.

"There's no reason for you to assume that," Nemesis stated, shaking her head slowly. "There is much that you know that I am unfamiliar with. That's why I have come to you. The information that you have supplied corresponds to my earlier suspicions that the potamoi are under an influence that is external to them."

Hecate paused, studying her conversation partner. Nemesis was the goddess of retribution, of justice. There was no questioning her reasoning: if she was alerted to a slight, she would take swift action to resolve it. She had no cohorts, no servants to care for her needs, cults devoted to her worship were so few and far between that they were practically non-existent, and, to Hecate's knowledge, Nemesis had no sexual companion. Her cold isolation and antisocial behavior were well known amongst the gods. While Hecate was oftentimes overlooked by the Olympians, Nemesis didn't care to be included. The fact that she was coming to Hecate now seemed out of character, from everything that Hecate knew about Nemesis. That made her slightly cautious. Nemesis was incorruptible and, yet, Hecate was suspicious of her motives.

"Why does this concern you?" Hecate asked, pointedly. "Do you feel that the potamoi are being done an injustice? Or do you feel that their characteristics are causing them to be unjust, themselves?"

Nemesis nodded. "The later," she confirmed. "Their actions were what alerted me to the situation in the first place: acts of violence and ritual killings, in and around local habitations."

"Potamoi don't leave the swamps," Hecate insisted.

"Were it not for that situational property, I would not need your assistance," Nemesis said. "I would simply dispense justice, dealing with the problem alone. I am coming to you, because it seems as though the potamoi are being influenced by another force, outside of Achelous, and the source seems mystical in nature."

This made Hecate smile. One always appreciates when their talents are appreciated.

"So," she nodded, "since I am well-familiar with mystical enchantments and, as it would seem, the Maeotian swamps, you came to me for assistance?"

If it were possible for Nemesis, the cold and unfeeling sword of justice, to look embarrassed, Hecate could have sworn that she did. "I hope that my request doesn't seem presumptuous," she answered, her voice devoid of emotion, even if her eyes flickered very slightly.

"Horace," Hecate addressed the eunuch, as he stood, patiently waiting, "it appears that I will be gone for a short time. Please instruct the servants to care for the home and the ground as though I were still here."

"It will be as you have instructed," Horace said, bowing his head and leaving the garden.

Potamoi, like naiads and dryads, were the spirits of their respective elements. When they appeared, however seldom that may be, it was in the body of an attractive woman. While they were fiercely protective of their natural environment, be that water, wood, or swamp, they typically remained docile in most other instances, unless threatened. That was fortunate, since very few weapons had the ability to do them any harm.

If the potamoi were growing restless, it was a situation that needed to be dealt with. If they chose to wage war on the world, the Earth would end up much worse for wear.

While it had its problems, Hecate had grown quite fond of Earth. She would prefer to live there as long as possible.

CHAPTER ONE

Nemesis hated having to come to someone else for aid, but the situation called for it. As the Sword of Justice, she should be able to function alone, without the aid of other parties. Aligning with others meant that she had the potential of forming bonds, both social and psychological, with that individual. That could lead to complications, should that person ever stand in the way of Nemesis' pursuit. Nemesis trusted that she would be able to separate herself from her emotional attachment should such an instance arise, but there was really very little need to test those boundaries. It was just easier to do things by herself.

Looking now at the lithe blonde woman with sparkling blue eyes, Nemesis sighed, inwardly. Hecate was very different than she was, embracing life and others, always ready with a disarming smile and willing to provide aid, if the situation called for it. Nemesis was aware that Hecate was strong, even dangerous, under the right circumstances, but those properties were difficult to distinguish at that moment. Right now, it was difficult to take Hecate seriously, and Nemesis resented needing her help even more.

As the two of them approached the Quaesturas area, where the disturbances had originated, Nemesis saw Hecate making a motion with her hand. As she stopped to view the goddess, she noticed that her formerly-sandaled feet were now protected by thick leather boots, rising to her mid-thigh. When Hecate noticed Nemesis examining her, she stopped advancing, blushing slightly. Nemesis nodded to her feet.

"That was an interesting trick," Nemesis said. "Did you conjure those from the air, or were they with you all along, but invisible?"

Hecate shrugged. "I guess they were with me all along," she admitted. "Technically, the boots are another form of the sandals, since they're composed of the same leather. All I did was isolate the properties of the sandal leather, then multiply and expand them, until they formed boots. Since we're headed into a swamp area, boots seemed to be more appropriate attire."

Nemesis cocked her head curiously. "To hear you describe the process, I would assume that it was a simple thing to do," she said, carefully concealing the degree to which she was impressed. "I would imagine that, if I were to attempt the same technique, I would be sadly disappointed."

Hecate smiled as she advanced toward the swamp's quagmire. "Thank you," she laughed. "I'd offer to show you how to do it, but I doubt you'd be interested. The process isn't that complicated."

Nemesis followed Hecate closely, wondering about the irony in her statement. To the outside observer, magic was likely one of the most mystifying and fascinating subjects possible. To hear Hecate speak of it, it was similar to weaving or farming. Magic was just something that she did, and she shrugged off the complexity of her gift. Nemesis began to wonder how much of her personality was modesty and how much was a disguise to conceal her true motives. Hecate was clearly very powerful.

Stepping into the swamp's quagmire, Nemesis quickly took an inventory of all the new sensations which were being introduced. There was the smell of disease, which she had been expecting, and which she was able to identify immediately. The wet, melancholy smell of entropy, combined with the uncomfortably moist aroma of decaying wood gave the environment a precise signature. The buzzing in the air intensified with each step that Nemesis took, and she tried to think about which disease each of the insects would be carrying. Scampering and slithering all around her, Nemesis could sense forms of life that she had never encountered before and, with any luck, never would again. Damp ground beneath her feet provided her with the awkward sensation that, with each new step, she may be swallowed by the bayou. Through her brief passage, no step had fulfilled that promise, but that only made the hesitation to take another stronger; were she to become complacent, the next step would be the one that would hold its guarantee, and she would be lost in the quagmire.

Looking to her partner, she was surprised to see Hecate advancing forward bravely, with a slight sparkle in her eyes. Arching an eyebrow, Nemesis observed her momentarily. She was confident, as though she knew the environment well and it was welcoming her as treasured company. Nemesis knew that Hecate had more experience with Maeotian swamp than she did, which had been the reason behind Nemesis' desired association with her. The level of comfort that Hecate had with a world that Nemesis found completely repugnant, however, gave her pause.

"You've been here before," Nemesis noted, as the two of them advanced through the swamp, both unsure of what they should be looking for.

"I have," Hecate confirmed. As she spoke, a large dragonfly landed on her shoulder, bare beneath the hem of her blouse. Instead of swatting it away in repulsion, she reached up, pet the large insect affectionately, and it flew off towards its next perch.

"It's peaceful," she continued, stepping forward again, casually knowing exactly where to step without even thinking.

"I don't know if I could relate to that," Nemesis replied, as she carefully calculated each footstep that she took. "All that I can sense is disease, rot, and the death which comes with it."

Hecate nodded. "That's understandable," she said. "There is an abundance of all three of those elements in this environment. There's also life, and it's a world that thrives in spite of those things. They've found a balance, existing alongside one another, embracing the community which has made them neighbors.

"And besides," she concluded, "there's nothing more peaceful than death."

Nemesis raised her eyebrows, partially in surprise, partly in admiration. "You didn't strike me as one to wax poetic," she admitted.

Hecate laughed. "Given the right outlet," she said, "I think everyone has the potential to sing."

Nemesis declined to join in the laughter, choosing instead to sink into contemplation. At that moment, there were too many other things to think about, but whenever she had a moment, she would need to consider how seriously she was taking Hecate. It was clear that the goddess was very powerful, and yet, she chose to belittle her abilities, perhaps in an attempt to disarm onlookers. While others may have found her comforting presence through the swamp to be endearing, even charming, Nemesis found her casual acquaintance with death to be unsettling. Up to this point, Hecate had proved to be nothing but a pleasant, if a bit eager, partner. Nemesis could not afford to trust her yet, though. Only through trust does betrayal strike.

The two continued their exploration of the swamp for nearly an hour before Hecate stopped, her eyes locked on something in the swamp ground. Dropping to her knees, she pushed aside foliage, digging about in the dirt, before finding what she had been looking for. Cupping her hands, she pulled it carefully from the ground, lifting it to her nose for examination. Nemesis stopped beside her to see what she was holding.

In the palms of Hecate's hands sat a strange, light green mushroom, emblazoned with purple stripes and speckled with spots of an even darker green. Nemesis looked at it skeptically, wondering why such an object would draw so much attention. Hecate looked up at her with her soft blue eyes and shook her head gently.

"This doesn't belong here," she explained, as if reading Nemesis' mind.

"A fungus doesn't seem out of place in this environment," Nemesis critiqued.

Lifting the mushroom to eye-level, Hecate began to spin the object in her fingers, as a contemplative frown creased her brow. "This isn't a fungus," she said, quietly, as if to herself. "I mean, it is, but it isn't one that I've seen before. There are several types of fungi in the swamp, and I am familiar with all of them. This type of mushroom is not among that number, and I don't know how it came to be."

Nemesis saw how perplexed Hecate was by the mushroom but resisted the urge to feel sympathy. Hecate felt comfortable in this area because she knew the properties, and she could quickly identify everything that lived there. Finding something alien in the vicinity must have been equivalent to coming home and finding an intruder, seated in your guest house. Nemesis quickly balanced the odds of Hecate, feigning distress in order to gain the upper hand, against those of Hecate's authenticity, and she found that Hecate's discomfort was likely true. Nemesis then considered words which could bring Hecate comfort in this situation, but she knew nothing she thought of would bring any calm.

Suddenly, as if signaled by something external to it, the mushroom began to vibrate, shaking violently against Hecate's fingers. She yelped in surprise and almost dropped it.

"Get rid of it!" Nemesis shouted urgently, staring at the mushroom with surprise and frantic suspicion.

A shrill wheeze suddenly began to emit from the mushroom and, it seemed, from several other places in various areas of the swamp ground. Quickly, Hecate threw the fungus away from her as hard as she could. As the mushroom crested through the air, it erupted into a cloud of vapor, colored a nauseating yellow. Both Hecate and Nemesis stared at the area in a mixture of repulsion and fascination, wondering what the outcome would be, and being sickened by the disturbing odor which accompanied the vapor. It reminded Hecate of something that had grown in damp areas, never saw the sun, and had died long ago, while Nemesis was reminded of rotten corpses, lain in the sun, and set to whither and dry. The two goddesses looked at each other; Hecate with wide-eyed curiosity, and Nemesis with a dark scowl.

"That was certainly unexpected," Nemesis admitted.

Hecate coughed. "I could have done without the smell," she admitted.

Nemesis opened her mouth, as if to say something, but she was interrupted by loud rustlings coming from the area where the vapor had emitted, from the swamp depths, and the surrounding trees. As she turned to see what was making the noise, she was witness to something astonishing. It almost terrified her, and it made her reach for her weapon.

Rising out of the bog, bursting from within vines, the bodies of women began to appear. At least, Nemesis assumed they were women, based on their assets. Their naked skin glistened a disturbing shade of green which looked, somehow, both completely natural and strangely alien simultaneously. Two orb-like eyes, colored a strange, heart-scouring lime, pulsed from behind tangled messes of black hair. Their bodies were thin, but muscular, and each was clothed only in vines.

The creatures held no conventional weaponry, yet, somehow, Nemesis felt threatened. She counted six figures, and none of them seemed very happy with them. Of course, it was difficult to gauge emotion from a pupil-less eye, but Nemesis surmised from their posturing. Everything about these women, from their stance and formation to the cruel snarl on their thin lips, suggested aggression.

Nemesis turned to Hecate: "Are these potamoi?"

Hecate nodded, examining the battle line which was quickly forming amongst the six new parties.

Nemesis frowned, curiously. "They look as though they want to kill us," she observed.

"They certainly do," Hecate confirmed, as she sank into a defensive stance, waving her hands through the air with fluid but deliberate motions.

"Ah," Nemesis reached over her right shoulder and pulled her sword from its invisible scabbard, before taking a stance of her own. "That's unfortunate."

The potamoi screamed shrilly in one voice, and began to advance. Nemesis prepared for the strike.

The ensuing combat was chaotic and surreal. The potamoi attacked as though they were one creature with many limbs. They needed no weaponry, it seemed, since their vines served as both defense and offense. As they advanced on Nemesis, the vines provided a protective shield around their bodies, constantly swirling and crawling, to both cause disorienting distraction and to obstruct oncoming attacks to their most vulnerable areas. Coming closer, Nemesis found that she was onset by an assaulting ivy, which sprang from the vines with stinging nettles. Her armor protected her from the majority of the attack, but a few of the stingers found a way through the shields into her skin. There, they burned, as if on fire.

Swinging her sword with exact precision, Nemesis struck at the ivy as it advanced toward her. She was beginning to feel as though she were on the defensive, and Nemesis did not like that feeling. She also hated that the more that she chopped at the attacking ivy, the more of it seemed to be coming, as if it were some sort of hydra weed: she would sever one vine and two more would take its place. With the vines attempting to strangle and sting her, Nemesis momentarily lost sight of the fact that she was, in fact, combating the potamoi. The ivy was a distraction, supplied by these swamp dryads. They were the source, and she was combating the symptoms. As she continued to thrash at the ivy, in the back of her mind, she wondered how Hecate was holding up against these creatures. She thought about how Hecate had shown no physical weapon, and she considered that maybe the goddess had an invisible one, much like her sword. Hecate's boots stuck in her brain, and she wondered if, perhaps, Hecate could form a sword from the air in a similar manner.

A sudden wave of heat brushed past her, and the ivy which had been attacking her burst into flame. Nemesis jumped back in surprise, recovered quickly, and looked toward Hecate, only a few feet away. She was preoccupied with her own combat, but their eyes locked momentarily, and Nemesis saw her weapon, as Hecate ignited the air around her, channeling flame toward the ivy. She moved with the fluid motion of water, smooth and seamless, dancing in the wind as a serpent in the dirt. The fire provided the venom in her strike, and instantly, Nemesis was both impressed and wary. The strength of this woman's power should not be taken lightly, yet it seemed that all of Olympus had done exactly that. Nemesis considered whether that had been the plan all along.

Returning her focus to the battlefield, Nemesis saw that Hecate's flames had left the potamoi temporarily vulnerable. Before it had a chance to regrow its defense to full capacity, Nemesis jumped at the nearest creature, swinging her sword at its neck. The creature dodged the swing and parried with a stabbing punch to Nemesis' side. The punch connected with Nemesis' armor with such minor impact that she hardly realized that she was struck at all. Spinning in response to the dodge, Nemesis plunged her sword into the potamide's body.

The blade sunk in deeply, yet the potamide showed no sign of pain. As Nemesis began to retract her blade, she was met with resistance. From inside of the blade's entry point, the oozing innards crept, almost cognitively, around the sword, holding it in place. Nemesis grit her teeth and scowled in frustration, as she pulled at the sword with heightened strength. The sword began to give, and finally, Nemesis was able to wrench it free, bringing what seemed to be half of the potamide's viscera with it. The hollowed creature collapsed into the ground, melting into the swamp in a fashion similar to the way it had emerged.

Turning to face the next attacker, Nemesis was pleased to see that Hecate's magic seemed to be doing an apt job at keeping the potamoi busy. She seemed to have dispatched two of them in the time that it had taken Nemesis to terminate one, leaving three creatures left to be dealt with. While Hecate was avoiding vines and igniting fire in the faces of the remaining potamoi, Nemesis snuck up behind one and plunged her blade into the creature's back between its shoulder blades, dragging the tip downward along the spine. As its bodily contents spilled into the swamp, the potamide screamed. Whether it came as a result of the pain or its intention was to alert the two remaining potamoi to Nemesis' presence was undetermined. Nemesis was thankful for it though, since it disguised her own pained gasp.

Nemesis had been surprised when, as she lunged at the potamide's back, a stabbing pain pierced her side. Now that the potamide was dispatched, she glanced to her side and was surprised by what she found. In the area where the first potamide had punched her, there was a hole in her armor, and it was rapidly widening, as though it were dissolving in acid. The effect was rubbing against her skin and causing irritation. Nemesis had to think quickly, since one of the remaining potamoi had turned their attention away from Hecate to her. Not knowing the extent of the damage which the irritation would do to her skin, Nemesis quickly tore off her upper armor, discarding it in the swamp. She was bare beneath the armor, and that made her feel a bit more vulnerable. Since the other option held a much larger threat, however, she would have to deal with the slight compromise.

The potamide who had been advancing on her thrust the attacking vines toward Nemesis. Nemesis dodged them quickly, considering how much easier it was to do when she was only dealing with a singular attacker. She also quickly became conscious of her naked chest, especially when being attacked by stinging nettles. A few of the needles buried themselves in her skin, and the insertion points burned fiercely. There was no time to consider superficial wounds, however. The attacker needed to be dealt with.

Spinning away from the vines and toward the attacker, Nemesis swung her sword fiercely. The blow pierced through air as the potamide dodged the attack artfully. She then lunged at Nemesis, reaching for her exposed body. A rare moment of fear stuck in Nemesis' mind, as she considered the effect that this touch would have on her flesh. She danced clear of the potamide's reach, parrying with a strike to the potamide's extended appendage. Her sword sliced through the arm as though it was soft cheese; it fell to the swamp's floor and melted into the moist ground, similar in method to the fallen potamoi. Nemesis looked toward the potamide, preparing to strike again, but what she saw surprised her.

She and the potamide locked eyes, and Nemesis saw the pain that she was in. It wasn't a physical pain, although the potamide was likely in that as well, but a mental draining. Nemesis saw that the potamide didn't like what she was doing: she knew what she was doing, and she was ashamed of it. Something, on the outside, was influencing her. To her surprise, Nemesis suddenly began to feel sympathy for her.

As quickly as the feelings emerged, they melted, as Hecate's magic tore through the potamide's body. She became one with the swamp once more, and Nemesis looked around herself for further threats. She and Hecate stood together, once again, alone. As she quickly sized up the panting spectacle before her, Nemesis was forced to reassess her initial impression of Hecate once again. Now, wearing torn clothes, dirtied from the swamp's filth, cut and bleeding in several places, this Hecate hardly resembled the dour, sweet, individual that Nemesis had met prior to the excursion. As Hecate caught her breath, the clouds of mania began to fade from her soft, blue eyes, and Nemesis could see the gentle creature whom she had formerly met emerging again. She looked at Nemesis with concern, which did very little to lower her guard.

"The potamoi are being coerced and manipulated by outside forces," Nemesis stated quickly, before the point was lost in the swamp.

Hecate nodded, reaching toward Nemesis' wounds. "You're hurt," she said, revealing the obvious. "Let me help you."

"Are you not listening to me?" Nemesis snapped, flinching back, out of Hecate's reach. "They are the victims. We dispatched them as though they were the enemy, but they were not in control of their actions. We have done them an injustice."

"We were defending ourselves," Hecate responded, looking at Nemesis' wounds with concern. "Had we not done so, the potamoi would have killed us and, likely, they would not have stopped with that. Whether they were acting of their own accord or through the influence of another makes no difference, really."

Nemesis hated that she could see the rationale in that reasoning. As Hecate tended to her wounds, pulling the burning needles out of her skin, Nemesis thought about the debt of justice which she now owed these strange swamp creatures. Nemesis watched as Hecate formed a salve from elements that she found in the swamp and, as she rubbed it over the afflicted areas, Nemesis trusted that she would find the source of the influence.

"I feel as though the potamoi's reaction had something to do with the mushrooms," Hecate said, after she had finished treating Nemesis' wounds. "If we can find a way to carry one back to my temple, I would like to study it closer."

Nemesis nodded. She would have responded, but she could not think of anything to say. Hecate stepped away from Nemesis for a moment, as she scanned the area for samples of the fungus that she could take, while Nemesis remained in her stance. She replaced her sword in her invisible sheath and pondered whether her feeling of vulnerability was based more on her naked torso or her conflicted feelings toward the actions that she had just taken.

As she was considering her actions, she noticed a slight stirring in the swamp near her. Nemesis frowned and turned toward the sound. She was surprised to see a strange man, hiding behind one of the trees. He was dressed in strange fabrics, featuring a weave that she wasn't familiar with, stained with extravagant colors and the filth of the swamp. The top of his head resembled a desert plain, producing no growth, to the point that she could see the rocks and crevasses which his skull produced. The long and tangled beard which hung from his chin concealed his age, but the bags under his eyes and the shadows in his gray, darting eyes revealed much that he probably would have preferred to keep hidden. He looked ashamed but, more than that, he looked afraid. Nemesis knew immediately that he did not belong there.

"Hail, stranger," Nemesis greeted the man, who was still attempting to remain unseen. She hadn't meant to sound as cold and suspicious as she did, but the man stepped out of hiding regardless.

"H-Hail, strong woman," the man stuttered, nervously. "I h-have seen what y-you and the o-other w-oman have done w-with the...the strange women who come fro-om the sw-amp. Y-you defeated them! I-i did not think anyone could defeat them!"

Nemesis examined the man closely. He was hiding something, but so was everyone. She could not determine whether or not she felt sympathy for the man. She only knew that she didn't trust him.

"What are you doing here?" she asked, probing the man as gently as she could.

"I have been held captive by those...those women for longer than I can recall," the man said, more confident in his oration now. "Those women, they...they have done horrible things to me. I do not wish to recount what they have done, since I will be reliving it in my nightmares, I have no doubt. I only know that I am grateful to you...you and your associate for defeating them. I, undoubtedly, owe you my life. Had I been forced to stay with them for a longer period of time, I undoubtedly would have taken that, of my own accord."

Hecate returned to Nemesis then, holding a small jar. Nemesis thought to ask her what the jar contained, but she realized that she already knew the answer. The look of anxious satisfaction on Hecate's face was all the answer she needed, anyway. Hecate looked to the strange man, then back to Nemesis with curiosity.

"It seems I've discovered a victim," Nemesis answered the unasked question, carefully avoiding cynicism.

Hecate turned to the man, wide-eyed and fascinated. "Hail, good sir," Hecate greeted him with more warmth than Nemesis was comfortable with. "Might I ask for your business within the swamp?"

"He claims that the potamoi have held him captive," Nemesis answered for him. "According to his tale, they have been taking advantage of him."

Hecate frowned and looked to Nemesis. Nemesis nodded, and their suspicion was shared.

"I-I-I owe you my li-life," the man insisted, his stammer returning. "There-there was no escape from these-these-women. I would have surely—"

"You would have surely died," Nemesis completed his statement. "You have insinuated as much already. Well, now the creatures who have tormented you have been dispatched. You are free to leave and, I would venture, never return."

The man stared back at Nemesis and Hecate with a look of desperation and tension. "You cannot leave me alone," the man begged. "The swamp women, they will return. If I stay too long away from you, they will come and take me prisoner again, I'm sure of it. Please, fair warriors, do not leave me alone. I ask only that you escort me away from here, staying in my company for a time."

Nemesis looked to Hecate, who returned the look with similar feeling. Neither of them trusted this man, it was clear, but neither wanted to be the reason for his captivity either. Having supposedly freed him from the potamoi's clutches, there was an argument to suggest that he was now their responsibility.

"Please," the man continued his lament. "I have no family and only a small home; it's not far from here. Allow me to stay with you for a short time, I beg of you. I will do for you what you desire, and it will be done of my own will. Surely, your needs will not be as craven as those of these swamp women, and I will satisfy them willingly. Please, I beg you, do not leave me alone!"

As Nemesis watched, she was disappointed to see Hecate's guard beginning to drop, replaced with a look of pity. This man was not to be trusted, but that did not mean that he did not need their guidance. Nemesis resisted the urge for her own heart to soften, perhaps in recompense for the unjust actions against the potamoi. She did not want to stay in the company of this man any longer than was necessary, but perhaps he needed them for a short time. If he had been done an injustice, it was her duty to make sure that he was now safe.

"I will not leave you," Hecate answered the man's request, only for herself.

"Neither will I," Nemesis sighed, reluctantly.

"Thank you!" the man sighed with exaggerated relief. "You will not be sorry, and I swear that I will not overstay your company. May I beg upon the names of my sacred avengers?"

"This is Nemesis, the goddess of divine retribution," Hecate said, motioning toward her, "and I am Hecate, goddess of magic. What are you called, lost traveler?"

"My name..." the man fumbled with his words, as he advanced through the swamp to stand between Nemesis and Hecate, "has been lost. It feels a lifetime since I have said it out loud. There was a time, I seem to remember, when people called me Prospero."

CHAPTER TWO

HECATE STEPPED UP HER PACE TO WALK BESIDE NEMESIS; Prospero followed them, a few feet behind. The more time that she spent with this man, the more weary she became of his stability. He was constantly muttering to himself. Hecate could only pick up random words, since she was not in the business of eavesdropping on private conversations, even those held between oneself. Of the few words that she picked up, the terms 'potion's potency', 'reevaluate standard range', and 'eliminate distractions' stood out. Hecate hated to jump to conclusions, and nothing that she overheard was sufficient enough reason to suspect that Prospero was anything more than a troubled, mentally traumatized, old man. The fact that he was talking to himself only seemed to validate those assumptions. Still, she wanted to confer with Nemesis and get her perspective.

"You are reconsidering our offer to remain in this man's company," Nemesis noted, once Hecate stepped in line beside her. Her eyes remained fixed on the path before them, as the party of three approached Hecate's temple. "I've been wondering if our agreement was made in haste as well, based on the overheard exchanges that this individual has been holding with himself."

Hecate nodded. "I've no reason to doubt his tortured statement," she replied in a hushed tone, "for he does, indeed, seem troubled. Still, his mannerisms and the dialogue which he holds with himself do not seem to hold with the tale he told. He seems more frustrated than traumatized, as if a plot which he had formed has failed."

Nemesis remained transfixed on the road. With each step that she took, she further considered her reasoning behind allowing this man to accompany them. He had begged, yes, and if his statements held any truth, he had the right to be uncomfortable with solitude. She could not have left him alone in the swamp, after all. One unarmed man could not hold against even one potamide, based on her interactions with them. If he truly was the victim that he claimed to be, an escort was not without reason. Still, something in her mind seemed to suggest that removing him from the swamp was as much in the interest of the potamoi as it was his.

The man had no visible wounds. That, along with his claim to have been tortured, raised suspicion. While Prospero's robes were filthy, they weren't torn or damaged in any visible way. His eyes shone with a madness that came from torture, but insanity was caused by many things. Torture had been the most obvious source, especially after dealing with the potamoi and hearing Prospero's tale, but there were many options that had been unexplored.

As they approached Hecate's entryway, Nemesis saw Horace, patiently awaiting their arrival. When he saw Nemesis' bare breasts, since she had been unable to find suitable clothing within the swamp, his expression did not change. Even the most chaste man would react to a woman's breasts. Horace, however, was not a chaste man. He was a eunuch, and he was dedicated completely to Hecate. That made Nemesis consider something.

"Sexual union is not within a potamide's list of desires," she spoke quietly to Hecate, "is it?"

Hecate shook her head. "Not typically," she replied in the same quiet voice. "They are the swamp, and the swamp does not seek congress with men. Disregarding that, Achelous is a jealous ruler. He would become angry to the point of wrath should one of his numbers stray from him."

In her mind's eye, Nemesis considered Prospero, following them with his head lowered, still talking to himself. Something was wrong with the situation.

"Sweet mistress," Horace's face burst into a smile as Hecate and Nemesis walked through the gates. "I have cared for your temple in your absence, and I hope that my services have not been unsatisfactory. Seeing you return safely is all the thanks that I require."

Hecate flew to Horace, and embraced him lavishly. "I have every faith in you, dearest," she told him, happily.

Draping her arm across Horace's shoulders, she turned to face Nemesis and Prospero once more. She pointed, "This is a man who we met in the swamp. His name is Prospero, and he is to be treated as a guest in this house. I have some things to take care of in the garden. Will you please make sure that our guests are made comfortable and that Nemesis has access to any clothing that she may require?"

Horace nodded, "As you wish, lady Hecate."

Hecate smiled widely, kissing Horace with all the affection that one can have for a pet.

At the mention of Hecate's garden, Prospero's eyes lit up. He turned his full attention to her, and Nemesis could practically feel how anxious he was to enter that world. She frowned as she watched him. She ought to be deciphering more about him by now, but she felt as though the secrets were compounding.

"I should like to join you in the garden," Prospero said with a confidence that seemed uncharacteristic, based on what Nemesis had observed from him to this point. "Plants were, at one point, a passion of mine."

Nemesis' brow furrowed as she considered his statement.

Hecate smiled at Prospero warmly. "I'm afraid that I must take care of some things alone," she informed him. "Perhaps, in another time, we could arrange an encounter there. For now, though, you will stay here."

"But," Prospero continued his plea, his infliction changing from eager to near panic, "I cannot be alone. P-p-please d-don't leave m-me alone."

The stutter returned in time to convey weakness and vulnerability. Nemesis took note.

Hecate laughed, somewhat nervously. "The things that I do must be done in private," she insisted. "You are safe within my temple, have no fear."

Nemesis stepped to the elder man, placing a hand upon his shoulder, before he could further beg for access to Hecate's garden. "I will remain with you," she assured him. "You will not be left alone."

Prospero turned to Nemesis with eyes of venom, but a wide and grateful smile. "I will, of course, feel safe with you," he said, his demeanor heavy with defeat.

"Perhaps I will see your garden another time," he sighed, turning back to Hecate with the same smile.

Hecate and Nemesis locked eyes with each other, sharing a private exchange. Neither of them trusted Prospero any longer. While Nemesis would have exiled him, Hecate was not ready to give up hope. Hecate needed to study the mushroom, which she had brought back with her from the swamp, and Nemesis needed to keep an eye of Prospero while she was doing so.

Horace was, of course, privy to this exchange. He wasn't surprised: he'd disliked Prospero from the first moment he saw the lecherous old beast.

CHAPTER THREE

THE SOIL IN HER GARDEN DID NOT LIKE THE MUSHROOM. FROM the moment that Hecate stepped into the area, it screamed out to her, as though the fungus were an attacking force. It was something unnatural, yet it was attempting to appear organic, and perhaps that was the element that the soil objected to the most. It screamed at Hecate, begging her to remove the foreign insurgent. It condemned the mushroom for its existence and, by association, Hecate for bringing it close. Hecate had to ignore the angry tirades, and hope that her soil would forgive her at some point. She had work to do.

Stepping to her work table, hidden within the shade of a stone pine, Hecate removed the mushroom from the box which she had been containing it in and lay it on the table for further investigation. Running her fingers lithely through the air, she formed a precise blade from the light. Lowering the point to the body of the mushroom, she carefully sliced the body down the center, dividing it into halves. She had been anticipating a release of the vapors as they had seen in the swamps, and she had prepared a containment hex, hardening the air around it so that the steam could not escape. It was not necessary, though. The mushroom fell apart, revealing it's interior with no ill effect. Hecate frowned as she examined the properties. It no longer looked like a mushroom.

Inside, Hecate could see the tiny, venom-filled corpuscles pulsing, as if with their own heartbeat. The indigo shade of the formula contrasted against the thin, blood-red membrane of the sack itself, which was strained to capacity, covered in a network of deep crimson stress veins. The corpuscles were confined to the top of what once was a mushroom, filling the pileus and lining the lamellae. Hecate's scowl deepened as she drew her eyes closer to the structure of the item. Aside from the venom, the body of the strange plant was hollow. The roots, which lay tangling from the base, could not draw any nutrients and, even if they could, there would be nothing to draw them toward. They served only to hold the apparatus in place. Perplexed, Hecate waved her hand over the enigmatic element, trying to divine the properties of the former mushroom. She opened her mind to receive the information.

Her eyes widened as she discovered the secrets. Focusing her thoughts with a tighter precision, she took a deeper look at the formula within the thin membranes. Dark, angry shadows filtered through her eyes as she discovered the design and purpose.

Even before entering her garden, Hecate had suspected that the item was of magic origin. A further examination of the properties confirmed that suspicion. More than that, it showed her the truth. The potamoi were, in fact, the victims. She now had a good suspicion as to who the predator was.

CHAPTER FOUR

NEMESIS HAD BEEN WATCHING PROSPERO CLOSELY, ESPECIALLY while Hecate had been absent. The moment that she had left the scene, he had begun to pace nervously, alternating between walking back-and-forth and walking in circles in a frantic, unpredictable tempo. The chaotic conversation with himself began again, and Nemesis tried not to listen to the comments, since they had rapidly descended into madness. Nemesis analyzed his movements and tendencies, taking note that he seemed incapable of relaxing. That was understandable, considering the ordeal that he had described to them but, if anything, his mania had only increased since exiting the swamp. Ever since learning that Hecate was examining the mushroom, he had virtually lost all interest in Nemesis, preferring instead to retreat into his mind, dancing with his misshapen thoughts.

There was no pattern to his pacing. Nemesis had been observing Prospero for quite a while, trying to determine a formula, but there was none to be found. She resisted the urge to be fascinated by that.

When Hecate's voice had sounded in her mind, Nemesis was startled. She attempted to conceal her surprise, although Prospero did not seem overly concerned with her activities.

"Nemesis," she had said. *"I've had a chance to analyze the object, and I have a better idea of what is going on. We need to return to the swamp and deal with the situation before it escalates."*

The lack of information which Hecate transmitted had given Nemesis some concern, as well as the vague nature of the transmission. The message had seemed urgent in nature, yet Hecate's tone was calm, almost sedate. Since this was the first time that Nemesis had received a message directly through brainwave, she chose not to over-analyze. Perhaps that was simply something that happened.

What had given her the most concern was Hecate referring to the mushroom as "product".

"It's not a mushroom," Hecate had replied, as if hearing Nemesis' thoughts. *"I have more reason now to be suspicious of Prospero, which is why I am sending you these thoughts directly, to avoid interception. For the time, I would like to keep this information as quiet as possible, so please avoid reaction. We may also need Prospero to be alive in order to alleviate the damage. Please do not kill him."*

From anyone else, Nemesis may have resented the thought that she would immediately resort to violence but, when coming from Hecate's calming voice, she had been forced to consider her motivations. Was she allowing her desire for justice to cloud her vision? If it were proven that Prospero had betrayed them, how would she respond? It was difficult for her to consider the idea that an injustice might be done against herself. No one had ever dared to do that, and the thought had filled her with anger. Prospero had continued with his maddening, unpredictable pacing, and Nemesis had avoided even looking at him until Hecate returned from her garden, for fear of what her emotional reaction would be.

Now, Hecate and Prospero were walking with her, back into the swamp. The journey from Hecate's temple to the swamp had been uncomfortably quiet, even for the usually introverted Nemesis. Prospero had avoided meeting either of their gazes, choosing to remain locked in his own conversation instead. He seemed to have dropped the guise of nervous apprehension and decided to adopt a new one: madness.

Once the three of them entered the swamp, Hecate turned to Nemesis, as if she were attempting to tell her something. Nemesis listened with her mind as well as she could. She still did not understand how Hecate had entered her mind, and maybe that was for the best. No conversation could be heard this time, and Nemesis was not sure if she had been listening right.

The swamp seemed darker than Nemesis had remembered it being. Whether this was because of the time of day or because she now knew what the swamp contained was up for debate. The ivy no longer seemed like a beautiful affectation on the trees, it now seemed like weaponry, waiting to strike if she were to give it an opening. The quagmire was no longer simply a foul-smelling swill, it was a threatening bog which would drag her into its depths should she dare to step into it. Even the buzzing of insects that persisted all around her seemed to be a hidden language, telling her to leave. Scanning the landscape told her very little new information about the environment. The only thing that she was able to glean was that she did not belong there.

Hecate advanced to a specific area, producing the box which had held the mushroom that was not a mushroom. She seemed somehow heavier than she had, as though something were weighing her down. Nemesis considered the individual that she had come to at first, so youthful and willing to help. This grimly serious individual stood in juxtaposition to her. She had aged, not physically but mentally. The grim sneer on her lips revealed as much.

"Very good," she said, sighing heavily. Hecate knew what she needed to say, and she was not looking forward to the reaction. An analysis of the venom had revealed that it was a reactive blend of specific compounds which, when inhaled, were designed to activate the most primal urges in the brain, be they savage, carnal, or defensive. Certain aspects of the formula suggested that it had been tailored specifically to interact with a specific species. Hecate did not have enough information to say specifically which species that was, but based on the evidence, she had a fairly good idea.

Hecate held the box aloft, gently opening the lid. She was stalling, and she knew that all of the present company were aware of that. Still, she was scrambling as she thought about the different ways to broach the subject.

"I have studied the mushroom," she declared. "What I discovered was more than a little surprising."

"Perhaps," Prospero grumbled, "if I had come to study the 'mushroom' with you, the discovery wouldn't have been so shocking."

Nemesis reached her hand behind her head, gripping the invisible hilt of her sword. Watching Prospero's actions and body positioning carefully, she prepared to strike.

Hecate relaxed a bit, closing the box again, and cocked an eyebrow at Prospero with a sly grin. "Really?" she queried. "What exactly could you have informed me of?"

"Well, for one thing," Prospero began, his voice suddenly filled with a formerly-unheard confidence, "you're not examining a mushroom. You're actually holding a rare enchantment, embodied in an object, constructed to resemble a mushroom. Perhaps, if you had allowed me to come into the garden with you, we could have saved ourselves both time and energy. I could have explained everything that you needed to know there, and I could have taken care of some things more succinctly. Now, it's just going to be awkward."

Prospero made a move to advance on Hecate, but Nemesis stopped him with a firm hand on his shoulder. The thin, bald, short man stared up into the chilling eyes of the tall, agile, intimidating goddess, and he scoffed.

"There's no need for your caution," he laughed. "I was not going to hurt the woman. I simply sought to hold my creation before I explained it to you. However, an explanation can be done just as well from here."

Hecate looked around the area and, to her surprise, found a few of the other enchantments, similar to the one that her box was holding, sprouting out of the ground as she watched. That did cause her some alarm, since she had never seen enchantments replicate and spread in this fashion before. Her brow furrowed, as she began to calculate the best way to deal with the situation that was unraveling.

"You already know my name, since I felt no need to lie about that," Prospero began, standing up straighter, adding about two inches to his frame. "What have I been keeping from you is the fact that I am, in reality, a very strong magician. I know that you would not know it to look at me in this form, but there was a time when I was respected, even feared, for my talents. I studied in Babylon, in a time before you existed, where I unraveled mysteries beyond your comprehension. Kings and rulers from across the world would come to me, and they would offer me land, or riches, or women, or livestock, or anything that I wanted, if only I would side with them and lend them my talents. There was a time, when I—"

Hecate would have been content to allow him to continue talking, since eventually he would become comfortable and over-confident, revealing a weakness. Nemesis, however, was not so patient. Her glare intensified, and she took a step toward Prospero. Prospero held up a cautionary hand, the action of a mouse warning a hawk to keep their distance and met her gaze unblinking. He did, however, take a step backward. Hecate smiled to herself. He was still intimidated by Nemesis.

"Stay your hand, woman," Prospero warned, in a strong voice, with only a slight quiver. "It is not your time."

"Then I would suggest you get to the point quickly," Nemesis hissed. Her eyes dripped with venom, her ivory skin vibrant with restrained energy; even the length of her hair seemed to reach toward Prospero as if to strangle the shriveled, old man before her.

"As I was saying," Prospero continued, clearing his throat, the confidence in his voice shaking for only a brief moment, "I came to this swamp to search for the same thing that you two were hunting: the Gem of Illecebra. I've not found the gem yet, but I found something more valuable than that: an endless supply of enticing—"

Hecate was no longer listening to Prospero. When she had heard "Gem of Illecebra", her mind had locked onto it. It could not be in this swamp. The gem had been lost to the seas when Atlantis had been swallowed. That is, if the gem had ever existed in the first place. A lot of text suggested that it did, but there was no evidence that it actually did. If there ever was any proof, it too was swimming beneath the waves. The gem did not exist, it could not have and never would have existed. No one, not even the most power-mad sorcerer on Atlantis would ever think to create something so dangerous. Prospero was a madman, searching for treasure where there was nothing. That was all.

Except, Hecate was beginning to wonder if, perhaps, the madman had been on to something.

"—developed my enchantment and disguised it," Prospero continued his explanation, "in the form of a mushroom. As I saw you witnessing, it effects the women in a very primal way. On one hand, they become savage and violent but, on the other hand, they become aggressively passionate."

If Nemesis were having an emotional reaction, it could not be read through her drawn face. The rage which had been there had drained, to the point that Hecate wondered if she were still connected with the situation or if, like herself, she had drifted into her thoughts at the mention of the fabled gem. That question was answered when Nemesis spoke.

"You saw a woman that you could not bed," Nemesis spoke in a voice so chilling that Gaea herself would need to redefine the term 'cold', "but rather than accept it and move on, you developed an enchantment to make her more susceptible to your advances."

It was not a question, yet Prospero shook his head. "It was not just one woman, it was an entire group of women," he corrected her with a pompous thrust of his chin. "And it was not simply that they would not have intercourse with me. They refused to acknowledge my existence at all. That could not be permitted to stand! I am Prospero, the magician! Kings and queens will—"

"Stop speaking now," Nemesis ordered him.

"These are not women," Hecate gasped. "They are potamoi! Their purpose is to protect the swamp!"

"If they are not women," Prospero sneered, "perhaps they ought not to appear so attractive."

Hecate looked to Nemesis with a look of horrified repulsion, and Nemesis returned the gaze with one of resolute hatred.

"Do not speak or respond," Hecate's voice sounded in Nemesis' mind once again, and she fought the urge to resent being told what to do. Hecate was not her enemy, after all.

"If I'm able to isolate the properties of the enchantment," Hecate continued, as her gaze stared into Nemesis, unblinking, *"I may be able to unravel its effects. He would need to enact the spell again but, unless I miss my guess, he seems to be preparing to do that very thing. While I am disabling the spell, I will likely be less than useful in combat."*

After that, Hecate broke her gaze, and the voice in her mind was silent. Nemesis' instinct was to nod, in order to affirm that she had received the transmission, but she resisted the urge. It wasn't until then that she realized Prospero had never stopped speaking. They did not appear to have missed that much information, though.

"—impressed," he was saying, his intonations suggesting that he had been expecting them to admire his work. "I mean, the formula that I used in my spell was fairly precise and intricate. It's pretty impressive, if I might say. If you take the time to appreciate the artwork, perhaps the two of you would be less upset."

"You expect us to admire your work?" Nemesis asked, in a voice as devoid of emotion as she could manage. "The spell that you created robs these creatures of their free mind, thus forcibly making them victims and endangering the lives of any who were in contact with them while under the influence of your spell."

"Yes," Prospero nodded. "Still, you have to admit, the formula and the conduit were impressive."

"You care nothing for the lives which were affected by your

devices," Hecate joined the ridicule, unable to disguise as much emotion as Nemesis had done, disdain dripping from the corners of her mouth. "You are a miserable, evil, old man."

"Spare me your moral lectures," Prospero huffed, "I'm a Corinthian. Well, as they say, those who fail to appreciate art, they will fall victim to it."

Nemesis shook her head, "Nobody says that."

"Well, they should," Prospero shouted, thrusting his hands into the air, and muttering strange words, which neither Hecate nor Nemesis could identify. The two of them exchanged looks, preparing for what was coming.

From all around them, the mushrooms which had not stopped multiplying began to burst open. The sickening odor of dead fish filled the air, and Hecate coughed, resisting the urge to breath in very deeply. As quickly as she could, she brought her hands up and began to analyze the formula. Despite herself, she found herself appreciating the finesse of the enchantment. Prospero may have been a sick, old man, but he was certainly creative.

The potamoi had begun to emerge from the foliage, and Hecate tried not to get distracted. She noticed Nemesis fighting them, struggling to maintain her presence. She seemed reluctant to strike with force this time, as if reluctant to damage these creatures. That technique would have worked just fine, if the potamoi not been fully willing and anxious to damage Nemesis. Hecate understood that Nemesis was reacting as such because she felt as if damaging them would be doing them an injustice. Still, that rationale was going to get her killed. Hecate focused her mind on unraveling the spell.

Opening her mind, she reached into the formula. She saw it there, a tangled chaos of enticement, digging its way into their brains, pushing them toward desire, pulling them from lucidity. She could smell the density, the sweet smell of mania, like honey dripping over fermented fruits. Hecate felt the strands of spider silk, weaving a complex tapestry, making sense in the disorder, while bringing chaos. There was no beginning to the design, as it wound about in soft angles, and Hecate found herself being drawn into the midst. Refocusing her mind, she resisted the pull.

There was no way to destroy the spell without risking the potamoi. It violated their minds in an intricate, detailed way, making the removal a delicate process, and Hecate did not have the time to even begin it. She would need to find a way to counteract the effects. Mentally, she intertwined her fingers and cracked her knuckles. Her mind furrowed, as she began to examine the spell.

CHAPTER FIVE

THERE WERE ONLY TWO OF THEM TO BEGIN WITH. POTAMOI emerged from the swamp, rage pulsing from their eyes, and Nemesis prepared for an attack. Pulling her sword from her sheath, Nemesis held it in front of her, defensively. These potamoi were being done an injustice; they needed to be defended as much as she did. Of course, as she wielded her sword against the vines which were thrust at her violently, it was clear that the potamoi would not think twice before spilling her blood.

Nemesis danced and parried each attack, the vines bouncing off and wrapping around her sword. Flurries of stinging needles showered her, as Nemesis ducked, blocked, and thrust away. Many of the needles were deflected, some of them stuck in her armor, and a few of them sunk into her skin. Where they entered her body, a burning sensation emerged, and her mind blazed with the pain. Nemesis resisted the urge to cry out, using the pain to fuel her defense. Looking out, she saw the two potamoi, algae-green and clothed in vines, advancing toward her, eyes filled with darkness.

A third attacker came out of the foliage, striking a direct line toward where Hecate was meditating. Nemesis dove quickly into her path, blocking the advancement. The potamide snarled at her and reached for her face. Nemesis dodged her touch, sinking near to the ground, and sweeping the potamide's legs out from under her. She began to fall, but danced and regained her footing, as Nemesis rose, driving her shoulder into the potamide's torso. The potamide doubled over and sank to the ground, panting.

Before Nemesis could turn and face another attacker, two sets of fingers were placed on her shoulders. Vines wrapped under her armpits between the gaps in her armor, grazing her flesh. She was unable to prevent the scream this time, as she was forced to her knees, her body burning with an unearthly pain, administered from outside, but somehow originating inside. Reluctant tears filled her eyes as more vines began to wrap around her, pushing her downward to the ground. She saw four potamoi, staring down at her in a blind rage, preparing to eliminate her. No matter how Nemesis pulled away from the ground, the vines held her even tighter. No matter how she resisted, the force holding her down only increased.

No matter how she searched, she could see nothing put sadism in the potamoi's eyes.

No matter how she tried to ignore it, she could not block out Prospero's mocking laughter.

The potamoi each extended a hand toward her, and vines began to advance from them toward her face. Nemesis closed her mouth tightly, knowing that this would have little effect. The vines would find an opening, and they would tear her apart, savagely, until her body was unrecognizable. She would decompose and become one with the swamp, her quest for justice coming to an end. Nemesis closed her eyes, tears burning as they dripped down her cheeks, and made peace with the situation.

The strike never came. The pressure holding her down weakened, then vanished. The laughter changed to frustrated orders, as Prospero commanded the potamoi to kill her. Nemesis opened her eyes in confusion, seeing the potamoi standing around her, appearing disoriented. Remaining on the ground, Nemesis took a moment to peer into a sky that she had never thought to see again as she tried to figure out what had happened.

Almost immediately, her answer came, as Hecate's innocent smile appeared over her, her head encircled by a halo of sunlight. She offered her hand, and Nemesis accepted it, standing to her feet. Shaking her head, she tried to orient her thoughts.

"The spell?" was all that she could think to mutter, still shaken from the attack.

Hecate nodded. "The spell," she confirmed. "It was a tremendously intricate thing but, once I figured out the idea behind it, it was not all that difficult to modify. All I needed to do was—"

Nemesis lay a weary hand on Hecate's shoulder, cutting her off. She sighed as she smiled tiredly. "Perhaps, now is not the moment for you to explain your technique to me," she said.

"Right you are," Hecate laughed.

Nemesis heard sounds all around her, gentle rustlings and sounds of emergence. Looking out, she saw potamoi, dozens of them, coming from the swamp and out of the quagmire. Their eyes were no longer filled with blind rage, changing instead to a very focused hatred. There was very little question as to who the focus of that emotion was.

"No!" Prospero screamed. "You will not strike me! I have made you compliant!"

He waved his hand and several mushrooms exploded into vapor. Nemesis looked to Hecate, but Hecate merely smiled.

"I countered the spell," she laughed. "Those are just explosive mushrooms now. They're actually kind of pretty when you remove the damaging effects."

Prospero continued screaming, commanding the potamoi to heed his will. The number of potamoi continued to grow as they advanced on the wizard; a sea of anger, fueled by vengeance. Nemesis and Hecate continued to watch, as the potamoi fell on Prospero, savagely and mercilessly tearing him apart. His screams subsided, once the vines tore through his throat, but his eyes remained alert long after.

Only when his blood flowed, thick and red, into the bowels of the swamp, and viscera seeped generously from his ears and down his neck, did his eyes cloud over as sense left him.

Nemesis joined Hecate's smile with one of her own. Justice had been done.

CHAPTER SIX

THEY LEFT THE SWAMP, SIDE BY SIDE. HECATE HAD OFFERED Nemesis a place of rest in her temple, along with some treatment for her wounds, and Nemesis had been quick to accept. The two walked in silence for a time, thinking about what they had just experienced together.

Hecate broke the tension first. She sighed, "Thank you for including me in this venture," she said. "I have always admired your work but, now, I feel like I appreciate it more. What you do is truly a gift."

Nemesis resisted the urge to respond emotionally. "You have no reason to thank me," she said. "This excursion would have been impossible without you."

I owe you my life, Nemesis added in her mind. She could not bring herself to say it aloud, but she suspected that Hecate already knew that.

The two walked in silence for another few steps.

"Prospero mentioned something," Hecate, once again, spoke. "He said that he had originally come to the swamp in search of the Gem of Illecebra."

Nemesis nodded, "I remember that being said. It is curious that he would be searching for something that does not exist, but he was a madman. Perhaps it was in character."

"Yes," Hecate nodded. "But, on the chance that the gem exists, do you not think that it would be beneficial to investigate?"

Nemesis shook her head. "It would be futile," she said. "The gem is a myth."

Hecate sighed. "I suppose you're right," she said. "It was just a thought."

The two goddesses walked together, content with one another's company.

CHAPTER SEVEN

A LONG, LONG TIME AGO...

HE DIDN'T CARE WHAT THEY HAD TOLD HIM ANY LONGER. THIS gem was going to be his masterpiece, and there was no one who could argue with that.

He had been studying the properties of the unicorn's horn for an age, and it's magic still captivated him. Its mineral was dense and complex, stronger than any other which he had identified. This made modifying it more complicated, if not impossible. Still, he had staked his reputation on discovery, and he would be damned if he allowed anything to get in his way.

Since killing a unicorn simply to recover its horn was still considered a condemnable offense, even if the purpose was for science, he had needed to conduct his research in secret, revealing his progress to very few colleagues. Even amongst those few, two of them had been horrified by his conduct, and he had been forced to eliminate them. Right now, all that the greater magi community of Atlantis knew was that he was on the verge of a great discovery. That was all they needed to know. Once he had accomplished his goals, his crimes would be justified, and he would be celebrated, rather than condemned.

There had been multiple crimes, of course. Advancement required the bending of the rules, after all. He had needed to come into possession of a large amount of centaur blood, preferably from a single source. If he had asked the centaur community for the blood, they doubtless would have wanted to know its purpose, and his crime would have been discovered. Also, there was no assurance that they would have supplied the blood or that the blood would have come from a single donation. He had needed to find the blood in an unconventional way, and he had done so in the easiest way that he could. No one would miss Jkelph, he had made sure of that.

Now, as he held the un-tempered unicorn horn above the large vat of centaur blood, with its heat slowly rising to a critical temperature, he was forced to consider the moral ramifications of what he was doing. With a shudder, he shrugged his morality off. If he were to begin considering things from an ethical perspective, he ought to have done so long ago.

"What you have done is wrong, Iago," a female voice cautioned him, from the doorway to his laboratory.

Iago laid the unicorn horn beside the vat then spun to face the speaker. He had locked the doorway, he knew that he had. Still, locked doors had never stopped Xilfim before: there was no reason to think that they would now. She stood there, matronly with her long, silver, hair and wizened, blue eyes, bearing a concerned scowl on her weathered face. At one point, Iago had embraced the guidance and love which she supplied. That time had come and gone, though. This was now his time.

He took what remained of his affection for Xilfim and translated it into resentment. "What I am doing is for the good of Atlantis," he retorted. "You are no longer my mentor, Xilfim. I don't expect you to understand what it is that I'm doing, but soon, you and all of Atlantis will."

"You are not doing anything for the good of Atlantis, you are doing this only for your pride," Xilfim informed Iago, advancing into the lab, her condemning scowl never flickering. "The Atlantian counsel would never have approved of your experiments, nor would the counsel of magi agreed to the testing necessary. You are an accomplished magus, Iago. You ought to be using your strengths elsewhere in a more beneficial arena. Come, step away from this ridiculous task, and return to the world of science. We will discuss what to do about your crimes at a later time."

Turning back to the vat, Iago lifted the horn once more. Holding it horizontally across his palms, he felt it vibrate, pulsing within grasp. It was as though she wanted him to use her. Examining the vat, he saw that the heat had risen to an acceptable level. Before he could think himself out of it, he dropped the horn into the vat.

Xilfim gasped and rushed toward him, her portly figure moving faster than Iago had ever remembered seeing her move. She stood beside him, watching as the horn was swallowed by the blood, eyes filled with horror.

"You ought not to have done that," she sighed. "The magical properties in those two sources are still largely untested, and there is no way of telling how they will interact."

Xilfim's horror was juxtaposed by the satisfied look of Iago. "I suppose now, we'll make a new discovery," he said, a smile creeping onto his lips.

The two magi stood together, watching the centaur blood boil. The refinement process had begun.

CHAPTER EIGHT

A LONG, LONG TIME AGO, BUT NOT AS LONG AGO AS BEFORE...

THE TIME OF OLYMPUS WAS COMING TO AN END. THE WORLD was expanding, and new gods were appearing, many of whom were not happy with the Olympians. War was approaching; indeed, it had already begun. There seemed to be powers, strong and foreign magics, working against them. Hecate had recognized the dark arts, of course, and she had attempted to identify their source. Strangely, however, their path had been hidden by a magic stronger than her own. That ought not to have surprised or offended her. She had known that, somewhere, there were likely some who had magics that were stronger than her own. She should not be bothered by that fact. After all, what was she? She was simply the goddess of magic. That didn't mean that she was automatically the best.

Try as she might, she could not decipher the trail. It was as though it was transmitted from another world. Hecate had fought the urge to become frustrated. She continued searching for something she could use to identify those who were antagonizing the Olympians.

She continued searching for a way to sway the war in the Olympians favor.

There had to be something that could be used to ensure the future of Mount Olympus.

As Hecate prepared for her venture, Horace watched her with concern.

"Mistress, I beg you to reconsider," he spoke eventually, as Hecate struggled to pull leather armaments over her legs, fitting tightly, like a second skin. "When last you traveled to the Maeotian swamp, you were accompanied by the lady, Nemesis. Even so, you returned with that wretched man, the man who later endangered your life. The situation is too dangerous for you to be attempting alone; I would implore you to stay out of the Maeotian swamp, or at least to not venture in alone. Perhaps contact Nemesis before attempting to journey forth?"

Hecate sighed as she covered her torso in protective clothing. "Prospero mentioned the Gem of Illecebra," she repeated to Horace once more, for perhaps the seventh time. "Nemesis dismissed his claim as nonsense. It would be illogical for me to think that she would accompany me."

"It is illogical for you to be searching for the gem at all," Horace retorted. "Since the gem may not even exist, there is no purpose to you endangering your life."

"I have to do something!" Hecate shouted, feeling the angst and frustration that she had been stifling threatening to burst. She looked to her eunuch and saw pain in his gray eyes, shadowing the concern and love which he held for her. She never shouted at him, and she had never intended to hurt him. The look in his eyes was enough to mellow her a bit.

Stepping to him, she embraced Horace tightly, laying her head against his chest. "I love you, sweet Horace," she whispered gently. "I need to do this, though. If there is even a chance that the gem is in the swamp, I need to retrieve it. Olympus is being threatened, and the

Gem of Illecebra could sway the battle in our favor. If there is a chance for this, I must take it."

She felt Horace's body convulsing as he attempted to contain his sobs. She held him tighter, feeling the soft fabrics of his robe against her still-naked breasts, with the occasional drop of salty water falling to her exposed shoulders. Her affection for Horace and his devotion to her was almost enough to make her reconsider her venture. Perhaps it was a fool's errand. Maybe she was being naive, thinking that a gem whose existence had never been proven could be found. She was chasing a rumor, the causal inference of a madman. The gem likely did not exist at all.

She had to know. If she did not at least search, she would never be able to let it go.

CHAPTER NINE

THE SWAMP WAS DARKER, MORE STAGNANT, THAN SHE remembered. The oppression that weighed down on her pushed, demanding that she buckle, forcing her toward the sludge. The putrescence which she trudged through stuck to her legs, drawing her into its depth, refusing to let her go. Maybe this was because of the associations that she had with the area now, or perhaps it was because of what she was intending to do. Either way, with each cautious step Hecate took through the muck, the trepidation that she felt grew, as did the feeling of isolation. She ought not to have done this alone.

Thinking back, she could have asked Horace to come with her, and that would have satisfied both his angst and her need for companionship. She would not have wanted to risk his safety, though. At least, that was how she excused it to herself. In truth, she would not have wanted to hear his lamenting and protective language. Hecate knew that Horace loved her, and his protective nature was one way in which he translated that. It did become tedious now and then, though. Hecate loved Horace as well, but their relationship needed to become less codependent. There were times when she needed to be alone. She hated to hurt Horace. Each time she told him that she needed time to herself, the look of pain and abandonment that crossed his face was enough to tear her apart.

Thus, when the opportunity had come for her to get away from the castle for a bit by herself with her own thoughts, she had taken it. It probably would have been better if the opportunity had been in a less endangering atmosphere, but she had to take what was supplied.

This trip into the swamp needed to follow a more rigid protocol than the former excursion. Hecate was not protecting the swamp this time. She was exploring and potentially removing something from it. For that, she would need to gain permission from this area's ruler, the lord Achelous. It was important for her to follow the rules of the community, especially in respect to Achelous. Hecate had heard tales of the things that had happened to those whom he had perceived disrespect from.

Hecate approached the specific area carefully, registering each step with precise accuracy. She turned to the right, to the left, finding her place in the exact area between two dogwood trees: one, alive and green, the other, dead and decayed. The foliage around the trunk of the dead tree was green and vibrant, as if the tree had given its life to provide care for the growth around it, while the living tree seemed to have drained all of the nutrients out of the surrounding area, making sure that it was fulfilled. The prevailing sensation in the area was complete silence. No wind twisted through the branches, no birds sang in the air, and there were no insects buzzing, spreading their disease. The air practically rippled with black magic, and the smell of death reeked, representing a deeper meaning than simply the absence of life. Hecate smiled. This was where she needed to be.

Removing the elements from her pouch, Hecate began to sprinkle sage into the soil. "*Illustrant iter,*" she began to chant, as she paced in the clockwise circle around the area, "*ad praetorium regem.*"

Reaching into her pouch again, she removed a small vial filled with frankincense. She continued to circle as she opened the vial, splashed a small amount against her face and the skin of her chest, and emptied the rest into the soil.

"*Illustrant iter ad praetorium regem,*" she repeated, as the pungent smell of funeral ceremony clutched at her senses, threatening to make her wretch.

Almost immediately, the ground beneath her feet began to swirl. Hecate's first instinct was to jump away and avoid the strange motion. Instead, she reminded herself to continue pacing in a circular motion.

"*Illustrant iter ad praetorium regem,*" she repeated a third and final time, in as balanced a voice as she could manage, while struggling to keep her pace relaxed and unhurried.

The soil began to draw her down, sucking her into its depths. She struggled to take a breath before she was swallowed completely. Her attempt was too late. Pain and repulsion were the last sensations she felt, as her mouth was filled by moist earth.

The feeling of drowning evaporated almost as quickly as it had come on. Hecate sank to her knees, gasping for air, and was surprised to find marble flooring beneath her. She ought not to have been surprised, since she knew that it would happen. Still, this was the first time that she had entered Archelous' court, so the experience was new to her. It was not one that she wished to repeat at any point in the future.

Hecate had closed her eyes on impulse as she had been drawn into the ground. She had not reopened them since emerging on the other side. Once the retching had subsided, she straightened her back, opened her eyes, and rose to her feet. Looking around her, Hecate resisted the urge to gasp with amazement. She was standing before the throne of Archelous, within the bowels of the swamp. The ornate pillars which held the domed ceiling aloft were engraved with precious stones that Hecate did not recognize, each of them shining with a beautiful and distinct polish. Around the gems, ivy wound up the columns, reminding any who viewed them of exactly where they were. Behind Hecate stood a tall archway, leading into a long hallway to somewhere that she could not determine. The flooring beneath her was marble, cold and unyielding, beautiful in its frigid nature.

Looking before her, Hecate saw Archelous, seated on his throne. Very little about him seemed recognizable from a biological perspective. His face, if one could call it as a face, was only defined by two, dark green orbs, both oozing a thick pus, which Hecate assumed functioned as eyes. Between the eyes, a long trunk swayed and pulsed, beating with a singular rhythm, as though it were absorbing oxygen through osmosis rather than breathing it in. Below his head, his body sat, simply a tangled mass of tentacles. He had taken the basic shape of a human, but Hecate felt that this was more out of convenience and comfort than necessity. He filled his throne to capacity, and maybe a bit beyond. He wore no clothing, nor was any necessitated. He was Archelous. He was king here, and there was no denying that.

On either side of him stood a potamide. They looked much different than they had when last Hecate had encountered them. The ravenous, crazed look was gone from their dark eyes and thin lips. What remained was an empty expression, completely docile, willingly subservient to Archelous. These were the potamoi that Hecate was familiar with. They carried out the wills of Archelous.

"A female approaches," the one on Archelous' left spoke, her musical voice sounding automated and emotionless.

"The goddess Hecate, friend to the potamoi," the potamide on the right elaborated, in a similar, chilling tone. "She seeks the audience of our king."

"She would levy her past deeds to support her, attempting to gain our kings favor," the left replied so evenly that the cynicism was difficult to detect. "This will not bode well for her."

"Likewise, it will not bode poorly," the right countered.

"Archelous will grant an audience to the goddess, Hecate," the two potamoi spoke, in unison.

Hecate took a moment to compose herself and, while doing so, she examined the potamoi. They appeared beautiful and lavish as she had suspected they would, with their thin, female bodies clothed only in vines. Their flawless skin was a shade of light green, the shade of growth and health. Their hair was black, thick and full, hanging down their bodies like drapery.

"I seek an audience with Archelous," Hecate heard herself say, before she was able to stop herself.

"This has been established," the right reminded her.

"The purpose of her audience has not," the left insisted.

Hecate breathed in deeply, realizing quickly that she was frightened and intimidated. "I have heard rumor," she continued, attempting to state her argument succinctly, "of a certain gem's residency within the swamp. I seek Archelous' permission to search for it."

"She seeks the Gem of Illecebra," the left stated. It startled Hecate to hear the words said out loud so distinctly, even before she had identified the gem herself.

"Lord Archelous has no use for the gem," the right continued the thought.

"The goddess has use for the gem," the left countered.

Silence filled the hall then, and Hecate felt three sets of eyes boring into her where she stood. "I would not abuse the gem," Hecate said after a moment of awkward silence. "The Olympians are at war right now, and the gem, if it is here, could balance the power into our favor. Lord Archelous may not be an Olympian, but it is to his benefit that the Olympians remain the dominant force. His kingdom would remain unchallenged. It is unlikely that he will receive a similar agreement from foreign pantheons."

"The goddess uses logic to sway our thoughts," the right argued.

"Diplomacy is not manipulation," the left countered. "Her logic stands."

"It would be to all of our benefit, should I be permitted to remove the gem, and supply its power to Zeus and the Olympians," Hecate argued. She allowed herself to feel some hope for the first time since she had entered the swamp. She allowed herself to believe that this may work out after all.

She almost believed that the gem was actually in the swamp, as Prospero had suspected.

"The goddess could keep the gem for herself," the left suggested.

"I wouldn't do that," Hecate insisted quickly.

"The goddess should be silent," the right replied.

"Archelous will deliberate," the left concluded.

Hecate could deny it no longer, and her weak knees would have betrayed her even if she had. She was afraid. Before this moment, it had been easy to hide her fear, since there were things that she could distract herself with. Now, there was nothing to hide behind. If her request was approved, she would return to the swamp, in order to search for something that might not be there. Even if it was there, it was likely hidden and protected by forces that she would have to fight against in order to remove it. If her request was denied, Archelous would almost surely have her killed.

Each moment that Hecate considered the situation, the more convinced she became that this entire venture had been a huge mistake.

She stood for a short eternity before she saw Archelous raise his trunk. His mouth, formerly invisible beneath the trunk, opened, and Archelous bellowed with a strong, bone-chilling roar. Hecate shuddered, feeling the warmth of Archelous' breath forcing her back, smelling the stench of quagmire which it carried. She closed her eyes tightly, attempting not to tear up from the intensity of the smell. When she opened her eyes once more, the three sets of eyes were boring into her once more.

"The goddess has been a friend to the potamoi," the right informed her.

"The goddess has been a friend to Lord Archelous," the left continued.

"The request has been approved."

"The goddess will require training."

"Training has been approved."

"Hail, Lord Archelous," both potamoi chorused together.

Hecate dropped to one knee, bowing her head in supplication. She breathed a heavy sigh of relief, as all the tension that she had formerly felt melted from her, replaced by nervous excitement.

A hand landed on her shoulder, and she looked up, into the eyes of a third potamide. "Come," she said, her voice carrying more warmth and personality than Hecate had heard previously (although that was likely only because of the company which she had been in, only moments before). "You will be trained, and you will be prepared."

Hecate stood to her feet and followed the potamide, away from the throne where Archelous continued to watch her, down the hall that held an unknown destination. She felt safe and confident. It was an illusion, but it was one that she would capitalize on for the time being.

CHAPTER TEN

HECATE WAS LED DOWN THE HALL, WALKING A FEW STEPS behind the potamide. Watching the way she walked was similar to watching water, flowing through a stream. The fluid motion which naturally slid her hips from side-to-side with each step made Hecate self-conscious about her own walk. The potamide was just walking, and nothing about her was threatening or pompous. Hecate realized that, and yet she was still intimidated by the effortless grace which this creature had.

The potamide slid to a specific chamber, where she stopped and motioned that Hecate should enter. Before doing so, Hecate looked into the chamber to examine its contents. The room held a small pool of water. The room appeared to be a bathing chamber.

"Enter the room," the potamide instructed Hecate, "remove your clothing and submerge yourself in the waters. Your conditioning will commence momentarily."

Hecate took a hesitant step through the door. She assured herself that she was not simply doing this because she had been instructed to, but rather, because she was choosing to. After all, it made logical sense to comply, since it was in line with her ultimate goal. Once in the chamber, Hecate peeled off the leathers which had protected her body and stepped into the pool. The feeling of cleansing water against her naked body was nothing short of euphoric. Closing her eyes, Hecate allowed herself to become submerged in the fluids. As she lay back, allowing the liquids to envelope her, she smelled fragrances and aromas that she didn't recognize. They were natural, or derived from a natural source, but the identity of that was alien to her.

Opening her eyes, Hecate saw the graceful potamide, walking around the pool. There were three stoves, each housing a fire, placed at key points around the pool, and the potamide seemed to be tending to each of them. With each time that she cared for one of them, a smoke of a different color erupted from the stove, each holding a unique scent. Hecate fought the urge to feel naked, even though that was her current state, and she reminded herself that this was what had been asked of her. The potamide's body was elegant and flawless, enough to make any woman feel a bit self-conscious, but Hecate was more concerned with the smoke.

"Excuse me?" Hecate called out to the potamide.

The potamide ignored her, continuing to tend to the stoves.

"Can you hear me?" Hecate asked, raising the volume of her voice slightly.

"The woman should not be speaking," the potamide replied. "The woman ought to be relaxing. Her training is about to begin."

"What are these smokes that I keep seeing?" Hecate continued to push for answers. "They hold aromas that I'm not familiar with."

The potamide remained silent, refusing to even look at Hecate.

Hecate was about to reassert herself, speaking louder and with more authority, when a sudden wave of nausea swept through her mind, causing the world around her to feel as though it were spinning. She inhaled deeply, trying to find her center, but she found that with the more she breathed, the more disassociated she became. There was something in the smoke, something that must be causing this. There were elements in the water, elements that were creeping into her skin. There was something in her mind, something that needed to be freed. Hecate relaxed into the water, knowing that there was nothing that she needed to do. Where she was now was a place that she wanted to stay in, and she wanted to be there for as long as she could. She closed her eyes, allowing her mind to transverse into another world.

When Hecate opened her eyes once more, she found that she was standing in the center of a gladiatorial arena. It was hardly a shock; if she were honest, the transition had felt natural. Looking down at her body, she found that she was no longer naked. She, instead, was clothed in a tight, simple strophlon, which held her breasts in place, but covered them hardly enough to provide any protection or modesty. Her thin midsection was bare, revealing her most vulnerable areas to any who wished to see them, while her body beneath her navel was protected only by an immodest loincloth.

This had to be a part of the test. Looking up at the stands surrounding the arena, she saw thousands of people, staring down at her. Most of them were jeering at her, anxious to see her fail. A few of them were smiling at her, their eyes filled with lust, and Hecate felt as though she were a spectacle rather than an individual. Every one of the viewers seemed impatient for the entertainment to begin. The entertainment, it seemed, involved more parties than simply herself. In order for her to continue the dance, she would need a partner.

That partner was supplied moments later, when a loud roaring was heard from the other end of the arena. The jeering changed to loud cheers of excitement as Hecate turned toward the new sound, preparing herself for an advisory of gigantic proportions. Her eyes fell upon a lion, large and angry, its tail twitching with anxious energy. She frowned, almost disappointed, since dealing with a lion ought to be no challenge at all. As the lion pawed the ground, preparing to attack, Hecate reached into the air, searching for magic with which to defend herself. Her search came back empty: there was no magic to be found.

The crowd cheered loudly as the lion charged at her. For the first time, Hecate felt fear, as she danced around the oncoming creature's charge, hardly able to avoid its talons. There was no magic for her to use, and she had no other weapon. The lion landed, mere feet away, turned to her and smelled her fear. Maddening rage boiled in its eyes and it sized her up, preparing to devour her whole. Hecate searched her mind for a rational option, begging herself to decide what she ought to do. The only option that she found was flight. Hecate turned away from the lion, and she ran.

The lion gave chase and, very quickly, Hecate realized how foolish the idea had been. The lion overtook her quickly, swatting her to the ground with one strike of its large paw. Pain seared through her, radiating out of the newly opened wounds on her back, and the smell of blood filled the air. Hecate screamed out, her cries drowned by the mocking laughter of the spectators, and rolled onto her back. The pain shifted from stabbing to burning, as the sand from the ground mixed itself into the open wounds, but Hecate had other things to contemplate. Chief amongst them, the hungry lion, staring down at her with a ferocious snarl.

Someone in the crowd, unwilling to allow the entertainment to be finished so quickly, threw a weapon into the ring: a long, crude, wooden bow with no blade and no structure. Hecate rolled toward where she had heard it fall, seized it, and sprang to her feet quickly. She held the bow as a barrier between herself and the lion, crouching behind it defensively, as the crowd laughed at her from behind, and the lion stared at her with malicious curiosity from her front. It took only a moment for the lion's fascination to abate, and it was on her once again, charging angrily toward her, its mouth filled with the sounds of death.

Hecate jabbed the bow into the lion's large, open mouth, forcing it as far down the creature's throat as she could. The lion struck at her with its front paws, and Hecate was forced to release the bow as she dove away from the attacks. The open wounds in her back widened and the pain increased as she danced away from the creature. Turning quickly, she saw the lion struggling with the bow, which was still engaged with its maw.

Sensing her opportunity, Hecate reached to the arena floor and cupped a handful of sand. Charging quickly, she cried out savagely and, when the lion looked toward her, she thrust the sand into its eyes. The lion roared and thrashed about madly. Hecate dove around the thrashing, danced to the rear of the beast and leaped on the large cat's back. There, she thrust her arms about the creature's neck and held on tightly, obstructing the lion's oxygen flow.

The lion panicked, desperately attempting to throw Hecate from its back. Hecate held on desperately for as long as she was able. After far too long of a time, the lion's struggling began to subside, and it fell to the ground. There it lay, unconscious, struggling to find its breath.

Another weapon entered the arena, this time a blade. As Hecate dismounted the lion, she considered the supplied weapon. The crowd in the arena had begun to chant, encouraging her to kill the beast, emerging from the arena as a champion. Hecate walked to the blade, holding it aloft, mad energy coursing through her veins. Everything in her mind wanted to finish the beast. She would be justified in doing so. The beast had, after all, tried to kill her.

Walking toward the creature, clutching the blade tightly, she noticed imprints on the lion's side. Its ribs and its mane were mated with dried blood, its fur barely covering scars. This creature had been tortured, trained to hate, starved to the point of madness. Hecate turned, thrusting the blade away from her. The crowd booed angrily at the anticlimactic conclusion, but Hecate did not care what they thought. She would not contribute to this creature's pain.

The lightheaded feeling returned, and the world began to melt once more.

When she opened her eyes, Hecate found herself seated on a throne. She was clothed in royal robes of crimson and indigo. On her head, a crown weighed down on her heavily. She removed the crown and examined it quickly: it shone with a golden hue, complemented by a plethora of rare and beautiful gems. Each was more beautiful than the last, and she imagined that the crown itself was worth a fortune, a small kingdom. As she placed it on her head, she almost felt guilty wearing something so elaborate and expensive.

Her robes were soft and embraced her with their warmth and comfort. Looking down, she could see their silken texture. The sleeves and collar were lined with a white fur that she could not identify. The textures which she felt against her skin reminded her of a feline, perhaps an exotic leopard that she had never seen before. She had never worn clothing composed of fur. The idea of slaying an animal simply for the sake of fashion repulsed her. As she sat on the throne, she considered casting the robe to the ground, simply for ethical reasons, but it was comfortable. She hated it, but she enjoyed the feeling it supplied where the fur touched her skin.

She saw that she was in a court. People were seated all around her, and most of them were staring at her. She looked at the faces in the crowd. It may have been her imagination, but she thought that she recognized some of them from the arena. They were silent at the moment but, in her mind, she still heard them jeering and mocking her. She expected that some of them were still angry at her for sparing the lion's life.

Standing before her, expectantly waiting to present their case, stood two figures: a wealthy man, wearing expensive clothing and holding himself in high regard, and a woman, dressed in little more than rags, her face fallen with shame.

"This woman," the man jumped at the chance to be heard first, "has stolen from me. I found her in my home, taking part in the bread that my servants had baked. She also drank from the water, which my servants had drawn from my well only an hour before."

"I beg your pardon, my liege," the woman replied weakly. "I was hungry, yes, since I had not eaten more than a crust for three days. The water that I had drank was foul and quenched my thirst only slightly, making me sicker than I already was. It was all that I could do. I chose to steal from this man, since my only other option was death."

"That is no fault of mine," the man replied in a heartless manner. "The woman asked me for something to eat on the day prior to this, and I had turned her away. She knew that I was unwilling to supply sustenance for her, yet she took it from me anyway."

"I am alone," the woman cried. "My husband has died, and my children have all left me. I have no trade with which to make money and, therefore, I have nothing to trade for food. I am sorry that I had to steal. I know that I was breaking the law. If I am to be thrown into prison, I accept it. At least there, I will be supplied with some food."

"You see?" the man pointed at the forsaken woman. "You see how this woman admits to her crimes? I demand that justice be served."

Hecate's heart broke for the woman. She was clearly starving, at the end of her wits. Hecate could see by her demeanor that she had been on the streets for far too long. She wore the stench of the back alleys as though it were perfume, and filth was the only compliment which she had for her skin. She was repulsive, both in presentation and in spirit. It was clear that she had stolen only out of desperation, but that did not justify her actions.

Hecate examined the wealthy man. "What would you have me do with this woman?" she asked, already knowing his answer.

The man scoffed. "Jail would be a step up in her social position," he huffed. "I require reimbursement for the items that she has stolen. I demand that this woman be stripped of the clothing which she wears on her back, and of everything that she lays claim to. Cast her, naked, into the streets, to live amongst the dogs, if they would have her. Her trials are not my responsibility to cure. Knowing that she lives in even more misery than she did before she chose to steal from me is payment enough."

The woman fell into quiet, shameful tears as she heard the man speaking. Hecate was at a loss for what to do. She knew that she ought to uphold the law, since she was the monarch here. Her heart was filled with compassion, though, and she did not wish to strip the woman of any more than the world had already taken from her. The woman had no dignity left to be taken, and her shame lay on the courtroom floor. This man, acting as though he was the one who was in the moral right, was behaving in a reprehensible fashion. Still, he was the one who had been wronged.

Hecate turned to the crowd, all of whom were looking at her expectantly. "What should be done with this woman?" she called out, seeking the opinion of the court. The onlookers replied in a mixed voice, some asking for mercy toward the woman, others demanding justice for the man. There was no conclusive answer. No matter what Hecate chose, she would risk angering a portion of the crowd.

The decision had to be her own. She was the arbitrator of justice, the final voice of the law. The people would hear her voice, and abide by what she said. Hecate looked to the man.

"You were robbed," she said in a cold voice. "You deserve to be compensated for your loss."

Reaching to her head, Hecate removed the crown. She then motioned for the crestfallen woman to approach the throne. Hesitantly, the woman stepped forward. Hecate handed her crown to the woman, and the woman accepted it cautiously, hardly able to hold its weight due to her weakness. The crowd around her gasped, realizing what was happening.

"One of the gems within this crown will more than compensate this man for his losses," she said, meeting the woman's pain-filled eyes boldly. "He will be satisfied with that as payment. After you have paid the man, you will sell the remaining gems for whatever profit you are able to, and you will use the remaining gold to clothe and educate yourself."

The man looked at Hecate with horror in his eyes. "Am I to understand that this woman will now be rewarded for her crimes?" he cried out in disbelief.

"As you have said," Hecate answered him evenly, "her situation is not your concern. She is a resident in my kingdom, though. That makes her situation my concern. You will be more than reimbursed for your losses, even beyond what you have lost. If I choose to give from my own wealth to a woman who has already lost more than any can repay, what concern is it of yours?"

The crowd around her cheered with approval at her decision, even as the man continued to complain that the verdict was unjust. Hecate smiled, her head feeling lighter without the crown, even lighter than it had been before the crown was upon it.

The unanimous cheering from the crowd assured her that she had chosen correctly.

Her head swam with contented glee and, once again, the scenery changed.

Her eyesight never focused. Everything before her appeared as a haze, as though she were viewing the world through a field of smoke. Her body felt strange, as though it were covered in thousands of crawling insects. Looking down, she saw that it was not. In fact, her body was covered in nothing. She was completely naked.

All around her, she heard noises: growling, snarling, angry noises, threatening her and challenging her. Along with this, voices called out to her, whispering to her, telling her who she was, reminding her of who she was not, instructing her as to the ways of the world, hinting that the world no longer existed.

She tried to move, but could not. There was no purpose to move anyway, since there was nowhere to go. Even if she could have gone somewhere, there would have been no point, since the world was trying to kill her, and any movement that she made would have only brought her closer to that end.

Who are you?

She tried to speak, but had no tongue. Speaking would have been useless, in any regard, since there was nothing to say. Since she had no name, there was no reason for her to claim an identity. She was useless, stripped of identity, serving no purpose, simply taking up valuable space.

Why are you here?

She had no answer for the questions which were whispered to her from out of the smoke. Even if she could have supplied an answer, there would have been no point. She was void of identity, unable to move. Why would her answer have meant anything? She was naked, covered in insects, surrounded by hungry predators. Surely, she was not long for this world.

(you) Are (some)one.

The snarling sounds drew nearer, now seemingly next to her. If she could move, she had little doubt that she could reach out and touch one of the attacking swarm.

Be some(one)

The insects on her body began to bite. They began to devour her naked flesh.

A lie (ve)

There is no point.

Nothing matters.

All is naught.

Dust to—

Hecate took hold of the thoughts which clouded her vision. This was a test, she reminded herself. She was real. Her nudity, the crawling insects, the smoke, even the predators were an illusion. The only thing that was real was her.

She was Hecate, and she knew who she was.

She answered the whispered questions in her mind, and her tongue was loosened.

She rebuked the insects on her flesh, and her body moved.

Hecate took her name, declaring it to the wind, and she was clothed.

Taking hold of her magic, Hecate commanded the smoke to clear, and it parted before her.

There were no snarling predators left to be seen. They had all run away from the power which she held.

Closing her eyes, Hecate smiled. She was confident that she had passed the test.

Hecate found herself in the pool again, back in Archelous' temple. The potamide was watching her now, and Hecate imagined that she saw a slight smile. While Hecate was still naked in the water, she no longer felt vulnerable. The potamide had not become any less beautiful, but Hecate no longer felt intimidated.

"The woman has survived her training," the potamide informed her. "She will exit the pool, clothe herself, and she is free to begin her journey through Archelous' kingdom."

Without saying another word, the potamide turned and left the bathing chamber. Hecate frowned as she considered what had just been said. Since the potamide suggested that she had survived, that suggested that there was a chance that she would not. She wondered how she would have reacted differently, if she had known that death was an option the entire time.

As she left the pool and clothed herself once more, the option of death seemed to loom over her, like a bright, shining beacon.

CHAPTER ELEVEN

UPON RETURNING TO THE SWAMP AFTER HER TIME WITH Archelous, Hecate embraced the atmosphere like a child, craving her mother's milk. She could feel the magic as she breathed in the air, infiltrating her body, rubbing against her skin. Her fingertips began to tingle at the renewed sensation, as though her body had been completely numb for a time but, suddenly, circulation was restored. For the first time since entering Archelous' court, Hecate felt clothed.

While Archelous had given her permission to search for the gem in his kingdom, virtually confirming that it existed somewhere within the swamp, neither he nor the potamoi had given her a direction to search in. This left her with a curious conundrum. While the Maeotian swamp was not large in comparison to other areas, canvasing the entire area for something like a gem would be tedious and time consuming. With a frown, Hecate breathed into the air, asking it for direction.

An answer appeared in the back of her mind. It was such an obvious solution that Hecate almost resented herself for not thinking of it sooner. Sitting beneath a withered birch tree, Hecate began to meditate. As she did so, her mind lifted into the air, so that she was able to see the entirety of the swamp. Closing her mind's eye, she was left only with an imprint of the area. She drew a mental grid across the imprint, dividing the area into hexagonal districts. After that, she began to search each district for magical activity. She would not be able to identify the source of the magic through this method, but it would give her a place to start looking.

She began her investigation. Even doing this would require an extreme output of energy, and she would leave herself completely vulnerable while in meditation, but it was necessary if she intended to complete her task. Entering the first area, she sifted through all of the innate and natural magics which were present in every part of the swamp, since there was nothing especially significant about them. Once she was able to see through that, any alien activity should have been clear. She combed through the area carefully, desperately searching for any discrepancy. She found none. Disappointed, she moved onto the next zone.

Almost immediately, a strange magic stuck out at her, so glaring that it was almost painful. Excitedly, she began to examine the location. To her surprise, Hecate found that the source was not pinned to a specific area. Instead, it was running about, as though it were a mobile creature. This meant that either something had picked up the gem and was running about with it or (more likely) the source belonged to something other than the gem. Hecate made a note to investigate the source later but, for the time being, she needed to continue her search.

Moving to the third area bore similar results, with multiple signatures of the mobile magic sources, but nothing stationary. The same held for the fourth area. The strain of the search had been building up in Hecate ever since she had begun, and now, as she began to search the fifth area, her defenses began to collapse. She realized that, if she continued to extend as much effort as she was during her meditation, she was at risk of doing irreparable damage to her mind. Hecate was about to pull out of her meditation in order to gather her wits and find nutrients to renew her strength when she saw it. There, in the fifth area, was a stationary source of magic, stronger than any of the other sources that she had been seeing. It was strong and blazing, like a beacon, calling to her, challenging her to come and play. The source begged her to come and rescue it, it warned her to look away. It could be nothing else: this was the Gem of Illecebra.

When Hecate pulled herself out of her meditative state, feeling alive and full of motivation, she found that the day had passed without her noticing, and half the night as well. While she could have gone exploring in the darkness, it didn't seem to make logical sense. Hecate placed a barrier tent around herself, twisting the air to form a shield, lay back, and closed her eyes.

When she awoke the following morning, Hecate prepared herself for her venture. Her clothing, while a bit filthy, was still in good enough condition to protect her from the elements. Simply to be on the safe side, Hecate strengthened the leather which covered her lower extremities and wrapped the fabric which held her breasts in place a bit tighter. She tied her golden hair back tightly, so that it wouldn't interfere with her vision, and prepared all the defensive incantations which she anticipated needing. After consuming some nutrients from the flora which surrounded her, she was prepared to go.

The map that she had investigated before surrendering to sleep was still vivid in her mind. She knew the path that she would need to take in order to find the place where she had sensed the magic. If she tracked through the first, being the sector that she was currently in, and the third sector, she could find it easiest. Setting out, she anticipated the worst, especially considering that she still had no information about the mobile magic sources which she had seen.

She passed through the first sector without much interaction. A few snakes, some of them venomous, crossed her path. Flies swarmed around her, but she knew every one of them, so she was not frightened. Rodents scampered about, fish swam through the stagnant water, and plants tried to draw what nutrients they could from the swamp. Hecate was slightly enchanted by the beauty there was in the depraved infrastructure of the swamp. Even in filth and stench, there was an equilibrium. The more time she spent there, the more she was growing to appreciate it.

Hecate had always been attune to nature. While others may have called what she did magic, she would have defined it as simply natural. After all, nothing that she did was beyond the scope of what anyone else could have done, given the appropriate talent. The only difference was that she knew how things were composed and how to manipulate them into her own definition. If there were others who could do the same, they would have had no problem doing exactly what she did, and even greater things still. The power in nature was beyond any that existed in the metaphysical world. That was one of the reasons why Hecate had never taken an apprentice. While she trusted herself to not abuse the powers, finding another whom she trusted equally would have been difficult. Through her long existence, she had seen how intensely power corrupted even the most benign soul, and also how much damage the abuse of power could inflict. For that reason, she had been hesitant to train another in that knowledge.

The only other individual who she would have been comfortable sharing that part of herself with would have been Nemesis. Ironically, Nemesis was likely the only individual who had no interest in those properties.

The journey through the first sector was as uneventful as she had anticipated it being. Before she entered the third sector, Hecate ran a sensory test over the area to see where the magical high points were. There were several of them, and they all roamed freely with no immediately predictable pattern, as though they were animals or living creatures of some sort. Interacting with the air around her, she created a light reflecting shield, which would allow her to pass through the area unseen. Still, she stepped daintily, being careful to not leave any evidence of her trek. After only a short time, she saw how valuable that defensive technique was.

She first saw the magical creature as it bored in and out of the ground. When she noticed it, she recoiled in shock, and only strong restraint prevented her from crying out in surprise. There before her, as unassuming and casual as a man in his private bathhouse, was a creature that she had never seen before. It stood upright, so that it might have resembled a man, had it not been for the tight coat of scales, which shown with a deep blood red, and a long, prehensile tail. The tongue which darted out of its long, pointed mouth and the talons on its hands and feet suggested that it was a lizard, and Hecate would have accepted that it was, had the creature not stood upright and held a long spear within its claws. Hecate examined it closer, witnessing it moving about in both an upright position, standing as though human, and a slither, as if it were a lizard.

Hecate considered the creature for only a moment, before a second, similar creature joined it, also armed with a spear. The two hissed at one another as they approached each other, but it didn't seem as though it were an overly aggressive noise. Instead, the two creatures raised their spears and tapped the tips of their weapons together before wrapping their tails together briefly, in a sort of manufactured salute. Hecate marveled at the creatures' civility, both toward each other and in their nature. She pondered on whether or not these creatures could be the source of the mobile magic signatures that she had noticed. She wondered who else knew about these strange, oddly civilized creatures. She considered what she ought to call them, realizing that they were hardly dragons, but neither were they salamanders. Giggling silently to herself, Hecate named them dramanders, on the off-chance that no one had named their species before.

The second dramander began to approach her position. Hecate quietly stepped out of its way, unwilling to reveal herself to these creatures yet. As the dramander drew past her area, he froze. Quickly dropping to all fours in a clearly defensive stance, he began to flick his tongue into the air, rapidly rotating his head to investigate a wider area. Hecate realized that the creature had smelled her. While her shield may be refracting light and reflection, it could not eliminate scent. The dramander locked eyes with the other, as though silently communicating with it, and the other dropped to all fours, before slithering over to join his brother in his investigation.

Thinking quickly, Hecate moved as silently as she could to the base of a tree. She was startled when she saw the heads of the dramanders following her movement, as though they were watching her directly. While carefully maintaining her shield, Hecate refined the air around her to create a reflective bubble. After doing that, she made the bubble itself lighter than air.

Her shield prevented her from dropping out of the bubble as it floated with the wind. Hecate used the trees for stability and guidance as she floated through the air, generally in the direction of the fifth quadrant. The dramanders watched her movement, until she floated out of their field of vision, but they did not pursue her. The only thing that continued to bother her was that they now had her scent. They clearly had a way of communicating with each other. Hecate had little doubt that they would transmit the information to their larger community.

As she continued to float toward her destination, seeing no point in lowering herself to the ground yet, Hecate was not exactly astonished to see many other dramanders roaming the area, many of whom looked up at her invisible bubble with a curious flick of their tongue. That was concerning, but Hecate could not become overly obsessed with that thought. After all, while the dramanders were fascinating and potentially dangerous, they could not be her concern at that moment.

Moving into the fifth quadrant through the air, Hecate lowered herself to the ground once more. She eliminated the bubble that she had been floating in, and only then did she realize how much energy and magic she had been draining from herself keeping the bubble in place around her. It was as if a weight had been lifted from her back, a weight that she hadn't realized she'd been carrying. Maintaining the two spells simultaneously must have been more trying than she had realized.

Fortunately, there didn't seem to be any dramanders in the area, so Hecate felt secure enough to let her shield down. She approached the source of the magic, the one that she was convinced was the gem, in full view, with confidence. As she drew closer to it, the ground around her became rougher, and Hecate noticed that an entire network of roots lay just beneath the surface. She could feel the twisting knots, the complicated weaving, all of it coming from one origin. When she eventually came into sight of that source, she smiled.

The tree was massive, as Hecate had imagined it would be, with a truck the size of a castle, and branches that spread out into infinity. It breathed life and energy, and its power made Hecate's skin quiver with glee. Everything about the tree seemed to pull her toward it, and she never wanted to be away from it. Its beauty and its strength were the only things that were missing from her life, and she could not be complete without the tree.

It took her a long moment to realize why this was: the gem was locked within the tree.

Hecate reached out with her magic, and she could feel the gem within the tree's trunk. She could remove it without damaging the tree very much at all, and she intended to do that. Focusing her magic into a precise point, she began to cast it deep into the body of the tree.

The moment that she attempted to do so, she found her magic rebuffed. Startled, she realized that something was preventing her from retrieving the gem. As the ground around her began to rumble, she realized that the tree's roots were moving beneath her, rising toward the surface.

This beautiful tree was holding the gem, and it was not willing to let it go. If Hecate wanted the gem, she was going to have to fight for it.

CHAPTER TWELVE

THE ROOTS BEGAN TO RUMBLE AND CHURN ANGRILY BENEATH her feet, and Hecate had to dance out of the way. She restored the shield, enveloping herself in protective energy, before returning to her work on the tree.

Almost immediately, Hecate felt an opposing power pushing hard against her, trying to tear her magic apart. She should have anticipated that. The tree, after all, was a strong and powerful magical signature, and she should have anticipated defensive properties. It took her by surprise though, and it nearly caused her to lose her concentration. The magics working against her were strong, it was true, but her magic was stronger. She had to focus on her goal.

Hecate could feel her goal within reach. Piercing the trunk of the tree had not been as difficult as she had thought and, while dividing her concentration between keeping her shield intact and reaching for the gem was extremely draining, she was getting closer to her goal than she had ever dreamed possible. Ecstasy was beginning to erupt in her mind: she was going to save the Olympians!

Of course, she had thought too soon. Just as she could feel the gem practically between her magical fingers, a wall of repulsion struck her, pushing her back. It had appeared from nowhere and taken her completely by surprise. Hecate fell back in shock, both magically and physically, feeling her magics crumble and the unforgiving firmness of the hard Earth beneath her backside.

She began to stand again, but found that she was prevented from doing so. Her magical shield had been dismantled, and the roots were taking advantage of that. Reaching out of the ground, they wrapped around her legs, securing her to the spot. Another root rose from between her feet, crawling up the inside of her thigh, quickly reaching her pelvis, then her torso, then her neck. It fastened a collar around her throat, and constricted, choking her.

Hecate resisted the urge to panic as her mind raced for a solution. Reaching into the aether, she found flammable aspects to the air around her. Igniting them, Hecate set the roots that had held her legs aflame. As she had anticipated, they retreated, releasing her extremities. The chord about her throat was thinner but more precise. Planting her feet against the ground, she wrapped her hands about it and ripped it savagely from the Earth. Once the root had been torn from its life force, the constriction about her throat ceased, and she was able to disregard the root easily.

As she did so, small roots began to wrap their way around her feet, preventing her retreat. Fortunately, they had not been secured, and Hecate was easily able to tear them up through the power of her feet alone. The moment that her foot was free, Hecate revived the shield around her, rose about a foot into the air, and returned her focus toward the gem.

The tree's magic reacted even stronger this time. At almost the exact area where she had been struck before, it lashed out at her again. She had been anticipating it this time, however, and while she was still thrust from the tree, she was able to maintain her shield. It was fortunate that she had, since she could see the roots beneath her, throbbing with an inhumane lust to hold her down and crush the life out of her.

Before Hecate resumed her advance into the tree, she considered her situation. There had to be another area to attack from. Once again, she created a bubble around herself, made it weightless, and she began to float into the air. Grasping at branches as she climbed into the atmosphere, Hecate found it more and more difficult to maintain the integrity of the bubble around herself, especially since it seemed as though the branches themselves seem set on compromising it. Of course, after thinking on that for only a moment, she realized that they likely were. This tree was trying to prevent her from retrieving the gem, so of course it was attempting to break down her protections. Hecate had thought that rising into the air would give her a better attack point, but it seemed that she had only given the tree another weapon which it could use against her.

Not wanting her efforts to be completely in vain, Hecate reached into the tree while she was still afloat. She bored into the tree, reaching for the gem. Then, before the magical repulsion could strike her again, she considered that thought. If she were struck while in the air, the magic would surely burst the bubble which protected her at the moment and she would fall from a great height. Even if the fall didn't kill her, the roots were waiting for her at the ground. This was probably not the best option.

As she was considering the best way to proceed, the wall of repulsive magic burst forth. She felt its power around her, but it didn't interact with her. She had stopped her invasive force just short of the area where it had struck her before. It was curious that the magic had initiated so early, unless it had been triggered and failed to anticipate her stoppage. If that were true, it meant that Hecate had just avoided the field by sheer luck. If it were untrue, and Hecate continued her invasion, she was damning herself.

Hecate continued her reach for the gem carefully, aware with each inch that she may be struck and killed at any moment. She did not have to be afraid for very long: she reached the gem quickly. There it was before her, and she could see it with her mind's eye. It shone with a glistening, deep red energy, cut into angles which hadn't been defined, radiating with power beyond what any man should have. It was smaller than Hecate had anticipated it being but larger than it probably needed to be. The elements of the gem were magical, but primal, yet mystical, foreign, and completely domestic. It seemed to contradict everything that had ever been known, while confirming the truth, simply through its existence.

Hecate understood then why the tree had fought so hard to protect it. Everything in her wanted to understand the gem and to have it with her at all times.

Wrapping her magics around the gem, she wrenched at it, pulling it from the body of the tree. The tree reacted, trying desperately to hold onto it, but it simply became a battle of wills after that, and Hecate's was stronger. She pulled the gem, and the tree pulled back. She wrenched at the gem, and the tree grasped at the element that she was now holding. After a time, she succeeded at wrenching the gem free. To her shock and awe, she began to remove the gem from the tree.

Once she got past the initial struggle, the removal process came with little resistance. It was as if the tree had known that the gem was lost. She felt the tree weeping, begging her to return the gem to its place, and that tugged at her heart. She hated the feeling of betrayal that she felt from the tree, and she despised the trembling guilt which flooded her now. Without the gem, the tree had lost its purpose. Its entire identity was wrapped into the gem, and it felt as though it would die without it. Hecate felt her own magic tremble as reluctant tears filled her eyes. The tree felt as though she was killing it, and she hated that. Was she not a goddess of the Earth? How could she betray an Earth element like this?

It had to be done. That sentiment did little to relieve her guilt, but the fact remained. She needed the gem. More than that, Olympus needed the gem.

The gem came free of the tree moments later. As it burst from the tree's trunk, Hecate felt the tree's magic crumble. She lowered herself to the ground with the gem in tow. Once there, she lowered her protective shield, placing the gem within her hand. The gem's power pulsed through her fingers, and she shuddered at what she felt. Turning away, Hecate began to leave to the swamp, hearing the wails of the tree after her, accusing her of killing it, begging her to stay close.

Hecate was holding the Gem of Illecebra. She needed to get it out of her hands as quickly as possible. Its magic was already beginning to take hold of her mind.

CHAPTER THIRTEEN

I<small>NSIDE</small> O<small>BLIVION</small>, D<small>IONYSUS</small>' <small>BAR, THE OCCUPANTS WOULD HAVE</small> said that they were having the time of their lives. That would have been ironic, since time didn't exist within Oblivion.

Being the god of wine and theater, Dionysus naturally had wanted to run an establishment that his customers would never want to leave. That was not difficult for him to manufacture. After all, he was the epitome of charm, and he knew how to please a crowd. The complications came when people who didn't want to leave were required to, thanks to scheduling conflicts. It took him a bit of time to figure out how to deal with that but, eventually, a solution came to him. With the guarantee that he would supply a significant amount of the best wine in his stock to Olympus, Dionysus was granted permission from Zeus to construct a bar in an area where time didn't pass. While the world continued to spin on the outside of the bar, Oblivion's occupants were not affected by the passing of time.

While it was true that the smarter customers still kept track of time while they were in Oblivion, it was surprisingly easy to get them to forget about those things after two or three chalices of wine.

Donating the wine to Olympus as a form of rent was a pain, since it meant that he couldn't sell it to his customers, but Dionysus quickly realized that Zeus didn't know much about wine. As long as Dionysus sang the praises of a certain vintage loudly enough, Zeus would either believe that it was spectacular or he would be too embarrassed to admit that he didn't care for it.

Oblivion was absolutely the place to be. Inside, one would find dryads and nymphs, satyrs and sirens, Olympians, and emissaries from pantheons far away. In one corner, one could possibly find the Norse goddess Sif exchanging fashion advice with Aphrodite, while somewhere else, Persephone debated the moral principles of the afterlife with the Egyptian god, Set. On the stage, there was usually entertainment of some sort, or there was about to be, and it was always of the highest quality. Somewhere, one was almost guaranteed to find Cthulhu, slowly nursing the darkest, richest of wines, dreaming of worlds to devour.

Oblivion really was the time of a lifetime. It was ironic.

Hecate didn't go to Oblivion all that often. It was not as if she didn't enjoy drinking with the other Olympians, or anyone else really. It was simply that she rarely took the opportunity to escape from time. It actually seemed to her to be a dangerous prospect, and one that could easily be abused. Still, Dionysus seemed to be running a fairly solid establishment. She had not heard of anything overly bad occurring there.

Plus, after what she had just gone through, she needed a strong drink.

After leaving the swamp, Hecate had returned to her temple and changed clothes. Horace had, of course, been overjoyed at seeing her and amazed by the acquisition of the Gem of Illecebra. After changing into her usual social clothing, a soft, white chiton and a pair of sandals, Hecate considered leaving the gem behind. She then realized that nobody would ever believe that she had found it without her carrying it with her and, since a large part of her going to the bar was to seek advice on how best to use it, she would need proof of her accomplishment. That being the case, Hecate wrapped in the gem in a small pouch and hung it from her hip.

Walking into the bar, Hecate had to admit that she was impressed. Pan was currently on the stage, playing his flute, and the music he was supplying was enchanting. Behind him, Orpheus was playing the lyre, just for support, while one of the Gemini brothers played percussion, and a naiad was singing beautifully, but the focus was obviously Pan. Every eye was turned toward the stage, and every ear was tuned to the music. It flowed through the atmosphere like soft silk, and the audience hung on every note. After a refrain, Pan lowered his flute, and began to sing.

In history, there are lies when poets stop to rhyme
In time, there is abuse when vocalists don't sing
Historians don't record those crimes
Books won't remember a thing
Remember me when this song ends
When music stops, and lyrics cease
Remember who I am
In history

The music ended softly, but it hung in the atmosphere for several moments after the song had finished. Hecate was filled with amazement at the gift that this satyr had just given the bar. It was a magic all of his own, more powerful in some ways than anything Hecate could do. In the music, she had felt pain, longing, memories of lost love, pleadings for future events, and so much else. Before this, she had never thought of Pan as anything but a trickster, and maybe even a nuisance at times. That song forced her to reevaluate everything that she knew about him. As the crowd applauded, Hecate made her way through the mass toward the bar, her head still ringing with the impact of the music.

As she took a seat at the bar, Dionysus slid up to her, wearing his signature, generous smile. "A new song from Pan, and a rare visit from the goddess Hecate," he laughed. "This really is a great night for me!"

"Is it night, though?" Hecate smiled back, allowing her eyes to flirt with the bartender, playfully. "I thought the charm of this place was that night never came."

"That's true," Dionysus replied, his eyebrows dancing seductively. "It's also true that the night's never over. It all depends on how you'd like to define this reality."

Hecate laughed, laying her hand on Dionysus arm, affectionately. "That's a very good point, sir," she giggled.

The moment that Hecate's hand touched Dionysus, she felt electricity surge through her fingers, sparking against his skin. At the touch, Dionysus jumped with surprise and, for the first time in their relationship, Hecate saw his charm pause. It was only for a brief moment, but she noticed it, and it frightened her. Hesitantly, she took her hand back.

"Wow," Dionysus shook his head, as if clearing cobwebs, "that was some punch you've got there!"

Reaching under the bar, he removed a bottle of red wine, popped it open, and poured a glass, which he pushed toward Hecate. "It's on the house," he informed her. "Now, why don't you tell me what you've gotten yourself into?"

Hecate took a deep breath, and sipped the wine. Dry tones and fruity textures flooded her senses, as she tried to find the words to explain the situation. She sighed.

"I," she began haltingly, "found something."

"That's fairly obvious," Dionysus said, lowering his voice, leaning across the bar toward her. "What did you find?"

"I found the Gem of Illecebra."

"Don't lie," Dionysus sneered, his eyes growing slanted with disbelief. "That gem doesn't exist."

Hecate brought the pouch that held the gem up and placed it on the bar counter. Dionysus carefully opened the pouch and peered inside. His jaw dropped in astonishment, and his eyes practically sprang from his skull. Hecate watched with a mixture of fascination, surprise, and fear at the range of emotions which rapidly flickered across Dionysus' face.

The act of wrenching his eyes away from the gem seemed to place Dionysus in physical pain. "Put that away," he gasped, once he was able to form words. "Seriously, you don't want to attract attention. Put it away."

Hecate closed the pouch, and slipped it back to its place against her hip. Dionysus shook his head as his eye refocused, and his reality filtered back into place. Once he had breath again, he laughed.

"I can't believe you found it," he chuckled as he poured himself a glass of wine from the same bottle he had offered Hecate. "No one else will either. You are unbelievable. That gem...what you have done...you are unbelievable."

Hecate felt herself blush a bit at the compliment. "Thank you," she said, smiling modestly. "I didn't do it for the praise, I did it for Olympus. Since we are at war, I thought that this was the way to sway the war in our favor. What do you think that I should do with it?"

Dionysus cringed as he considered the question. "The business man in me wants you to just leave it here, since it would draw an incredible crowd," he muttered, behind darting, nervous eyes. "I know that your motivations are pure, though, and mine wouldn't be."

After a quick scan of the room, his eyes fell on a center table. At the table sat a petite woman, covered in a purple shawl, which deftly covered the chain armor beneath it. Her hazel eyes pierced the souls of those who looked into them, as her hair, the shade of the night sky, shimmered with the light of forgotten stars, trapped within its swirling mass. She sat alone, nursing a glass of red wine. On her shoulder sat an owl, who scanned the room casually, his head turning about in a circle. Dionysus considered her, smiled a casual smirk, and nodded.

"Athena," he stated, directing Hecate's vision toward the woman.

"She's the goddess of wisdom, after all. I have little doubt that she'd be able to guide you to where you need to be."

Hecate nodded, finished the last of her drink, and reached into her coin purse to pay for the beverage. Dionysus smiled slyly, refusing her money, and Hecate leaned across the bar to embrace him affectionately on the cheek. The tender kiss created sparks that took both parties by surprise, and Dionysus stepped back, wide-eyed.

"I, um," he stammered, uncharacteristically lost for words, "I think you need to get rid of that thing...quickly..."

Hecate nodded, her own eyes growing large with a mixture of surprise and fear. Standing from the bar, she turned toward Athena's table. Before she was half-way there, the owl on Athena's shoulder turned to her. Hecate felt his eyes peering into her, and she paused in her advance. Athena straightened her back and turned to Hecate. Her eyes gleamed with a cold, calculated depth, but her full, red lips smiled warmly. She nodded to the empty seat at her table.

"Join me, Hecate," she spoke across the loud bar. "I have a feeling that we have items to discuss."

Hecate nodded and took the offered seat. Something about the way that the owl had looked at her hinted that he had already determined the subject of conversation, but that would have been impossible. While Hecate had been associated with Athena in the past, it was never in an intimate forum, and there was no way that she could have known about her venture. The owl was not psychic. There was no way that she had any idea what Hecate currently carried with her.

Still, as the goddess looked at her across the table, eyes twinkling with an otherworldly energy, Hecate still felt as if she knew.

"So," Athena asked in a low tone, warm but serious, "what is this matter you'd like my advice on?"

"The Olympians are at war with the foreign pantheons," Hecate inquired. It was a statement, since she knew it to be true, but she found herself intimidated by Athena, so the statement came out more as an inquiry.

Athena nodded. "That is true," she confirmed. "Only half of us will admit it, but the war is real. Nothing can change that."

"Perhaps something can," Hecate muttered, taking the pouch which contained the gem from her hip and beginning to open it.

"Stop," Athena commanded her, all warmth draining from her voice.

Hecate froze in surprise, her fingers clasping the drawstrings to the pouch. She looked at Athena with a confused frown. "I was just going to show you—" she began.

"I know what you were going to show me," Athena cut her off. "Yes, I know that it isn't a myth. I have always known. The reason that I haven't tried to gather it myself is because it is too powerful. It contributed to the downfall of Atlantis, and it will tear down any party that holds it for too long. You may be attempting to aid Olympus by providing it to Zeus, but you would cause more damage, indirectly."

Hecate closed the pouch securely, dropping it into her lap. She cocked her head at Athena. "You are wisdom," she said, in a mild, slightly curious voice. "I would be a fool to question you. What, then, should be done with the gem?"

"The gem cannot be destroyed," Athena said, lowering her head, and glancing around the room for potential listeners. "You must hide it. Hide it further away than it was hidden before. Hide it somewhere that it cannot be found again."

"How can I accomplish that?" Hecate queried. "Is there anywhere that can guarantee the gem's invisibility?"

"There is one place," Athena informed her.

Hecate opened her mouth to ask where, but closed it again as the answer occurred to her. The owl turned to her, as if confirming the realization. There was nowhere on Earth that was safe for the gem to be hidden, nowhere that man could not find it.

Hecate would have to hide the gem in time.

CHAPTER FOURTEEN

NEMESIS LOOKED DOWN ON THE WORLD FROM WHERE SHE perched, with a cold, analytical glare. Lifting the directional beacon that Hephaestus had given her from her hip, she saw it pointing her toward the middle of the city. This meant that she would need to blend in. Nemesis hated blending in.

Cupid had hung up with her after denying her invitation, but that was all right. He probably would have read too much into the invitation, anyway. Nemesis had no interest in developing a relationship, romantic or otherwise, with Cupid. His innate ability to sense and generate strong emotional fields would have made him a valuable companion on this venture though. Aside from that, it was easier for a woman to blend in when they were with a partner. Many men, when in a social arena, will see a woman with a partner, and never see them again. It was part of the game that men played, and Nemesis had decided to simply accept it as a symptom of their pathology. Disregarding the fact that it was subtly insulting, suggesting that she only existed if she was available for procreative activities, Nemesis found that it was easier to get her work done if men paid less attention to her.

Through the centuries, Nemesis had watched as her name faded into near obscurity; when one referred to "nemesis", it was in the form of an adjective, and the speaker was likely referencing their own or a third party's enemy. Nemesis realized that very few would care to remember the goddess of divine justice; after all, it wasn't as if she had done much to ingratiate herself into human culture. The fact that no one remembered her much didn't detract from her mission.

Nemesis was perched on the rooftop of a high rise, just outside the downtown area. The sun had set three hours ago, at about eight in the evening, and she would need to hurry if she wanted to complete her maneuver before the sunrise. Flexing her shoulders, she felt the outline of her sword hanging down her back. It would be invisible until she needed it, but she knew that it was there. The shoulder flex had become something of a habit that she used to center herself. Reminding herself that her sword was there gave her focus and drive, and it revealed to her what she needed to get done.

Currently, she was dressed in a skintight black bodysuit, constructed of a thin poly-blend, which Hephaestus had constructed. It would stop bullets, as if they were really a threat, but it wouldn't interfere with her movement. The suit clung to her curves like a second skin, hugging her athletic form tightly. Over the body suit, Nemesis wore a dark, hooded cowl, which made her feel a bit more modest, but still didn't obstruct her movement. This society was strange and conflicting, glorifying sex as though the very act were a god, yet shaming women for their bodies and the artistic ways which they displayed them. Sexuality had never been a concern for Nemesis, since she had never taken a suitor and she cared little for how she was perceived. Still. the duality of modern culture was something to consider. She would need to change into something more socially acceptable before descending into the city.

Crouching low, Nemesis leaped from the rooftop where she had been crouched in the direction of an adjacent building. Toward the apex of her leap, she reached to her hip and thrust a grappling hook in the direction that she was jumping. The hook deftly latched onto the other building's rooftop, and Nemesis climbed her way onto the roof with little effort. Hearing the sounds of traffic beneath her, she broke into a sprint, each footfall expertly landing with a cat's grace. She reached the building's edge and, once again and without pause, she leaped into the night.

The third building was a bit closer, and she hit the rooftop without the use of the grappling hook. Absorbing the impact of the landing, Nemesis dropped into a crouch, rolled, and hopped to her feet. A small gathering of pigeons who had been observing her with some interest coo-ed approvingly before flying into the air, unwilling to share their rooftop with such an agile force of nature. Standing up, Nemesis felt the chill of the evening air bite into the skin of her shrouded face. Lowering the hood, she allowed it to dance in her hair. There was no need to remain disguised here on the roof, since there was no one to see her anyway, save for the pigeons. Nemesis doubted that the pigeons would share their discovery.

Hades had first discovered the anomaly. After the Olympians had been forced into exile, he had set in place a system of triggers which would alert him to the emergence of any great objects of power directly tied to the Olympians. Of course, the triggers rarely worked as they were supposed to but, since mineralogy was tied to Hades' signature properties, they were particularly sensitive toward gemstones. When Hades learned about the sudden appearance of a new signature, it took him a little time to decipher its identity. After he had, he quickly told Persephone, his wife, and she relayed the news to Hephaestus. Hephaestus didn't believe it at first, but had shared the news with Nemesis anyway. That was why she was here now, on a building's rooftop, peering into the night, holding the device which Hephaestus had given her: she was tracking the Gem of Illecebra.

There was no time to contemplate the absurdity of her venture, searching for an item which had long been thought a myth, even among the Olympians who had, themselves, become myth amongst human culture. Right now, all that Nemesis could focus on was researching the signature. If the evidence was confirmed, then it complicated more than just the lives of the Olympians. Nemesis pushed those thoughts to the back of her head as she considered the city beneath her. Consulting the device, she saw that the signature was close at hand. It was time for her to descend into the city streets.

While on the rooftop, Nemesis changed into the outfit that she would wear in the city. It was less of a physical change, of course, and more of a change in the way that people perceive her. Instead of seeing a dark woman in a cowl, they would see an attractive woman in an expensive evening dress. Persephone had suggested the outfit: she had noted that the signature was coming from a more social area of downtown, and it was possibly located inside a dance club. Nemesis had accepted that determination, but under a few conditions.

Because she was not changing, physically, her maneuverability would not be compromised by the three-inch stilettos which appeared on her feet. Her armor remained in place, and her dignity unblemished by the tight, long, silver, gown, slit on either side from hem to mid-calf. Her ample breasts remained concealed as the gown rose to meet behind her neck, which revealed her strong shoulders. Dark eyes, a dainty nose, and full, deep lips filled out her face, and a gorgeous flowing mane of thick, black hair fell down her back in natural waves. The body which she wore was not as thin as she was usually, but broader hips gave her the impression of power and dominance. Her skin, a sultry shade of caramel, blended evenly over her bodily structure, flawless, save for a dark mark on the back of her right shoulder. The blemish had been important to Nemesis. In the form that Persephone had constructed for her, she appeared almost too perfect, and she didn't want to risk being identified.

Persephone had reminded her that humans no longer believed in the Olympians, thus making that hesitation a bit over-dramatized. Nemesis agreed that the risk was minimal, but she had insisted on the flaw regardless.

Walking to the edge of the roof, Nemesis stepped off of it and plummeted toward the ground with the freedom of wind. After falling three stories, Nemesis took hold of a ledge, stopping her free fall abruptly, before planting her feet against the building and propelling herself backward toward the ground once again. Nemesis repeated the process, with some modifications, until all seventeen stories of the building had been scaled. It wasn't until the fifth floor from the ground that Nemesis thought to make sure that no pedestrians were observing her. Quickly scoping the area, she found no peering eyes, but thought it prudent to land in the alley next to the building.

She landed deftly on the balls of her feet. As she looked around the area where she had landed, Nemesis found bags filled with various refuse, all in different degrees of decay. She found food that looked as though it had hardly been touched next to filthy rags and used diapers. With a cocked eyebrow, Nemesis considered that even the filth of this generation was still more sanitary (and smelled better) than Ancient Greece. Standing up straight, she rolled her shoulders back and secured her posture, before noticing movement in one area of the trash pile. Thinking that it might be a rat or another type of rodent, Nemesis took a step toward it, just to make sure. A disheveled, unshaven man, wearing the cologne of sewage, stepped from within the trash, holding a half-eaten pastry and looking at her curiously.

"Hello," he said, cautiously, a row of stained, unwashed teeth appearing behind his lips. "I hope you don't find me invasive, but where did you just come from?"

"I was just walking by, when I heard you moving about," Nemesis replied, as casually as possible. "I came to investigate the noise."

"You didn't, though," the man shook his head. "You fell out of the sky."

The man pointed toward the building which Nemesis had just come down, his finger tracing it upwards, as if to eliminate any suspicion that Nemesis might have as to which direction the sky was in.

91

Analyzing the man, Nemesis saw a certain wildness in his unfocused eyes. Were he to relate the story to anyone, they would never believe him, even though what he was saying was the truth. Telling him what happened would be easier than concocting an elaborate story to explain her appearance. She wasn't supposed to reveal herself to humans, but there was no avoiding it now.

"I am Nemesis, the goddess of divine retribution, enforcer of justice," she explained. "I've come here to search for the Gem of—"

"Oh, fuck off," the filthy man snarled, hurling his partially digested pastry at her. "I'm homeless, not stupid. Why don't you just scamper off to your nightclub or wine tasting, or whatever you rich bitches do, and get the hell out of my house?"

The pastry bounced off of Nemesis knee, and nearly ignited her temper. As the man turned from her, returning to his pile of trash to find more baked goods, she felt her anger stirring her to strike him down. Taking a deep breath, Nemesis turned from the alley, walking out onto the sidewalk. That reaction, after all, may have been the most fortunate thing to come from the situation.

Nemesis then was forced to consider whether she was more offended by the man's lack of belief in her story or the association which he implied, of her being upper class. Either way, the interaction had concluded, and further consideration wouldn't accomplish anything.

Walking the sidewalk, Nemesis checked the location device, disguised as a wristwatch. The signature directed her straight forward, toward an area surrounding a trendy-looking nightclub. Her walk never slowed, nor did she deviate as she approached the area.

It was Wednesday night. Wednesday was, perhaps, the least enticing night to be out on. Situated midway between workweek and weekend, finding a point to be out and social on Wednesday was difficult. After all, the depression of getting back to work that haunts Monday has faded to acceptance, and the excitement of the approaching weekend is not likely to set in until Thursday evening. What little enticement had existed when the night began faded quickly as the night progressed. By midnight, practically the only people out were the third-shift workers who were wishing they were in, homeless people who were wishing they had somewhere to be, and those few individuals who still believed that being in before one o'clock would somehow make them less relevant.

Bars and nightclubs who remained opened at one o'clock on Wednesday were typically empty or close to it. Managers often argued with owners over the sense of remaining open so late in the middle of the week and, rather than listen to their managers, the owners would insist on instating special discounts and drink deals to tempt the customers who were, more than likely, already in bed. None of these deals or temptations were ever enough to draw a substantial crowd.

That wasn't the case currently outside of Obsession. Obsession, a modest nightclub with an under-whelming physique, somehow had a line of people, waiting to gain entrance. There was such demand that the manager had actually needed to call in a doorman and extra security to prevent overcrowding. It's almost curious that the thought of supernatural influence had never once crossed the manager's mind. He just thought that he was running a cool club.

When Nemesis caught sight of Obsession, she knew that she had found what she had been searching for. Not only did the device which Hephaestus had given her explode with an almost red hot energy, but she could feel it, in her body and in her mind. There was something inside that club that she desperately needed. She would not be satisfied until she was inside.

Judging from the crowd outside of the club, she was not the only person feeling that way. Had she not been precisely attuned to the sensation, Nemesis might have thought that she was simply feeling an intense urge. Still, because she had been anticipating it, she knew what she was feeling: the Gem of Illecebra was drawing her. Since she was aware of it, the draw was intensified. Nemesis didn't understand how the gem worked, but she knew the effect when she felt it.

Stepping toward the club, Nemesis moved effortlessly through the crowd, which practically parted for her as though she were a bull driving through a mass of rabbits. Somewhere in the mass, a man reached out his hand to stop her. He gripped her shoulder, and Nemesis spun slowly to look him in the eye. The man (a tall, thin man, wearing eyeshadow, black leather pants, and who had shoulder length black hair, betrayed by dark brown roots) stared at her coldly for a moment, and Nemesis saw him. He was an accountant by day who had never been in a successful relationship, and he was afraid of his own fetishes. All he wanted was love, but he had settled for toleration so long that he thought love was unachievable. Nemesis saw him: he was weak and muted, with fantasies that made him blush. He was a pervert, he knew it. Now, Nemesis knew it as well.

She also saw that he had never, and would never, act on his desires. He was too ashamed of himself. As the man stared at her, his cautionary hand slipped from her shoulder. He dropped his gaze within seconds, apologizing for having the nerve to touch her. Nemesis nodded confidently and returned to her direct route toward the entrance.

The security guard at the entrance stepped into her way, as if he would halt her. Nemesis locked eyes with him. He was stronger than the former individual had been, but also less guarded with less shame. Nemesis saw the children who had bullied him in grade school for being large and clumsy. She saw the woman who had used him to play a joke on her real boyfriend, assuming that he understood the joke. Nemesis saw the unfinished Political Science degree, the stage acting experience, the woman whom he had cheated on, and the women who had cheated on him.

"Right this way, ma'am," he muttered, dropping his gaze and stepping aside. Nemesis smiled, raised her hand, and brushed it down the side of his face as she walked through the door. She rarely touched people, nor did she like to, but something about this man made her feel as though she ought to acknowledge him. As she heard the unhappy people, complaining about how she had gotten through while the rest of the crowd needed to wait in line, she felt some sympathy for his position. She smiled to herself as she felt his eyes, staring at her in wonder, as she walked away. Walking away was the point, though, and looking back was not an option.

The club was loud, and the music was pulsing. The occupants of the dance floor either clung desperately to their partner, hungrily striving to be seen, or they danced alone, complete in their solitude. Nemesis moved through the dancers, some chaotic and some rhythmic, with poise. She made her way to the wet bar against the back wall and sat down on one of the stools. Almost immediately, she felt alien eyes upon her.

"Hey," a voice with a slight slur broached her ears from over her shoulder. "Are you from around here?"

The aroma of cheap beer and cigarettes wafted through the air, and Nemesis breathed deeply. There was no point in even acknowledging the speaker, since he was not the purpose for her being there. She didn't need to see him. Instead, Nemesis signaled the bartender.

"Yeah, me neither," the speaker continued to press, this time sliding into a seat beside her. "I'm just passing through, and looking for things to do in the middle of the week. This place seemed like a big deal, so I came in, and found you."

Nemesis could tell that he was lying, but she had no idea why he would need to lie about something like that. He was local, perhaps 45 years old, and he probably had both a family and a career. At the moment, he was dressed in old jeans and a graphic t-shirt, but his mannerisms suggested that this was a disguise. Were she to look deeper into him, Nemesis could have all the answers to these questions, but she didn't have time to care. She would have to be satisfied with speculation for the moment.

"You can pretend like you don't see me," the man chuckled. "I kind of like when women play hard to get."

The bartender stepped up at that moment, asking Nemesis if she needed something to drink.

"I'd like a glass of Merlot," she replied "and a moment with your manager, if it's not too much trouble."

The bartender opened his mouth to ask about the subject of the meeting but reconsidered quickly. He went about preparing Nemesis' drink, and alerting his boss that there was someone here to see him.

"Merlot, huh?" the man beside her crooned, attempting to sound smooth as he slid closer to her. "Classy woman."

Nemesis rolled her eyes. "I wonder how that meeting with the manager is going to go," she sighed, loud enough for the man to hear. "There is so much that I need to discuss with him."

Surprisingly, the man took the hint, stood up, and relocated further down the bar, placing a handful of stools between the two of them. By that time, the bartender brought Nemesis her wine with the alert that the manager would be right out. Nemesis thanked him and sipped her wine delicately. It tasted strong and true.

CHAPTER FIFTEEN

NAMING A CLUB OBSESSION HAD SEEMED LIKE A LOGICAL thing. After all, if one were to insinuate that others ought to be obsessed with a location, it would at least pique a person's interest. That had been the idea when Adam Rizziole had first opened the location, in the less-savory side of Cleveland. He could have used his father's money, or the family connections to open it in a more successful district, but Adam had never shied away from a challenge.

The club had been robbed three times within the first five months of being opened. There had been a prostitution bust less than a block down the street, a handful of drug charges on patrons of his club, a few acts of violence, and a really bad dubstep DJ. It was about that time, when Adam had been mugged while walking to his car, that he decided, maybe, he needed a new location. Obsession closed its doors, having been open only seven months.

That, of course, did very little to slow Adam down. He found a new location in a more reputable place, and began construction on the club a month before the original location was shut down. For this one, he did have to ask his father for some collateral, and he hated that more than he could have imagined. It wasn't as if Guillermo

Rizziole was reluctant or begrudging toward the financial investment; quite the opposite, in fact. Guillermo had always rushed to help his son out anytime that Adam needed it. On top of that, Guillermo never asked for the money back, nor did he request "special favors". Adam was aware that his father had the best of intentions, but he wanted to do things for himself. He wanted to feel as though he had accomplished something.

Now, Obsession had been opened for two years, and Adam was feeling pretty good about things. He had paid his father back for the investment, and Guillermo had turned the money into an even larger investment, becoming a full partner. Adam had needed to accept that. His father had assured him that he would be a silent partner, staying out of the day-to-day work. It had worked out pretty well, up to that point.

Behind the bar there was a plaque, which held a picture of the original club. If one were to look at it closely, you could see the urban underbelly, the seedy clientele, and you would wonder why anyone would think to open a club in an area like that. Adam didn't see it that way. When he looked at the picture, he saw the first thing that he had done on his own.

Business was surprisingly good. Shockingly so, in fact. Adam had never expected to have a full house on a Wednesday night. Two weeks ago, he had even considered closing the club early on that night, since there was little business to be had. The few stragglers who drifted into the club after eleven at night weren't usually people that he wanted Obsession to be associated with. He had never wanted his club to be an elitist or bourgeois location, but when the patrons were stumbling in drunk, smelling as though they hadn't showered in a week, any business owner would reconsider their admission policy. That had all changed one day, about a week ago. Suddenly, every night was like Saturday night: people were lining up to be let into the club, stumbling over themselves, dancing to the music, and drinking at the bar. The tips were amazing, and the crowd was manageable. The extra security that had to be employed was actually respected and appreciated. It was almost as if the patrons, while desperate to get into the club, were nervous about doing anything that might be considered an offense to the establishment. Adam had never heard of anything like that happening at any club before.

He never once associated the timing of his positive insurgence with the acquisition of the gem, which he had bought from a street vendor, for Alice, his girlfriend. He just thought he was running a good club.

The gem hadn't been anything all that pretty, but Adam had felt drawn to it. Alice would like it; she liked obscure stones. The street vender had seemed adamant about his choosing that gem specifically, and Adam hadn't really argued. The woman had looked like a character from a Shakespearean play: a hunched crone in layers of clothing, complete with weathered skin, liver spots, and a prominent wart on her nose. Her hair had been ragged and tossed, her voice had been strained, and yet, somehow, her eyes had shone with a distinctive light, the bluest eyes that he had ever seen. If he were honest with himself, he would admit that he only bought the gem in order to see a twinkle of satisfaction in those eyes. He got his wish, and he had brought the gem back to the club. After placing the gem in his wall safe, he had set up his date with Alice. She would, undoubtedly, be thrilled with the gem.

Adam never once thought that, maybe, she was expecting to be proposed to that night, and was whispering to all of her girlfriends about how excited she was. He just thought that he was a pretty sweet boyfriend.

As Adam sat in his office, counting the till from the past two nights, he suddenly felt as though he were Scrooge McDuck, swimming through a pool of cash. All of the money that he was counting had been earned legally and through ethical business practices, but he still felt a small amount of guilt with each stack of bills that he went through. This was only the money that had come in on Monday and Tuesday night. The club was closed on Sunday, otherwise Adam was sure that his stack would be even higher still. On Sunday, Adam had been tempted to drive past the club, just to see if there was a line of potential customers, waiting to gain entrance to the establishment. He chose not to, since there would have been no point, except to add to the wonder of the situation. Had he driven past, he would not have been disappointed. There had been a long line of potential patrons outside his club, desperately staring at the CLOSED sign in the window, hoping that it would magically flip, and they would be granted access to a sacred land. Some had knocked on the windows, a few had yanked at the door, and a handful had even considered breaking the window, just to get through. The only reason that they hadn't was because, if they'd done so, they might have been denied entrance in the future.

Had Adam driven past the establishment and seen the line, he might have become suspicious, thinking that something strange was going on that he didn't understand. Adam was a logical man, though. He would never have suspected that his patrons were being drawn to his establishment through the supernatural influence of a strange rock which he had bought from a hunched old lady with pretty eyes.

When a knock sounded from his door, Adam jumped. His first instinct was to hide the piles of cash, and he had to remind himself that he had done nothing wrong.

"Come in," he called.

His surprisingly-intimidating bartender, Gregory MacAlister, stepped through the door, his fitted white shirt strained tightly against his toned musculature. Gregor, as he preferred to be called, stood 5'9" from the ground, but from his presence, he made it seem more like 6'5". A carefully maintained three-days-worth of stubble shrouded his chin with shadow, drawing attention away from the cleft in his chin, and stern, unsmiling lips hid the dimples on his cheeks. A black beret concealed a swiftly retreating hairline, and thick, scowling eyebrows betrayed the warmth which his soft, brown eyes held. Adam had never been fooled. He knew that Gregor would likely have a guilt trip over accidentally stepping on a praying mantis. When Gregor was not at work, he was likely caring for his ailing mother, and a portion of his paycheck went directly into a college fund, dedicated to the children of an ex-girlfriend whom he had never fallen out of love with.

Gregor cocked a curious eyebrow at the pile of money on Adam's desk. "Is that from last week?" he asked.

Adam shook his head. "This is just from Monday and Tuesday," he confessed, feeling slightly relieved to have someone else confirm how impressive it was. "We've been really pulling it down! If this keeps up, I might actually have to pay you what you're worth."

"A man can only dream," Gregor chuckled mirthlessly. "Look, there's a woman at the bar who wants to talk to you."

"All right," Adam began to collect the money, placing it in his desk and struggling to close the drawer. "Is it good or bad? Does she seem upset?"

"She seems serious," Gregor stated, after a moment of brief consideration. "She walked in, came right to the bar, ordered a glass of red wine, and asked to talk to you, right before shutting down Lurker Larry."

"Red wine at a dance club?" Adam raised his eyebrows as he stood and stepped from behind his desk. "Classy woman."

Gregor laughed loudly. "That's exactly what Lurker Larry said," he chuckled.

Adam blushed as he stepped to the office door. "Let's never mention that again," he grumbled.

Adam squinted against the flashing lights as he entered the club floor and walked toward the bar. One would think that he would be used to the sensations, after years of club management, but he had never grown accustomed to it. Coming from the office to the club floor had always felt a bit like he was a hermit, emerging from his cave for the first time in five years. As his eyes adjusted to the new lighting, he looked toward the bar and spied the woman who was seeking his audience: she was unbelievably beautiful. The soft caramel cream of her skin flowed elegantly, subtly contrasted by the silver of her dress. The sequins sewn into the fabric around her full, strong breasts caught the reflection from the lights above them, returning it from whence it had come, as if simultaneously drawing attention and denying exposure, while the skin of her exposed thigh embraced the attention, drawing hungry eyes to her with promised warmth. As Adam drew closer, he had to consciously readjust his line of vision, meeting her eyes, deep and dark, both threatening and enrapturing. He took a deep breath, begging his body not to burst into goosebumps.

"Hey, how are you, miss?" he asked, his face contorting into a smile which was probably too wide. Adam extended his hand, not sure if he was offering a handshake or begging her to touch him.

"My name's Adam," he continued his introduction, "and I own this sad excuse for a dive bar. I hear you wanted to speak with me?"

The woman accepted his hand confidently. "I'm Nemesis," she declared.

"Pleased to meet you, Nemesis," Adam said, clumsily flinching, trying to tell his mouth to stop talking before he said something foolish. "Do you have a last name, or shall I just call you Nemesis, like Cher or Beyonce?"

There it was. Adam felt his face, glowing with a pulsing radiance.

Nemesis frowned and cocked her head, curiously. "Nemesis will be fine," she replied in an even, unemotional tone. "I'm not as familiar with those other two individuals that you associated me with, but it makes no difference. There is something within your possession that should not be there."

The smile faded from Adam's face, as he immediately began to analyze everything that he had purchased in the past few days. For the first time, the gem stuck out in his mind. "Maybe we should talk about this further in my office."

Nemesis nodded, looking in the direction that Adam had come from. "I think that would be for the best," she replied.

Gregor watched as Adam led the woman toward his office, curious as to what was going on. As Adam held the door open for the woman to step through, Gregor frowned. It may have been a trick of light, but he could have sworn that he saw the faint outline of a sword, supported between the woman's shoulder blades.

Adam brought the woman, Nemesis, into his office, and immediately stepped behind his desk, making sure that the drawers were locked.

"Please," he said, motioning to the chair across from him, "have a seat."

Nemesis ignored him, as though she hadn't even heard him speak. She was looking about the room, as if scanning it, searching for something.

"Excuse me," he spoke, this time a bit louder, "have I done something wrong? Everything that you see is legal, in accordance with local precincts. I swear, even our bathrooms are sanitary. If there's something that you object to, please—"

Nemesis held up her hand to silence him as her eyes locked onto the safe in his wall. "You've violated no law that I'm familiar with," she said in a serious tone. "You are likely not even aware of what it was that you were coming into possession of. That does little to alter the fact that you ought not to be holding it."

Adam took a deep breath. "It's the stone, isn't it?" he gasped.

At mention of the stone, Nemesis turned to look at him sharply, her eyes full of accusation. Adam jumped to his feet, wide-eyed, as she continued to stare. Suddenly, all of his short-comings and failures popped into his mind, and he felt guilt for everything that he had ever done, from the test that he had cheated on in 4th grade, to the child who had been torn from him when his ex-girlfriend had broken up with him. He started to hate himself viciously, even as the look of condemnation from Nemesis began to soften.

"It is the gem," Nemesis nodded, her voice holding a bit more warmth than it had previously. "The Gem of Illecebra belongs to no one, and whoever holds it violates the natural order. I see that you had no intention of doing so when you came to have it, and you have been judged pure. You are an innocent victim, and I feel sorrow for having to take it away. Still, the gem is not yours to have."

"I didn't mean anything when I bought it, I swear," Adam pleaded, unsure what he was pleading for. "I bought it because I thought my girlfriend would like it. She collects stones. I thought she'd want to have it."

Nemesis nodded. "Perhaps there is a stone she would like to have more," she said, returning her attention to the wall safe.

As Nemesis reached over her shoulder, Adam considered that maybe it was time to propose. He would have considered it longer, if every thought hadn't suddenly dropped from his mind, as he watched Nemesis pull a long sword from thin air.

"Holy shit," he gasped. "What the hell is that? Where did that come from?!"

Nemesis didn't answer. She simply lowered her sword toward the safe and prepared to strike.

"Wait!" Adam cried out, jumping from behind the desk.

Nemesis paused, frowning as she inspected the man, diving from behind his desk. "I have told you," she said, matter-of-fact, "this gem does not belong to you. It belongs to no one, in fact. I need to relieve you of it. If you intend to stand in my way—"

"No, no," Adam raised his hands, fumbling over his words, "I'm not intending to stand in your way! It's just...I mean, if this gem is so important to you, I can just give it to you. You don't have to dig it out of my safe."

Nemesis lowered her sword, and Adam turned to the safe with quivering hands. He breathed deeply, as he tried to remember the combination that he had entered into the machine dozens of times without thinking. His fingers shook as he opened the safe, removing the bag that contained the gem. A thousand thoughts raced through Adam's head as he closed the safe, turning back toward Nemesis, handing her the bag. Chief amongst those thoughts was the curiosity of where the sword had come from, but he was also wondering what was so significant about the gem itself. Also, he was concerned about what he was going to give Alice now.

He was ready to propose, wasn't he?

As the bag landed in Nemesis' palm, a visible shudder ran through her body. She opened it and removed the gem, holding it up to closer examine it. Adam thought that he saw a shadow pass through her eyes as she stared at it, and he got the distinct impression that she both wanted to keep it as close as she could and get it as far away from her as possible. She breathed deeply, returned the gem to its bag, and dropped it quickly into her purse.

Adam frowned at her, mystified. "This gem is kind of a big deal, isn't it," he asked.

Nemesis nodded. She lifted her sword and replaced it in its scabbard, before Adam's descending jaw.

"How did you do that?" he asked. "Are you a magician? Like, do you have a card? I'd love to talk to you about putting together a show sometime."

Reaching into her dress, Nemesis produced a small, jingling pouch, which she handed to Adam. "I am sorry for the inconvenience of the evening," she said, meeting his eyes intensely. "Please accept this payment as recompense."

Adam opened the bag, and found five, large, golden coins. He wasn't sure how real they were, but they looked pure enough. Of course, that probably meant that they were fake, but he would concern himself with that later.

If Adam were to take these coins to a goldsmith, he would come to find that they were, in fact, real. They were extremely pure and very valuable. Keeping the gem inside of the club would have been, ultimately, more financially beneficial, but it was a fair trade, more so even.

When Adam looked up from the coins, Nemesis was gone from his office, disappearing as swiftly and as silently as the sword. Adam stared at the empty space for a moment or two, reminding himself that what he had just experienced had actually happened. Alice would never believe it. He probably wouldn't believe it himself when he woke up tomorrow morning.

A moment later, Gregor came to the door. "What was that all about?" he asked.

Adam shook his head, returning his mind to the club. "I have no idea," he said honestly. "She just wanted that rock which I picked up for Alice. She said it didn't belong to me or something, and she pulled out a sword."

"I thought I saw something!" Gregor exclaimed, wide-eyed, relieved that his mind wasn't playing tricks on him. "Are you okay?"

Adam nodded. "Yeah," he admitted, "she wasn't threatening me. I just gave her the rock, she gave me a pile of gold coins, and that was that. She just kind of vanished."

"I saw her walking out of the club," Gregor admitted. "Gold coins and enchanted gems? Did we, like, land in some kind of weird pirate video game?"

"God, I hope not," Adam sneered, as he opened the pouch and flicked one of the coins to Gregor. "I suck at video games."

Gregor caught the coin in midair and turned it over in his palm. He knew immediately that it was real, but something in his mind told him to keep that information to himself. Adam would likely have let him keep the coin, even knowing its value, but Gregor wasn't sure of that.

CHAPTER SIXTEEN

NEMESIS FELT THE EFFECTS OF THE GEM IMMEDIATELY. ALL the pressures that she had assumed would come with carrying the cursed object were stronger and more intimate than she had imagined. As she began to move across the dance floor as quickly as she could, she found her path constantly being obstructed by potential partners.

"Hey baby, why don't you come and grind over here?"

"Wow, you're pretty; can I get a dance?"

"So, how many drinks do I have to buy you before you think I'm attractive?"

Tactfully, Nemesis evaded groping hands and thrusting pelvis', as she weaved her way toward the exit. Everyone, from the trendy women to the lecherous men, seemed to want nothing more than to keep her in the club. She caught the eye of the bartender as she walked. His eyes practically begged her to come and have another drink, this time with him. She had seen into the bartender and found that he was a noble man. At another time, perhaps she would have been tempted to join him in his unspoken offer, but she doubted that he would have even noticed her at that time. After she finally reached the door, the man standing guard there made her a similar silent offer. Of course he did; she was irresistible with this gem in her pocket. The offer from the doorman was tempting, but not as tempting as the offer from the bartender. Nemesis walked from the club swiftly, moving toward her extraction point.

The streets were even emptier now than when she had entered the club, roughly an hour previously. She had imagined that, the moment that she stepped into public, the streets would fill with susceptible people, drawn by the strength of the gem, anxious to touch her, as though she had a great power for healing or possibly that she was a movie star. She was relieved when nothing like that happened, of course.

As she walked, the sounds of the night enveloped her. Nemesis was not sure if this was the gem in her pouch making her hyper-sensitive or if she was simply on the edge of her nerves, but it seemed as though everything was circling around her, trying to dig into her life. There was no one on the street for Nemesis to avoid. The scant cars which passed her did so without braking, as though they were not noticing her. Why would they slow down? It was not as if they knew she was holding an ancient artifact from the lost continent of Atlantis. They had no idea that the fusion of unicorn horn and centaur blood was rumored to have a powerful, subliminal effect on a person's psychic energy. If the amount of business in the club had been evidence, people did not need to be aware of the gem in order to be affected by it.

Nemesis wanted to see the gem destroyed. The power that it held was too strong for anyone to possess. The problem with that was that the unicorn horn was extremely strong, making a diamond seem like putty in comparison. The problem was that Nemesis had no idea how the gem was going to be eliminated.

Casting it away was clearly not good enough. Someone would inevitably find it. Individuals had always sought after the gem for as long as Nemesis could remember: politicians, thespians, random treasure hunters, and countless others. Thinking back, Nemesis remembered the incident in the swamp with Hecate, when the two of them had battled the mad man, Prospero. He had come to the swamp in search of this gem, had he not? After the incident, Nemesis had continued adventuring with Hecate on several occasions, since the two of them had complimented one another nicely, but there had been no further mention of the gem. In the swamp, Hecate had expressed interest in pursuing it. As Nemesis approached the nexus, she began to wonder if Hecate was, perhaps, involved in the gem's sudden appearance.

Pulling the gem from her pouch, Nemesis held it in the palm of her hand for a brief moment. A deep burgundy tint contrasted against the natural soft cream, as its smooth, oval shape embraced the moon's reflection hungrily. It really was beautiful.

With a shudder, Nemesis dropped it back into her bag and stepped through the nexus.

CHAPTER SEVENTEEN

OBLIVION, DIONYSUS' BAR, HAD CHANGED OVER THE CENTURIES, which seemed odd for a place like that. When Dionysus had first opened Oblivion, one of his clear specifications was that he wanted his patrons to be free from the restraints of time. As long as an individual stayed in Oblivion, they would not age, they would not wither, not even their hair follicles would increase. The world outside of the bar continued to spin, but not for the patrons of Oblivion. It was complicated, now and again, with individuals forgetting about their responsibilities, but that was not Dionysus' concern. Two patrons had accidentally spent 2,000+ years there, but that had only been a one-time thing. Since they had continued to buy drinks, Dionysus had no reason to kick them out!

Now, in modern ages, the bar had updated and expanded quite a bit. There were now pool tables and pinball machines in a room, adjacent to the main bar. A modest stage with florescent lights hosted live music now and again, and a brightly-lit dance floor allowed the more enthusiastic customers a venue to release their energy. Dionysus' library of liqueurs and fine drinks had expanded widely, now embracing nearly all available variates. Dionysus was always on the search for new blends, of course, and if he ever took time off, he was likely searching for those.

When Nemesis entered that night, her motivation was not to drink. She would order a drink, of course, out of respect for the house, but she came to speak with Dionysus. Due to Dionysus' search for new ways to intoxicate his customers, he had inadvertently become very well-traveled and learned. Nemesis wanted to destroy the gem. If anyone would know of something strong enough to perform that action, it would be Dionysus.

Entering Oblivion, Nemesis made a quick inventory of the occupants and other sensations. The expected smells of beer and pretzels blended with the smell of oak from the tables and chairs, with soft undertones of citrus provided by fruits strategically placed around the room. Loud sounds of multiple conversations filled the establishment, as Nemesis took inventory of those that she knew: Hades sat at a center table, dressed in a pinstriped blazer over a collarless Ramones tee-shirt. He was nursing a beer and fiddling with the latest technological toy, as his gorgeous bride, Persephone, sat across from him, sipping a crimson shaded cocktail. Hades looked up as Nemesis walked into Oblivion and locked eyes with her very quickly. Nemesis nodded to him briefly, hoping that the message would transmit. Hades nodded back, confirming that it had. Persephone witnessed the exchange, raising her eyebrows when she saw Nemesis. Nemesis could practically feel Persephone scanning her, searching for evidence of the gem. Nemesis shrugged it off. It made no difference in the outcome whether they saw the gem or not. All they would need to know is that it was destroyed.

Over the multiple conversations, live music could be heard from the stage, where a beautifully articulate woman was singing, accompanied by a hefty man playing a kettle drum, while a slender woman strummed an acoustic guitar.

Lies are what I hear when I listen to the wind
the world of man will fall, time will begin again
take my hand, my love; guide me to my life of sin
in tragedy, we are whole

It was melodramatic, but Nemesis could not help but enjoy it. Over the centuries, she had been exposed to countless music styles and several evolutions of different instruments. There were some that she appreciated, and some that she did not. Angst-y, frustrated, feminine music had always been a personal favorite of hers.

Dionysus was waiting for her as she approached the bar. "Out of all the bars in all the world, she walked into mine," he drawled in a sultry tone, as he filled a tall glass with deep red fluid. "How do you do, Nemesis? I assume we're still drinking Merlot?"

Nemesis tried her best to hide her reaction, but something about Dionysus always made her smile. "It has yet to let me down," she replied, hiding her reaction as best she could. "I see no reason to change a routine that has yet to be broken."

"Only the best for my girl," Dionysus winked at her lavishly as he slid the glass to her. "I think you'll like this particular vintage: very rare, very well aged, and very expensive."

Nemesis took a sip. The precise, dry, oaken textures of the drink mixed with the distinct tang supplied by a very singular grape caused goose flesh to creep across her arms, and dancing sparks to race down her spine. She raised her eyebrows to Dionysus in surprise, and he laughed loudly.

"That reaction is all I need in payment," he chuckled. "Now, my love, what brings you to my establishment?"

Nemesis frowned and took another sip. "Could I not simply be socializing?" she asked.

"Not in my experience, no," Dionysus shrugged. "Why? Are you being social?"

A touch of rose flushed on Nemesis' cheeks. "You know me better than that," she was forced to relent. "No, no, I do need your counsel on something."

Reaching into her pouch, Nemesis removed the Gem of Illecebra. Dionysus' face ran a gambit of emotions in a matter of seconds, ranging from curious to frightened to intensely fascinated. His eyes filled with mystified enchantment, and he reached out to touch the gem. Thinking better of it, Nemesis pulled the stone away, dropping it back into her pouch. Almost immediately, consciousness snapped back into Dionysus' mind, and he shook his head, as if clearing mental cobwebs.

"Phew," he breathed, talking in deep breaths. "You certainly do have something there."

Nemesis nodded her agreement. "You know what it is, then," she confirmed. "Do you have any suggestions as to what I should do with it?"

Dionysus considered this for a moment. "You should leave it here," he said in the most serious voice that he could manage. "I can make sure that it's taken care of, and I'll keep it away from anyone else."

Nemesis' raised eyebrow was all that was needed to break through Dionysus' professional veneer. He smiled sheepishly and shrugged, "Can't blame a guy for trying, right? I mean, it's...I don't even want to say its name, since it might sense that someone has found it and disappear again!"

"Aside from that," Nemesis chided him, "you don't want anyone to know what you have in the bar right now."

"Can you blame me?" Dionysus struggled to keep his voice hushed. "That gem is a myth, as in, it doesn't exist! For you to walk in with the gem in hand is beyond unthinkable! I mean, how did—"

Nemesis quickly brought her hand to her mouth to hide her gasp, but her dancing eyebrows gave her away. "You knew," she declared adamantly. "You knew the gem existed. You recognized it immediately, and you were not nearly surprised to see it as you would have been had you not known of its existence."

Dionysus nodded reluctantly. "Yeah, I knew," he admitted. "I haven't seen it in a very long time, but I knew it was somewhere out there. It doesn't matter now, does it? You have it, and I can't imagine you'll be using it for yours or anyone's advantage."

"I would see it destroyed," Nemesis admitted. "In your travels, have you found anything strong enough to handle that task?"

Dionysus struggled to remain composed. "Dude," he eventually sighed. "If the stories are correct, this gem is forged from a unicorn horn. Do you have any idea how dense unicorn horn is? Maybe there was something strong enough to work it on Atlantis where, you know, unicorns existed, but that place vanished a long time ago! Where would you expect me to—?

Dionysus paused. His brow furrowed with concentration, as his mind raced to find an answer.

"You've thought of something?" Nemesis pressed him after a patient moment of waiting.

"Hephaestus might have something," Dionysus answered, his voice thick with hesitance. "I mean, if there's something that could do a thing, he would have it. You should go talk to him."

Nemesis nodded her thanks to Dionysus. The answer that he had given had not been what she had hoped for, but it had been enough for her. This Dionysus was not the calm, collected Dionysus that she was familiar with; he seemed insecure and nervous. She considered whether it could be the gem that was affecting him or if there was something else at work. Either way, the concern was not hers at that moment. Tipping her wine glass back, she swallowed the last of her Merlot, and turned to leave. As she did so, she nearly collided with the satyr, Pan. Dressed in specially tailored jeans and a casual blazer over a Led Zeppelin tee-shirt, Pan stood a little over four feet from the floor. Nemesis had to resist the urge to be annoyed by his lack of stature, since there was nothing that he could have done to influence that. After all, it was her fault for not paying closer attention.

"I beg your pardon," she apologized, as she recovered her footing.

She placed a reassuring hand on Pan's shoulder and felt his heart-beat quicken, just from the slight touch.

"It's no problem," Pan chuckled. "I never mind being run over by attractive women."

"Hey, barkeep," Pan got Dionysus' attention casually. "I've got something cooked up for tomorrow night. Do you mind if I take a little longer of a set?"

Dionysus laughed. "Once again, time means nothing in Oblivion," he chuckled. Turning quickly to his schedule, he scanned the entries. "It looks as if no one wants to follow you, which I can't blame them for. You can take all the time you need. Are we getting some new material?"

Pan laughed. "There's never anything new in music, Dionysus," he replied, jovially. "It's just the same four chords, played with some deviations made to speed and arrangement."

Dionysus shook his head and chuckled. "Always the cynic," he laughed. "Take all the time you need tomorrow."

Nemesis considered Pan. As the producer and CEO of Panflute Records, he made a career of finding new and challenging musical acts. She knew that his heart was still in the creative process though. While Pan had never played the particular brand of music that she favored, Nemesis loved watching his act. She could feel the love that he had for the art practically flowing from the stage.

Pan turned to her with his impish smile and a playful twinkle in his eye. "Will you be coming to my set?" he asked. "I am playing some new songs, and you wouldn't want to miss that."

Despite her best efforts, Nemesis felt her lips curl into a smile. "I will do my best," she replied, feeling her will succumbing to his natural charm. "There are things that I must deal with but, should there be a moment, I will be there."

"That's all that I ask," Pan smiled widely.

Nemesis resisted the urge to feel seduced. Turning away from the bar, she advanced to the exit as naturally as she could. Walking out the door, she laughed to herself. Nemesis was not naturally someone to feel an attraction to anyone, much less a musician. Still, there was something about Pan that she adored.

CHAPTER EIGHTEEN

BUSINESS AT OBSESSION WAS WINDING TO A CLOSE. ADAM SAT IN his office, counting the night's take. It had been an impressive night, all the way around. Money had been good, and the morale had been high. Aside from the incident, regarding the woman and her invisible sword, not much had occurred. It had just been a good night all round.

After finishing with the counting, Adam took one of the gold coins out of his pocket. He held it between his fingers and considered it closely. It was a bit worn, but that probably didn't take anything away from the value. A brightly shining coin didn't mean that it was gold, and a dull one didn't mean that it was fake. The true value would be found in properties that were much deeper than that.

If the coins that he had been given were real, then the woman had done him an immense service. After all, he had paid less than $30 for the trinket. The fact that the woman had been so adamant about having it for herself did give him pause, but not enough to make him reconsider his choice. The only thing that gave him pause was that he would now need to find something else to give Alice. She liked jewels, yes, but Adam had given her those before. Maybe it was time to give her something a bit more impressionable.

Maybe it was time to give her a ring.

He was in love with her, and he wanted to be with her forever.

If these coins proved to have any value, maybe he could use them as a down payment on a ring.

Standing up, Adam was already seeing the ring in his mind. Locking his desk and his safe, he considered the size and purity that he could get. Walking toward the door to leave his office for the evening, he ran his fingers over the five gold coins that were in his pocket. If they were found to be pure gold, he could do a lot more than make a down payment. He wouldn't get his hopes up though.

As he approached the office door, he saw the door handle turning. He frowned at it with concern, as the door opened cautiously.

"Gregor?" he asked, cautiously.

There was no answer from his bartender. Instead, a petite woman stepped through the door. Adam was immediately stricken by how beautiful she was, reminding him of a spring flower. Golden hair fell from her head, covering her bare shoulders. Her torso was clothed in a white leather corset, revealing enough cleavage to be enticing, yet not enough to appear obscene. Her legs were shrouded in a wispy skirt, which flowed freely where it needed to and clung tightly in exactly the right areas. Her face displayed youth and allure, containing thick, full lips, a button nose, and bright eyes. There was something in the eyes that Adam recognized, but he could not place the association.

"H-hello," he greeted the woman haltingly. "I—I'm sorry, but we're closed. Is there something I can help you with?"

The woman looked at him with a stare that sent chills dancing down his spine. "Have you kept it safe?" she asked, playing the pronoun game, as though he ought to know exactly what she was talking about.

Surprisingly, Adam had a sneaking suspicion that he did know what she meant. Of course, he couldn't reveal that immediately. "I'm sorry," he apologized, feeling foolish for pretending to be naive. "What are you asking about?"

"The gem," the woman replied, her eyes burned into Adam, pulling at his mind to recognize where he had seen them before. "You bought a gem for your girlfriend. Have you kept it safe?"

With a shock, Adam suddenly recognized the eyes. "Oh my god," he gasped, stumbling backwards against the impossibility of what he was seeing. "You're—you're the old woman!"

The woman stepped forward, entering the office. "I'm sorry that you've been drawn into this," she said, her tone softening slightly. "I needed a place for the gem to be held for a brief time. Do you have it with you?"

Adam shook his head, blinking rapidly. "You," he gasped "sold me the gem. You were an old woman then. How did you—"

"It doesn't matter," the woman raised her hand, indicating that Adam should become silent. "I will return your investment, tenfold. Do you have the gem? Will you return it to me, willingly?"

"I don't," Adam replied, his eyes bulging out of his skull. "A woman came and took it from me earlier tonight. She had an invisible sword, and she was all, like, commanding. Should I not have given it to her?"

The woman's brow furrowed. "Nemesis," she sighed.

Adam nodded. "Yeah, that was her name," he admitted, staring around the room madly, in order to find the hidden cameras which were surely there to record the elaborate prank. "She has it now. Should I not have given it to her?"

The woman shook her head in disappointment and turned away from him. "I'm sorry for what will become of you now," she said. "I would have spared you from the consequences."

"What consequences are those?" Adam asked, suddenly feeling sick to his stomach.

The woman turned and walked from the office.

"Wait!" Adam called after her. "What's going on?"

He darted to the door after the woman. As he looked out into the bar, she was nowhere to be found. He saw only Gregor, with his back turned, behind the bar. It wasn't uncommon for Gregor to stay behind late in order to dust bottles. Adam walked to the bar.

"Phew," he sighed. "This has been a weird night. Did you just see a woman pass through here?"

Gregor didn't answer.

"Dude," Adam said cautiously "are you all right?"

His eyes fell to Gregor's hand, wrapped tightly around its contents. In it was a broken bottle of whiskey, shattered and jagged. Something in his mind clicked, and Adam suddenly knew that he was in danger.

"Um," he stammered as he rose from the bar and backed away, slowly. "I think I'm just going to leave now. I'll see you tomorrow night, okay?"

Gregor turned to face him then, his eyes dripping with dark rage. His arms were scratched and bleeding. His mouth was open, snarling.

"Never," he growled. "You never appreciated me."

"I did, bro," Adam quickly answered, moving toward the exit. "I always appreciated you!"

"Not enough," Gregor replied angrily.

Adam didn't understand what was going on. All he knew was that he was in danger now, and he needed to get out of the area. As Gregor charged at him savagely, Adam turned and dove for the door.

CHAPTER NINETEEN

As she approached Hephaestus' kiln, Nemesis considered everything that she respected about his character. After being rejected by his parents, Zeus and Hera themselves, he had always refused to be kept down. Even with his physical limitations, Hephaestus had become a vital part of the Olympian infrastructure. Now, with the rise of technological power, his position was more important than ever before.

Walking into the outer foyer, Nemesis heard the sounds of machines grinding, fire crackling, and the singing of a welding torch's flame coming from the next room. The smell of engine grease and gasoline was subtle, but it was there. There was a door, connecting the sitting area with the workshop, and Nemesis could see sparks and steam through a rounded, port window. She walked toward it and peaked through, feeling like a small child, spying on an elder, in order to gain some perspective as to what being an adult might be.

She could see Hephaestus, hunched over his work bench, his back to her. His massive shoulders shrugged with each movement of his muscular arms. The fabric of his shirt strained against the width of his back as he focused on his work. For a moment,

Nemesis wondered what it was that he was working on. Hephaestus was always working on something new, whether it was an interdimensional portal, which provided transport to and from separate realities, or a new form of can-opener, providing a more efficient transport for ravioli from can to plate. Nemesis considered approaching him, but thought better of it. Hephaestus was a genius and, while he might not be a classically "mad" one, it was probably best to let him finish his work in peace. Looking about the room, Nemesis noticed a couch, situated specifically for the purposes of waiting, and not disturbing. There was a large shelf of reading materials, ranging from popular novels and comic books to technical manuals and study guides. There was also a large, red button on an end table, next to the couch. Nemesis removed a copy of the latest Seanan McGuire novel and sat down on the couch. Examining the red button, she surmised that it could be used to alert Hephaestus when he had company. That being the case, she pressed the button. After doing so, she sat back, content to read while she waited.

She lost track of time as she was reading. When she heard the door opening, her mind snapped back into reality, and she realized that she had been there for almost an hour. She stood to her feet, marking her place in the book and placing it on the table. Hephaestus entered the room, noticing the book in the corner of his eye. He turned to Nemesis, and nodded his acknowledgment.

"Nemesis," he greeted her neutrally as he wiped his hands on the towel that he was holding. "It's been a long time."

Nemesis nodded, as she took a fraction of a second to take in his face. His long dark hair was pulled back into a crude ponytail, pulling it away from the strong angles of his face. One of his eyes stared with an intense, golden fire. The other, the mechanical one, flashed with nearly the same color, but Nemesis could see the difference. She had often considered whether she could actually tell the difference or whether it was the scarring around the false eye that gave it away, but she chose not to think about it too much. His jaw held a well-maintained beard, which Nemesis had never seen looking unruly or anything less than perfect.

"I hope that I haven't interrupted anything pressing," she said, remembering not to stare.

"Not at all," Hephaestus shrugged, as he casually tossed the towel aside. "I was actually just going to apologize to you for keeping you waiting so long. I was upgrading the mobile hotspot in my eye and installing a USB hub on my leg. Then, I got going, and I decided to upgrade my leg's hardware while strengthening the shell and saving all of the necessary data. To do that, I needed to go offline for a moment, which meant disconnecting—"

Nemesis glazed over, as Hephaestus went into great detail about the complex digital playground that he had created. She remembered when Hephaestus had first replaced both his withered arm and his gimp leg, almost a decade before he digitized his rotten eye. At that point, the limbs had been little more than replacements: placeholders, to compensate for the original's insufficiency. Hephaestus had been steadily upgrading the replacements as new technology became available. At first, Zeus had been repulsed by the idea, saying "no son of mine is going to turn himself into a computer." Hephaestus didn't even acknowledge that idea. After all, Zeus had never really been a great father-figure anyway.

"—then I just needed to reattach my leg," Hephaestus concluded his essay, then blushed and dropped his gaze.

"Sorry," he said. "I know you didn't ask for a detailed account of what I was doing."

"I did not," Nemesis confirmed, "and I only understood about a third of the information that you supplied. Still, I admire your passion and dedication to your craft. I always have."

A dark shadow passed over his face as his mind shifted back to the physical world. "Thank you," he replied. Nemesis knew that any mention of being appreciated was like twisting a dagger into Hephaestus' flesh, after the way that Zeus and Hera had treated him all through his life. For centuries, he had been the lame one, the one that Hera couldn't even bother to acknowledge. It had only been through wit and usefulness that he had earned a place on Olympus. Nemesis knew that, no matter how much she encouraged him, Hephaestus would probably always have that monkey on his back. The fact that Zeus only came to him, even now, when he needed something built or devised certainly didn't help. Hephaestus was really only comfortable when he was with machines.

Hephaestus walked to the couch and sat down comfortably, gesturing that Nemesis ought to do the same. She nodded, moved to the couch, and sat down next to him. The manly scents of sweat and technology wafted toward her, as Hephaestus turned his bionic eye toward her, scanning her for virus.

"I have something that I would like for you to take a look at," Nemesis said before her nerves could get the better of her. Opening her bag, she retrieved the Gem of Illecebra and handed it to him. As he took hold of it, his eyes grew wide with childish fascination and, as he turned the gem within his fingers, his lips turned upward and his jaw went slack as he uttered a soundless gasp of glee.

"Holy shit," he breathed, holding the gem as though he were a paleontologist holding a fossil from a newly discovered species. "This...is this unicorn horn?"

"It is," Nemesis replied, nodding. "At least, according to legend. I don't see why that portion of the tale would be false, though, when it would seem that the others are authentic. That is the Gem of Illecebra. It is rumored to have been forged on Atlantis, prior to the continent's sinking."

"Hell yeah, it was," Hephaestus practically cheered. "Forged from a unicorn horn with a centaur blood tarnish, created by the mad alchemist, Iago of Qirzel. It's said to hold some kind of magical sway over the people around it, drawing them to its holder."

"You speak as someone well-acquainted with the story," Nemesis arched an eyebrow, almost reconsidering her choice of confidants.

"Are you kidding me?" Hephaestus cried, his eyes never leaving the gem. "This is the Maltese Falcon! No, scratch that: this is more like the wardrobe portal to Narnia! The Gem of Illecebra doesn't exist! The only mention of it was from some random notes in Iago's rantings, where he talks about its construction and alludes to its power. Iago was insane though. Most of what he said was rambling, and—"

Nemesis, once again, felt her mind wandering. Hephaestus was passionate, it was true, and she was very aware of how intelligent he was. That was why she had brought the gem to him in the first place. She had not anticipated him having such an emotional response to the gem. She ought to have had, though. In her rush to destroy the gem, she had perhaps neglected the cultural significance of its very existence. That point had not been lost on Hephaestus, obviously.

Nemesis watched his reaction closely. He was thrilled to be holding the fabled gem, it was true. He did not, however, seem to be drawn to its power. That was encouraging.

'—is why, even if one is somehow able to find both a unicorn willing to discard their horn and a centaur willing to lose the amount of blood needed for the process, a stone of this caliber will never be created again," Hephaestus concluded his explanation. "It's so rare that there is an unrepeatable gemstone with such distinct properties. This, in fact, might be the only time that I've ever seen one."

Nemesis nodded. "I thought that it might be," she confirmed "and that makes me loath to request what I'm about to. I need to see it destroyed."

A pained look crossed his face, and Hephaestus made a whimpering sound, which was distinctly uncharacteristic for a man of his mass. "Why would you ever want to destroy something so beautiful?" he asked, pleading. "It's not as if it can be used to hurt anyone. It's just a gem! Nobody even believes it exists, so what harm is it doing?"

"The harm comes from the fact that it does exist," Nemesis explained. "You have heard the rumors surrounding the gem's properties. You undoubtedly know the extent that some will go to in order to possess an artifact of this power. You've heard that this stone was the element that brought destruction to Atlantis. I cannot allow that to occur again, especially in a world such as this. This is why it has to be destroyed."

Hephaestus shook his head gruffly. "Be a little pragmatic about this, Nemesis," he argued. "None but a select few even know that the gem exists. The stories have been lost and, even if they hadn't been, you can't seriously believe that this thing has supernatural power! It's like the Holy Grail: sure, it's fun and exciting to see but, at its core, it's just a cup! This gem has more significance because it's Atlantian and composed from the horn of a relatively extinct species. It's just a gem though! It should be preserved and treasured, not feared."

Nemesis considered the argument. Hephaestus, denying the gem's power, didn't raise any alerts in her mind, since Hephaestus was more grounded than most. He didn't believe in superstition. Nemesis suspected that the only reason he believed in magic was because he was himself a mythological being. Even with that being the case, Nemesis suspected that Hephaestus had devised a scientific algorithm to excuse the magical properties as a form of undiscovered science. What Nemesis hadn't been expecting was the romance that Hephaestus had formed with the stone, based on its mineral properties, rather than its supernatural power.

She considered the situation. "If I'm able to prove to you the destructive properties of the gem and the damage that it could potentially hold," Nemesis began cautiously, choosing her words with care, "will you consider aiding in its destruction?"

"I mean, I guess I'd have to," Hephaestus reluctantly agreed. "If, somehow, the stories which surround this gem are proven to be true. Rationally, if common sense and scientific reasoning are proven to be false, there's really no point in bringing logic into the mix. I don't even know if I have a device powerful enough to damage this, though, honestly. This is unicorn horn!"

"All right," Nemesis confirmed, "I will go, find proof of the danger that this gem holds, and I will return once that has been established."

Hephaestus' gaze remained fixed on the gem. "Maybe, if I heat it to a high enough temperature, like, center of the sun high, it'll compromise the gem, making it malleable enough for me to work with."

Nemesis opened her mouth to say something, then closed it again, realizing that she had nothing to contribute to the conversation that Hephaestus was having with himself.

"I wonder how it would respond to acid," he contemplated, his brow furrowing deeply as he analyzed the stone. "If I had a laser strong enough to drill a hole into it, maybe I could try dripping a small amount of sulfuric acid into the pores to test the reaction."

Nemesis' mind was racing as well, with a much more silent discourse. She needed to find proof of the gem's destructive properties, and she had no idea how she could do that. Logically, the first place that she should look would be the place where she had found the gem, by returning to downtown and searching the area for an environmental difference. She should also track down the woman that the club owner had bought the gem from, since she clearly had known what she was holding. Those were the logical places to start. She turned toward the door and began walking toward it.

"Wait," Hephaestus called after her, "are you leaving?"

Nemesis turned back to him, and the two locked eyes. "I'm going to find the proof which you require to solidify the gem's danger," she confirmed. "Will you keep the gem safe for me while I am away? I will return for it."

Hephaestus nodded. "Of course I will," he answered. "I'll start experimenting while you're gone, trying to find a suitable destructive technique, just in case."

The two bid their farewells, and Nemesis left, considering where to begin the search. The obvious choice was Obsession.

It didn't take her long to get back to the area surrounding Obsession. Once she got there, it took her even less time to realize that finding proof wouldn't be a difficult thing.

The scene was in shambles. Standing in the place where Obsession had been was only a burning commercial for the gem's power, complete with frayed electrical wires, a collapsed ceiling, and the crumbled remains of what had once been walls. The damage seemed to have been done from the exterior, which was not surprising, considering the two enormous cyclops who were currently standing in the street outside where the club had been, raining terror and destruction down on the morning commute. Each was armed with a primitive club, which they swung about madly, with complete disregard for property. Car horns and alarms were going off, people were screaming, sirens blared badly and, in the midst of it all, Nemesis spied the one person who might actually be able to make a difference. Even dressed in modern clothing, composed of jeans, a tank top, and boots, she still looked magical. Her golden hair tossed out with reckless abandon as she crafted her spells in the air, tossing them toward the cyclops, attempting to halt, or at least slow, their advances. Nemesis ran to her side, in order to see what she could do to help.

"Hey," Hecate greeted her, her face bursting into a warm smile. "Fancy meeting you here!"

Even in the face of such madness, Nemesis felt her spirit being lifted by Hecate's disarming smile. Suddenly, the situation didn't seem so dire.

CHAPTER TWENTY

Nemesis unsheathed her sword and prepared herself for battle. "Do you have any idea what is happening here?" she asked Hecate, before blocking a pile of rubble from falling on her head.

"Oh, straight to business then?" Hecate snapped back, as she twisted the air around falling debris, shifting it away from pedestrians, and thrusting it at one of the attacking cyclops instead. "No 'hail, sister, it's been a while', or 'sorry I haven't been about recently; perhaps we could get a drink sometime?'"

Nemesis dove to the ground, rolling away from a stomping foot. "Do you really think that now is the time to discuss our social etiquette?" she asked as she recovered from the dive, springing back to her feet and brandishing her sword defensively.

"Perhaps not," Hecate answered, isolating a portion of the fire and thrusting it toward the knee of the cyclops who had just stomped at Nemesis, "but once this is over, I think one of us owes the other a massage date."

The cyclops yelped at the fire as it burned the skin of his thigh. He stumbled backward, toward where Nemesis was standing.

"I've never had a massage before," Nemesis answered back, as she drove the shaft of her sword deep into the cyclops' leg, in the area where Hecate had just burned. "Are they pleasant?"

The cyclops roared with rage, swinging his weapon madly. Nemesis pulled her sword from its flesh and turned to see the body of the weapon coming directly toward her. Before she had time to react, the weapon hit an invisible barrier and was deflected backward. The reflected energy struck Nemesis like a large hand, pushing her backward. While it was likely much more gentle than the club would have been, it did take her off guard, and pushed her to the ground.

"Really?" Hecate critiqued, as she stepped to where Nemesis had fallen, lending her hand to aid her comrade from the ground. "All these years of existence, and you've never had a massage?"

Nemesis accepted the extended hand, climbing to her feet again. "I just never had the time, I guess," she said, facing the second cyclops, who was angrily posturing, seething, directly behind Hecate. "There always seemed to be something more important to address."

"There's always time for a massage," Hecate retorted, as she squared off to face the cyclops who was currently facing her, anger flashing in its eye, rage dripping from its lips. "On an unrelated note, this gentleman appears to be considering a charging attack on me."

Nemesis nodded. "Likewise," she replied quickly. "Ankles."

"What?" Hecate barely had time to assess the situation before the cyclops began its charge. Fortunately, she realized Nemesis' suggested move quickly. Diving to the ground, she rolled between the heels of the monstrosities' enormous feet, evading the advance.

Nemesis performed the same technique with a lithe dive, rolling forward and landing on her feet. The result was that the two cyclops collided with each other. Since they were of similar size, neither of them were pushed back, significantly. The attack did, however, redirect the focus of the cyclopean rage away from Nemesis and Hecate. Since cyclops have never been known for their over-abundance of mental fortitude, they began to see the other as their adversary.

Hecate barely had time to register the pain in her side before she had to begin evading savage footfalls from the two battling giants. She rolled away, and more pain radiated from her ribcage. Nemesis moved to her position quickly and helped her to her feet. Each movement brought painful, flashing lights to her eyes.

"Are you well?" Nemesis asked, steadying her shaky stance by placing securing hands on her hips.

Hecate placed a hand on the origin of the pain and felt the moisture that was there. The open wound was filled with gravel and contamination. There was also the sharp pain in her side, frustratingly close to her ribcage. Also, she had torn her tank top.

Hecate sighed. "I think I'm going to need that massage after this," she grumbled.

Nemesis regarded the two battling cyclops with a critical eye. "How did this happen?" she asked, then shook her head. "Never mind. How are we going to deal with this?"

Hecate quickly analyzed the situation. The two monsters were beating on each other, and neither appeared to be gaining an upper hand. As they struggled with each other, their feet were trampling the surrounding area. While traffic had stopped in the streets and most of the civilians had been removed from the area, they still presented a clear and present threat to human society. They needed to be dealt with swiftly.

"Brain stem," Hecate muttered.

Nemesis looked at her, curiously. "How do you propose we—"

Hecate held her hand up. "I used this technique on a tree once."

Before Nemesis could express her confusion or mention that trees didn't typically fight back, she found herself being elevated into the air. She panicked for only a brief moment before realizing that she was encapsulated in a protective shell. It also took her only a moment to realize that she was quickly moving toward the rear of one of the cyclops' heads.

She analyzed the movements of the beast quickly as she readied her blade. The two beasts were so engaged with each other that they hardly noticed her. As Nemesis rose, she located the precise area. As she floated closer, she drew her blade back. At the precise moment, she stabbed through the protective shell, sinking the shaft of her sword deeply into the flesh of the cyclops.

A disgusting cocktail of blood, viscera, and brain matter sprayed out of the wound, as if it were an untapped beer keg. Reactive, Nemesis shielded her eyes, but the barrier holding her aloft prevented any discharge from interacting with her directly. She withdrew her blade, observing as the cyclops turned and attempted to swat at her. The back of its hand connected with the bubble, and Nemesis felt herself propelled away at a great speed, then stopped abruptly. With a brief look toward Hecate, Nemesis could see her using all of her focus to control the bubble's movement. She seemed to be growing weak, and that concerned Nemesis.

Looking back to the cyclops whom she had just stabbed at, she was relieved to see it stumbling about clumsily, as the open wound on its neck continued to empty. As she began to float closer to the angry cyclops again, she saw the monster trip, falling to its knees. It struggled to stand up again, but the uninjured cyclops chose that moment to step up, smash its weapon into the damaged giant's head and, once it had collapsed to the ground again, stomp savagely on its neck. Nemesis heard the stomach-churning, wet, gurgling, snap of the cyclops' bones and the triumphant roar of the second's victory. Looking back to where Hecate was standing, she locked eyes with the goddess. At that moment, the two of them knew what they should do.

Quickly, Nemesis rose from three feet above the ground to nine, almost a foot higher than the beast. She came to a position, directly between the sun and the cyclops.

"Face me, beast," she roared out, hoping to be heard above its own chauvinistic, maniacal roaring. The cyclops turned toward her, following her instructions perfectly. As it squinted against the direct sunlight, Nemesis felt herself racing toward its face. She prepared a strike, but was unable to land one in time, as her protective bubble slammed into the cyclops' face. The cyclops stumbled backward in shock and attempted to regain its footing. Nemesis felt the integrity of her bubble compromise momentarily, and she fell for a brief moment, as she witnessed sparks erupting from the ground beneath the cyclops' fumbling feet. The beast yelped and danced as Nemesis' restored bubble flew at him once more, this time slamming into his back.

The cyclops fell to the ground, producing a triumphant cloud of ash and soot. As it struggled to stand once more, Nemesis landed on its back and drove her sword deeply into its neck. The monster stopped squirming quickly, and Nemesis stepped away from the fell beast. Turning, she saw Hecate kneeling, treating her own wound. Quickly, she raced toward her friend.

"Let me help you with that," she requested, once she was close enough.

Hecate held her hand up to dismiss the thought. "It's nothing, really," she insisted. "I just need to separate the gravel, cleanse the wound, then close it up. It shouldn't take a moment. It's a shame about the top, though; I really liked this tank."

Nemesis sighed as she sat next to Hecate. "It's only clothing," she said. "I'll take you to get a new one later."

"Yay, shopping spree," Hecate half-cheered, distractedly. As she focused her magic on the wound, the blood beneath the surface began to rumble slightly, forcing the debris out. She barely flinched as she sparked a purifying flame into the wound and closed it carefully, leaving only a slight scar on her delicate skin. After the process had been completed, she leaned back in the rubble.

"So, it turns out," she sighed, "the Gem of Illecebra is real."

"I know," Nemesis replied. "I retrieved it mere hours ago and delivered it to Hephaestus, in order to see it destroyed."

Hecate closed her eyes and sighed heavily. "This probably would have worked out better if we had coordinated our efforts from the beginning," she said.

Nemesis considered that statement. It was likely not a coincidence that Hecate was the other party involved in this incident. After all, she had been there when the magician, Prospero, had mentioned it being in the swamp area. She had even wanted to follow up on the lead after the incident involving the potamoi had concluded, but Nemesis had dismissed the rumors as the ravings of a madman.

As Nemesis looked to where Hecate sat, she wondered what information was being kept from her.

Standing, Nemesis offered her hand to Hecate, in order to facilitate her rising as well. "You should come with me back to Hephaestus' kiln," she said. "He required proof of the gem's mystical nature before he would destroy it. You will be able to provide that."

Hecate accepted Nemesis' offered hand and she stood to her feet. "Have you any idea how dense unicorn horn is?" she asked, cynically. "I didn't think it could be destroyed!"

Nemesis nodded. "Hephaestus had a similar argument. He was beginning to devise a plan, though, before I left in search of the proof which we are now able to provide."

"Speaking of proof," she continued, her eyes scanning the area of rubble and mayhem, now containing the fallen corpses of two cyclops, "how are we going to deal with this?"

Hecate shrugged. "They're humans," she said flippantly. "They'll figure out a way to explain it."

Nemesis watched as Hecate's fingers danced in the air, as she modified perceived images, and removed harmful properties. It probably would not have been helpful to societal growth if humanity were to come into contact with the blood of a cyclops.

CHAPTER TWENTY-ONE

Welcome back to Current News: I'm your commentator, James Novus. Traffic was obstructed today in downtown, when two large cranes went haywire. According to one observer, "it was like watching two fantasy giants fighting each other". The cranes destroyed one downtown nightclub and damaged the surrounding area, causing three accidents, six reported injured parties, and two deaths. The manager of the destroyed nightclub could not be reached for comment. Our thoughts and prayers are with the families of the victims, and we wish the survivors a speedy recovery.

In other news, the head of a local sorority is tired of being victimized by a society that refuses to conform to their standards. They have organized a movement, currently consisting of over

**one-hundred members, with the purpose of
removing the word "man" from common usage.
Their reasoning: the term has been used for too
long, and it has been a proxy for victimization
and abuse. More on this developing revolution
after these messages.**

NEMESIS AND HECATE WALKED TOWARD HEPHAESTUS' KILN
together, speaking on things with no particular meaning in an effort
to avoid discussing the gem. The subject hung over their head, like a
cartoon cloud that neither one of them wanted to acknowledge.
Finally, the pressure became too intense.

"The gem causes an intense magnetic attraction to the holder,"
Hecate broached the subject first.

"I surmised as much," Nemesis confirmed.

"The intensity of the attraction is increased the longer the holder
has possession of the gem," Hecate continued. "Once the holder loses
possession of the gem, they experience a period of repulsion, equal to
the level of attraction. That wave, oftentimes, destroys the holder."

Nemesis stopped her advance, turning to Hecate. "You seem to
know quite a bit about the gem and its power," she commented,
making an effort to not sound suspicious, yet failing slightly.

Hecate sighed. "Nemesis, it's a fabled object of powerful
magic," she replied, rolling her eyes. "I'm the goddess of magic; of
course, I know about it. My research into the gem began shortly
after we encountered Prospero and, once its existence had been
confirmed, I began to search for ways to counteract the gem's
properties."

"Oh," Nemesis nodded. "I suppose that makes sense."

After reaching Hephaestus' kiln, Nemesis walked into the lobby
and looked around.

"Anyway," Hecate picked up her explanation from the point

where she had been cut off. "I finally did find a way to simulate the gem's—"

Hecate stopped talking and looked to Nemesis with confusion. "What are you looking for?" she asked.

Nemesis' eyes darted about the room with a nervous energy, like a hawk who had spied movement on the ground and was ready for her meal. "Someone has been here," she muttered as she continued to canvas the room.

There were elements of the lobby that had been disturbed and then replaced, so that no one would even notice that they out of place unless they had seen them before. One of the couch cushions had been flipped and rotated. Some of the books on the shelf were out of order, and two of them were upside down. The carpet seemed as though it had been cleaned within the time that she had been gone, which seemed unreasonably odd.

Someone was attempting to cover their trail.

Even as she thought it, Nemesis realized that she was likely being overly paranoid. Stepping quickly to the door between the foyer and the workshop, she peered through. Hephaestus was not within eye shot.

Hecate's hand on her shoulder caused her to jump slightly. "What's going on?" she asked. "Are things all right here?"

"I don't think so," Nemesis replied, with a contemplative scowl.

Nemesis pressed the call button, but didn't wait for a response. She pushed the door open and walked into Hephaestus' temple, uninvited. Any trepidation that she had felt was quickly dismissed when she saw Hephaestus lying face-down on the ground. His body was covered in bruises and contusions.

Hecate gasped and rushed to him the moment that she saw his body. Kneeling beside him, she took his head in her hands. Hephaestus groaned as he woke back up, rolled over, and locked eyes with Nemesis.

"I think I'm ready to accept that the gem's dangerous now," he groaned.

Hecate helped him to his feet and supported him as best she could as they moved toward the couch. Nemesis stayed within the workshop, attempting to make sense of the situation. The workshop was in a much greater state of disarray than the foyer had been. Things were over-turned, machines were running without a purpose, and oil was puddled in various, unprotected areas. It was a complete mess, and nothing about the situation made any kind of sense.

One thing about it was clear: there was no gem in the workshop.

The Gem of Ilecebra was missing.

CHAPTER TWENTY-TWO

Hephaestus held the gem in his hand for a moment too long. He could feel it vibrating.

Every mineral had a vibrational signature, whether it was an innate, structural one, an endowed one based on the location, one that was gained through osmosis, based on the proximal location of other vibrations, or a combination of all those sources. Hephaestus spent enough time with stones and metals that he could identify some elements simply by the way that they felt. Of course, being a god might factor into that as well. None of the other Olympians claimed to have a similar trait though, so Hephaestus chose to believe that it was a talent which he had cultivated.

That was how he had known that the Gem of Illecebra was authentic: it had a foreign vibration. Nemesis had told him that it was magical and, while he had debated it with her, he had very little doubt that she was correct. He could virtually feel the magical nature pulsing out of its pores. Of course, he would never admit that it was magical; it was simply a vibrational property.

Nemesis wanted to have it destroyed, and the thought of

damaging something so perfectly unique and irreplaceable nearly brought tears to Hephaestus' eyes. He had given his word, though: if she were able to return with proof of the magical nature, he would aid her in the gem's destruction. He had very little doubt that she would return with proof. She was Nemesis, after all. Finding a way to destroy the gem, though, could be another situation.

As much as he hated to admit it, Hephaestus found a strange form of glee in the thought of destroying something that was both indestructible and irreplaceable. As he had suggested to Nemesis, heat could be an option. The problem was that it would need to be extremely, melting teeth enamel, frying eyeballs like scrambled eggs, hot. Unicorn horn was dense! Since they had practically become extinct, or severely endangered, when Atlantis sank, there had never been a need to create tools powerful enough to manipulate the mineral. The infusion of centaur blood only served to complicate things further because of all the properties that it added to the mixture.

Actually, Hephaestus had no idea what the centaur blood added, and the opportunity to discover those additions made him tingle with excitement. He seriously didn't want to destroy the gem but, if he needed to, he was going to have fun with it.

Stepping to the furnace, he fired it up. In order to get it to the hottest, most dangerous, skin-roasting temperature, the fire would need to be fed and coaxed for hours, possibly days. It would be too hot to be anywhere near the furnace, so Hephaestus would need to use insulated, heat-resistant drones to deposit the gem. That was frustrating, since Hephaestus had wanted to place the gem in the furnace himself. There was nothing to be done about that, though.

Finding unicorn horn, to a geeky kiln master, was like finding the philosopher's stone. Hephaestus remembered back to the expedition that he had formulated, he and Artemis, to hunt for that very object. He had been inspired by that video game series, the one with the attractive woman treasure hunter, but he had never mentioned that to Artemis. The two of them had done research and cryptography, formulating a massive plan to track down the fabled rock. Thinking back on it now, Hephaestus wondered if the philosopher's stone had merely been an excuse to adventure. The journey itself had been well worth it, and the adventures that the two of them endured together had formed a bond of companionship that Hephaestus treasured now. They had never found the philosopher's stone, although they had searched long and hard. By the end of the journey, while neither of them had wanted the adventure to end, they had both been forced to admit defeat. The elusive philosopher's stone remained a myth.

That is, until now. Hephaestus longed to share the gem with Artemis; he wanted to laugh with her and share the mythological item. Hephaestus had created many other technologies, crafting seemingly other-worldly objects from stone, wood, aluminum, cybernetic mesh, and virtually any other developmental element. He was the god of technology, after all: each new tech owed something to him, from the kiln, to the combustion engine, to binary code. Somehow, the one failure seemed to resonate with him more than the hundreds of successes. It probably wouldn't have been as bad if he had not failed in front of Artemis. That was likely why Hephaestus wanted to share the gem with her. Maybe then, he wouldn't be such a colossal failure.

He still had to find a way to destroy the gem, and involving Artemis would only complicate things. He would need to discover some other mythical item that supposedly didn't exist in order to impress her. Maybe he could find King Arthur's crown or something like that.

The furnace was heating as Hephaestus prepared the drones to pick up the gem. He needed to make sure that the drones were treated to resist the levels of heat that they would be experiencing. The gem itself was not heavy or overly cumbersome, weighing less than eighteen ounces with a smooth, oval shape. The shape measured no more than five inches from end to end, with a width of four inches, and a radius of, maybe, two and a half inches. Hephaestus had plenty of drones that were equipped to transport those weights, so that wouldn't be a problem. Any hesitation that Hephaestus felt right now was a result of him over-analyzing or reluctance to end his time with the gem.

Of course, Hephaestus would continue to analyze the situation as long as he could. He wanted to make sure that he got the formula right. After all, when one is destroying a priceless, irreplaceable, legendary artifact from a world that no longer exists, they want to make sure that it's done right.

The furnace was continuing to heat up, and Hephaestus was considering which acidic formula to drop into the softened body of the gem in order to quicken the destructive process, when he heard sounds in his lobby. Activating the camera in the Tablet, which was strapped to his forearm, he triggered synchronicity with the drones in the lobby. Four large men stood there, attempting to appear menacing in the most dated, cliché way possible. Each stood at a different height, ranging from maybe five and a half feet to nearly seven, but they all appeared to be slight variations on the same model. They all had a sculpted musculature, which they proudly displayed through tee-shirts with the arms torn off. Their legs were concealed by rugged and patched jeans, their feet were protected by large, heavy boots, and two of the four had wallet chains. A long, full mane of hair hung from each of their heads, each with a signature color pallet: some dark, some light. Hephaestus couldn't help but chuckle when he saw them. As much as he enjoyed Guns and Roses, he hadn't been expecting to see their cover band waiting in his lobby.

When the pounding started on the garage door, Hephaestus shifted from being amused to annoyed. All four of the men approached it and began to strike the door with force, almost simultaneously. The doorbell was very clearly posted! There was no reason for them to be attacking his door! Lifting the Tablet to his mouth, he activated the microphone.

"Step away from the door," he commanded with as much authority as he could muster. "I'll be with you in a moment."

The pounding continued, despite his rebuke. If anything, it increased in intensity.

"Slayer!" Hephaestus shouted, forgetting to temper his frustration for a moment. "Back the fuck off!"

The group of 80's hair band rejects didn't acknowledge him at all.

Hephaestus wasn't exactly worried about the group breaking through the door. After all, it was five inches of reinforced titanium steel, equipped with an electrical charge which would release if anyone but him tried to get through without his individual code. Hephaestus wouldn't even be able to hear the pounding if he hadn't installed sound amplifiers in the door; they were to prevent him getting lost in his work and letting guests go unnoticed (yes, he had the buzzer, but some of his guests were still uncomfortable with modern technology). It was the principle of the thing.

Hephaestus sighed. He was going to have to deal with this. Rolling his eyes, he set the gem aside with reluctance. There was very little doubt that this upcoming confrontation had something to do with the gem.

Hephaestus raised his bionic arm and programmed it to release an electrical current. Lifting his hand, he released it into the metal of the door. Chills danced over his spine as the electricity shot out through the conductive metal with a satisfying sizzle. The pounding stopped, and Hephaestus checked the camera. All four of the assailants had been hit by the surge, and it had launched them backward. Unfortunately, it didn't seem to have slowed them much. Their expressions didn't even change from their gruff, brutish snarls, as they picked themselves up and advanced toward the door once again. Hephaestus sighed. This was becoming problematic. It was time for him to take things into his own hands.

Signaling the door, he opened it before the first of the long-haired Iron Maiden groupies could reach it. Hephaestus hated physical confrontation, but when the situation demanded it, he was capable of it. Using the strength of his bionic leg to propel himself forward, he landed a punch with his organic hand into the first combatants torso.

It was like punching steel. Fortunately, Hephaestus was used to that feeling, and he recovered quickly. The man doubled over, and Hephaestus met his chin with a second strike, this time using his bionic fist.

In the confined space of his lobby, there wasn't much room to space out attacks or focus on one combatant at a time. The second and third came at him at almost the exact same time, and Hephaestus was forced to divide his attention. While clumsily blocking the attacks of the one, he launched an electrical pulse into the body of the other, which sent him careening backward into the chair, landing in an almost natural seated position. He then focused on the other, who was still attempting to strike him. Raising his organic knee sharply, he landed a blow to the assailants crotch. It was a cheap move, but it was desperate times. The assailant wheezed, which was the first sign of weakness that Hephaestus had witnessed, and bent over. Seizing the opportunity, Hephaestus grabbed a handful of greasy hair, spun him around, and savagely rammed his head into the metallic door frame. The assailant crumbled to the ground as Hephaestus sent another charge through the frame.

That, unfortunately, had left his back exposed. The fourth band member took advantage and began to beat on Hephaestus' shoulders as though they were a fitting replacement for the newly opened steel door. Each blow felt like a strike from a metal bat, and Hephaestus felt the damage inflicted through each strike as it vibrated through his inner organs. Spinning quickly, Hephaestus faced the new assailant, and tried to catch one of his strikes. The Motorhead-clone's expression never changed, nor did he stop attempting to beat on Hephaestus. Both hands attacked with ferocity, and Hephaestus was disappointed to find that he could not block each of the blows. He was also dismayed to find that he could hear the other two thugs approaching him from behind. He needed to come up with an idea, quickly.

He was Hephaestus, the god of the kiln. This was not a suitable fight for him. All technology was because of him. This situation was inappropriate. If Artemis ever found out that he got his ass kicked by a handful of power chords with mullets, she would never let him live it down. He could find a damn way out of this, he knew it. As the rain of fists powered down on him, he tried to think. He was now bleeding from at least five places. He could find a way to win this.

One of his ribs cracked. He could do it.

His vision shifted to red, as blood filled his organic eye. Why were they even attacking him?

He sank to his knees as a plan came to him. It would be draining, but he had no other choice.

Closing his organic eye was painful. Hephaestus needed to do it, in order to access the mechanics of his bionic eyeball. Fortunately, his assailants had not cracked the lens yet, although they had scratched it. In all his years with the eye, he had only ever used the laser capacity for work-related repairs and fusions. Using it as a weapon seemed a weird thought now, although (if he were Ares) it probably would have been the first thing to pop into his head. Blinking his eye three times, Hephaestus accessed the capacities, turned toward one of the assailants with his emotionless grimace, and triggered the laser. It tore through the creature's head as though it were cheese. The assailant collapsed to the ground, blood and viscera pouring from the hole in his head like a stream flowing down a mountain.

The two remaining attackers continued to strike, unaffected by the fate of their lead guitarist. As Hephaestus repeated the technique on another one of the attackers, yielding a similar result, he considered that these weren't actually people. They looked and bled like people, but their responses were automated, zombie-like. They showed no emotional depth, aside from anger and rage. Hephaestus resisted the urge to make social commentary on the characters. Instead, he dealt swiftly with the final aggressor. After the combat now, the solution seemed so easy. Hephaestus felt like an idiot for not thinking of it faster or, at least, before his ribs had been broken, he was drained of energy, and he was bleeding from several places.

His bionic eye was drained, and it shut down to recharge.

Hephaestus wiped the blood from his other eye, opening it carefully. The lobby was an absolute mess. He was likely going to need to have the carpet deep-cleaned, and he might need to replace the furniture. He couldn't think about that now though.

Standing to his feet took all the energy that he had left. Placing his weight primarily on the bionic leg, Hephaestus ran a biological scan of his body using the sensors connected to his arm. Aside from the obvious, superficial places that were still bleeding, there was significant bruising, including a handful of ribs. His inner organs did not seem to have taken much damage, and there was very little chance of a concussion. He was going to be in significant pain for the next few days, especially when he breathed. As the world stopped spinning in front of his one functional eye, Hephaestus looked around him. His lobby was in complete disarray, and the five bodies lay on the ground around him, drenching the carpet with the viscera that had spilled from the wounds that he had inflicted. An army of gnomes continued to pound away at his brain as he considered what he was going to do. Hephaestus sighed, turned, and walked back toward the incinerator.

Pausing, he considered throwing one of the bodies into the flames, just for fun and to see how quickly it would barbeque the flesh. He decided against it. He needed to focus on the gem for the moment.

Returning to where he had temporarily stored the gem, he retrieved it and examined it closely. It was still perfect, with the glean of the centaur blood accenting the curves and refinement of the gem's textures. He was going to have to destroy it. It wasn't safe to have in this world: Nemesis was right.

It still sucked.

As Hephaestus turned to close the metallic door again, he felt a pinch at the base of neck. Spinning quickly, he saw a slight fluctuation in the air, as if something unseen was moving. Frowning, he scanned the room, searching for the individual.

As his eyes began to blur, Hephaestus realized what the pinch had been. He had just been drugged. Desperately, he clung to consciousness, and he threw the gem toward the kiln in panic. As he fell to his knees, the world fading to darkness, he witnessed an invisible hand catching the gem in midair. He could barely focus on the panic in his compromised mind as he watched the gem walking away from him.

CHAPTER TWENTY-THREE

HECATE HAD NO IDEA WHAT SHE WAS TO FEEL. AS SHE KNELT BY Hephaestus, treating and examining his wounds, she listened to his story intently. It was a long, complicated story, one that it would have been difficult to concoct during the time frame that he had been granted. Also, Nemesis had given him the gem, which seemed to insinuate that he was trustworthy. The tale was difficult to believe, though, even after everything that Hecate had seen. Fighting two cyclops in downtown Cleveland was one thing. That had been verified and it was undeniable, after all. Being assaulted by a small group of assailants, dressed like a Def Leppard cover band, was different, especially when there was no evidence to support the claim.

Nemesis, standing over the couch with her arms crossed, was having similar concerns, it seemed. "Your lobby looks pristine," she critiqued, peaking an eyebrow. "If anything, I would argue that it looks cleaner now than when we left.

Hephaestus sighed and closed his eyes heavily. "Yeah, that I can't explain," he grumbled. "It was a mess when I passed out."

"I thought that you said you had been drugged," Nemesis' voice dropped an octave as her suspicion rose.

"I was," Hephaestus defended himself swiftly. "The drugs caused me to pass out but, before I did, this place was an absolute mess. There was blood in the carpet, broken furniture, and four lifeless bodies."

"Didn't you say there were five?" Hecate asked, testing him.

Hephaestus frowned, considering this for a moment. "No," he finally replied. "No, there were definitely four, unless we're counting the invisible twatwaffle who drugged me. Then, there were five."

Nemesis cocked her head to the side. "If the assailant were invisible," she said, coldly, "how do you know that they were a twatwaffle?"

Hephaestus sighed with exhaustion, and Hecate stifled a snicker. Nemesis frowned, realizing that she must have missed the joke.

"A twatwaffle is an inappropriate, childish, slang term for—" Hecate began to explain, then frowned as she contemplated what a twatwaffle actually was. "Well, do you know of anyone who is so annoying they make you question your entire reason for existence?"

Nemesis looked at Hecate cynically.

"The invisible bad person, Nemesis," Hephaestus blurted out in frustration. "The invisible bad person makes five assailants."

Hecate jumped at the emotional outburst from Hephaestus. She had been treating his wounds carefully, attempting to reconstruct the broken rib through her magic, before and during the recitation of the encounter, for which there was little evidence. The sudden surge of emotional energy had caused her to lose her concentration, and she all but lost control of the healing. Quickly, before any of the progress could be negated, she placed a stasis spell over Hephaestus' body.

"Calm yourself, Hephaestus," she said sweetly, laying a comforting hand on his shoulder. "I need to talk to Nemesis for a moment."

Hephaestus nodded, closed his eye, and began to breathe deeply. Hecate stood and looked down on him, sympathetically. It was strange, seeing this 6'3" figure, composed almost completely of steel and muscle, in such a compromised state. Hephaestus had always been a quiet, reserved individual, valuing enlightenment and technological advancement over anything. While he was tall and muscular, Hecate had never seen him as much of a fighter. She had always seen him as a kind, genuine, if distracted, individual. Looking at him now, with emotions boiling over and wounds covering most of his visible body, he looked so different from the person that she knew him as. Her mind went to the gem. Could this be a lingering effect of its presence?

Before she could think too long about it, she pulled Nemesis back, in order to have a private discussion with her. "He could be telling the truth," she informed her in a hushed tone.

"He could also be lying," Nemesis countered. "Judging from the state of his lobby, I would suggest that that is the more likely of the options."

Hecate nodded. "I agree it looks that way," she confirmed. "Still, with as smart as we both know Hephaestus to be, doesn't it seem as though he would come up with a better story than that to explain the gem's absence?"

"Or, perhaps he would have known that we would have expected a more convincing story," Nemesis stated in return. "So, therefore, the inconceivable nature of the story that he told was purposely rendered to throw us off guard."

"Okay," Hecate sighed "we're not in The Princess Bride right now, so before one of us decides to start a land war in Asia, I'm going to finish mending his wounds. Why don't you go and investigate the kiln area, so maybe we can find some evidence as to what actually happened."

"Why would we start a land—" Nemesis stopped herself, closed her eyes, and shook her head. "You really need to stop making references to things that I don't understand."

"Good grief, Nemesis," Hecate tossed her head back, smiling tiredly. "You and I are going to have a girl's night sometime soon. We'll get massages, eat chocolate ice cream, and watch all the movies that you should have watched over the past hundred years."

"I'm familiar with chocolate ice cream," Nemesis said, as she turned toward the kiln. "The 'night of girls' proposal sounds enjoyable."

Hecate watched the goddess advance toward the kiln, her hips moving rhythmically, her hair flowing like a sheet of fine ebony silk. It was easy to forget how beautiful she was with how brusk she tended to act. Hecate knew that she had a soft side, where affection and love cowered, desperately waiting for the day when they would be released. Nemesis liked her solitude but, like everyone, she needed people. Hecate considered herself lucky to be one of those people. She turned, returning her attention to Hephaestus, who was looking at her patiently.

"I'm sorry about losing my temper," he sighed as she returned to working on his wounds.

Hecate shrugged. "It happens," she replied. "You seem to have gone through quite a bit, so it's reasonable that you'd be stressed out."

Hephaestus nodded, allowing himself to relax a bit. "You believe me," he asked, "don't you?"

Hecate considered the question for a moment. "I want to," she admitted.

"I'll take what I can get," Hephaestus sighed.

Hecate continued mending the wounds, hoping desperately that Nemesis would find some evidence to validate Hephaestus' story. In her mind, she replayed all the instances in her past which had involved people that she had wanted to trust. She hoped that history was not about to repeat itself.

CHAPTER TWENTY-FOUR

NEMESIS WAS CAUTIOUS TO BELIEVE HEPHAESTUS. VERY FEW people even knew that she had the gem, and those few included Dionysus, Hades, and Persephone. She immediately dismissed Persephone, since she wouldn't have been interested in gaining power anyway. It was not as though power were not a strong enough draw, it was simply that she had all the power that she would have needed anyway. She was wed to the king of the underworld, and Hades would have done practically anything for her anyway. That left Hephaestus, Dionysus, and Hades.

There had been a fight in the lobby. The attacking party had done their best to cover it up, but Nemesis had seen subtle signs. The arm of the chair by the bookcase had been damaged, then repaired quickly. It hadn't looked that way when she had left, and Nemesis had taken note of it. Also, the books on the bookcase had been rearranged, and a couple of them were missing. While it had been covered up well, there was evidence of a burn on the ceiling, probably a result of Hephaestus' laser eye. These factors were the only reasons that Nemesis hadn't accused Hephaestus immediately, despite his wounds. The evidence of the fight, however, didn't relieve him as a suspect. It happened, yes, but that may have only given him a false alibi.

Hephaestus had described his attackers as thug-like humans. While that wasn't exactly out of Hades' realm of influence, it did kind of indicate his lack of involvement. Hades would likely have sent denizens from the underworld, and they could not have been confused with humans. They likely would have been fire denizens, which would have been made obvious by burn marks in the carpet. Since burning was more difficult to cover than standard damage, Nemesis would have noticed the modifications more readily. That did not eliminate Hades as a suspect, but it did drop him to the bottom of the list.

The kiln was still running, getting hotter by the moment. Nemesis' eyes shifted to the workbench, where she spied the drone that Hephaestus had been intending to use in order to deposit the gem into the burning inferno. Had Hephaestus simply been attempting to steal the gem for himself, he likely wouldn't have gone to such extremes to convince them that he was actually attempting to trying to destroy the artifact.

That left Dionysus as the chief suspect. He had joked about wanting to keep the gem in Oblivion, but Nemesis had never expected him to take drastic measures in order to obtain it. Dionysus was pretty content to run his bar with the amount of business that he had. It seemed illogical to think that he would turn to violence, just so he would get a little more business, especially since Dionysus was well aware of what would happen should he ever lose the gem. It didn't make sense.

Of course, very little about the transaction made sense.

Nemesis walked from the room, returning to the lobby, where Hecate was still in the process of healing Hephaestus' wounds.

"So, heat would actually strengthen the gem, right?" Hecate was quizzing Hephaestus. "How were you intending to use it, in order to weaken it?"

"I wasn't actually trying to weaken the gem," Hephaestus admitted. "I was trying to irritate the centaur blood that the gem is endowed with as it is susceptible to heat and, if I could get that to react, it might compromise the gem. It's a long shot but, I mean, we're talking about unicorn horn here. All we have are long shots."

Nemesis analyzed everything that Hephaestus was saying, watching for clues and indications as to whether or not he was lying. If he was, he was doing it very well. The look in his eyes betrayed a deep disappointment, and the tone in his voice held an authentic sadness. It didn't eliminate him from suspicion completely, but it did help to ease her mind a bit. Hearing the details of his plan also gave her some solace. When he had originally been reciting the story, her first thought had been that he was lying.

"The technique used in the gem's destruction doesn't matter right now," Nemesis informed the two of them as she advanced to the area where Hephaestus was lying. "I've investigated the area, and what Hephaestus has told us is confirmed: there was an altercation, and it's reasonable to assume that his recount of the events is true."

Hecate sighed loudly and hugged Hephaestus tightly. Hephaestus groaned in pain, but returned the hug briefly.

"So, I was thinking," he said, after Hecate had ended the embrace. "You originally tracked the gem through a magical signature. Is there a chance that you could use that technique again? I mean, I kind of designed the tracker, so I know it's possible. Do you still have it with you?"

Nemesis nodded and pulled the tracking device from her pack. She had thought of it, of course, but since Hephaestus had designed the device, she assumed that he could mask it as well. She had wanted to gather as much information as possible about whether or not Hephaestus had been to blame for the incident before she attempted it.

Hecate stood and walked toward where Nemesis was standing with the tracker. Hephaestus grunted as he sat up, clicked his bionic leg into active mode, and stood. He immediately sat back down again, his head sinking into his hands.

"Sorry," he grumbled. "Light-headed."

Nemesis nodded and walked toward the couch, with Hecate following. Standing, with the device fully in view of all involved parties, she clicked it on. It took a moment for the device to identify a trail but, once it had, it confirmed what she had been suspecting.

There was a very clear trail, leading away from Hephaestus' kiln, in the general direction of Oblivion.

CHAPTER TWENTY-FIVE

CHEIRON LOOKED WEIRD WITH HUMAN LEGS. HE WAS THE greatest trainer of heroes in the history of Greece and Rome, training champions like Achilles and Jason. He commanded respect and honor, and there was absolutely nothing less than that being reflected in his eyes, along with his gruff, chiseled visage. Still, there were many who thought that he might have been able to maintain an ever stronger image had he retained his centaur legs. After all, centaurs were noble and proud creatures simply by existence. He was still a centaur, and he was still proud. To remain in the world, though, he had needed to hide his hind legs.

Dionysus walked to the place where Cheiron was sitting and refilled his beer. He came to Oblivion often enough that Dionysus hardly noticed any difference now between his past visage and his current; a grizzled, yet fit, old man with ragged hair, well-maintained facial hair, and an exhausted look in his eyes. There weren't many students left to be taught any longer, so that left a lot more time for drinking. Cheiron took full advantage of that.

As he contemplated the now-full mug in front of him, Cheiron took a pack of cigarettes from his pocket, and he lit one. Inhaling, he puffed the smoke out his nose, while simultaneously lifting the mug of beer and swallowing deeply. Dionysus watched, then shook his head gently, snickering. Cheiron glared at him cynically.

"Don't mock my vices, bartender," he critiqued in good nature. "It's drunks like me that have kept you busy all these centuries."

"Oh, trust me, old man," Dionysus laughed, as he wiped down the counter, "I have no shortage of fools to serve my swill to."

Over the years, Dionysus and Cheiron had formed a strong bond, mostly communing over beer. There was a certain brotherhood that could only be found between a bartender and their patrons. Since Dionysus had always been more lover than fighter, he had never endured Cheiron's tutelage, so there was no history between the two of them. They had formed their relationship over one thing: debauchery. Now, they were brothers. Of course, Dionysus still charged Cheiron for the copious amount of beer that he drank, but that was just business.

Cheiron looked toward the stage, where the music was setting up. "Pan seems to be playing here a lot lately," he noted, as he lifted his growler to his lips and drank deeply from the contents.

Dionysus nodded. "Yeah, I think he mentioned something about uncovering a new sound," the bartender replied. "I don't know how that's going to happen, or why it needs to, honestly. Pan's just a good musician."

Cheiron nodded and sucked on his cigarette. "I mean, every artist needs to reevaluate themselves once in a while, right? They get tired of doing the same thing, over and over, *ad nauseam*."

Moving down the bar a bit, Dionysus refilled the mug of another patron, before sliding back toward Cheiron. "Pan has been a bit despondent lately," he admitted with a shrug. "There was that affair he had with the flutist, but that ended a few months ago, and he's never really taken those things too hard."

Shaking his head, Cheiron exhaled a cloud into the atmosphere. "I really thought they had something there," he sighed.

Dionsys laughed. "Dude, it's Pan," he chuckled.

Cheiron shrugged and returned to his beer.

Dionysus was about to continue his analysis of Pan's behavior, as the subject in question began to tune his guitar and perform a sound check, when a muffled disturbance from the direction of the door distracted him. Looking toward the altercation, Dionysus wished that he could have said he was surprised to see a feral version of Nemesis, tearing through the room. What did somewhat shock him was the death glare on her face, which seemed locked on himself.

"Where is it?" she demanded, when she was a few feet from the bar.

The gem, popped in his head immediately, followed by *oh shit, she thinks I stole it!*

Dionysus' mouth fell open, but he could think of nothing to say in response.

Reaching over her shoulder, Nemesis gripped something invisible, which history told Dionysus was her sword, but she seemingly reconsidered. "I don't need my sword," she growled.

"You really don't," Dionysus heard himself say.

"I would much rather strangle you with my bare hands."

"Oh, that's unfortunate."

Nemesis lunged across the bar savagely, her fingers stretching for Dionysus' neck. Dionysus ducked and dodged away from the attack, trying to determine the best method of escape. "It's not here!" he cried out desperately. "I don't have it!"

"What did you do with it?" Nemesis continued to advance toward Dionysus, beginning to climb over the bar. "I know that it's here, its trail led me straight to this location."

"What?!" Dionysus' eyes popped out of his skull. He couldn't explain how the trail could have led to Oblivion unless the gem was there. "Nemesis, you have to know that—"

"You, also, of all the parties who knew of the gem, had the most to gain from its possession."

That was probably also true. Dionysus didn't like how the

evidence was so clearly stacking up against him. "Why would I need the gem?" Dionysus pleaded. "Oblivion's doing just fine without it!"

Wow, that was a stupid response. Anyone who knew him at all would know that he never passed a chance to drive up business. Nemesis' feet landed on the other side of the bar, and Dionysus realized that he had nowhere to run. As she began to advance on him, he slunk away from her desperately.

A flurry of movement erupted from the bar and, quickly, Cheiron was between Nemesis and Dionysus, posturing defensively. "I don't know what the hell's going on here, Nemesis," he grumbled. "But if you want to get to Dionysus, you'll have to get through me."

Nemesis stopped her advance and studied Cheiron for a moment: "Do you think that would present a challenge, centaur?"

"Dionysus brings me beer," Cheiron retorted. "You never get between a centaur and his beer."

Nemesis reached over her shoulder again, and gripped the invisible sword that hung there. A quick glance from Cheiron revealed that, should martial combat ensue, he had already located three or four vulnerable places where he would strike in order to gain the upper hand. Both Cheiron and Nemesis were skilled combatants, and Dionysus couldn't determine which of them would be at a disadvantage. That only meant that the clearest victim of the conflict would be Oblivion itself. Quickly, Dionysus lay a hand on Cheiron's shoulder, hoping to de-escalate the conflict.

"Hold on, you two," he said, desperately trying to be diplomatic. "Let's take a second and talk this out."

"The time for talking was before you attempted to steal the gem," Nemesis snarled.

"Which gem is she talking about," Cheiron asked.

"It's nothing," Dionysus explained. "Certainly not something I'd want in Oblivion."

"It's the Gem of Illecebra," Nemesis announced, as she began to pull her sword from its scabbard. "You saw it, you wanted it, and you would have done anything to steal it."

"The Gem of—" Cheiron's eyes grew large. "That doesn't exist!"

"It actually does," Dionysus muttered quietly.

"It does," Nemesis confirmed, bringing her sword to the ready in front of her. "You were one of the few who knew of its existence."

"You found the Gem of Illecebra?!" Cheiron gasped in disbelief.

"I found it!" Nemesis declared, advancing a step toward Cheiron. "I entrusted him with the information, then took the gem to Hephaestus in order to have it destroyed. Dionysus was the only one who knew that I had done that!"

"Because I told you to!" Dionysus cried out, defensively.

"You knew where it was going to be!" Nemesis growled back. "You knew just when and where to attack in order to procure the gem for yourself!"

"Okay," Cheiron held his hand up "did this happen recently?"

"You know when it happened," Nemesis snarled. "Hephaestus is still recovering from the wounds which your goons inflected."

"Goons took out Hephaestus?" Cheiron was startled again. "Where the hell did—okay, setting aside the profoundly ridiculous idea that Dionysus had goons attack one of the most physically and mentally dominant individuals that any of us know, what advantage would it be for him to leave a trail leading you right back here?"

Nemesis paused in her advance.

"Plus," Cheiron continued "I can tell you with certainty that I have been here drinking for an extended period of time. Dionysus has not left the establishment."

Nemesis wasn't used to second-guessing herself. The facts that Cheiron had just laid out did, actually, make sense. It would have been illogical for Dionysus to bring the gem into Oblivion, especially since he would have known that this would have been the first location that Nemesis would come to. The fact remained, however, that the trail had led Nemesis here. Something suspicious was going on but, the more that she considered the situation, the more convinced she became that Dionysus was not behind it. Reluctantly, she sheathed her sword.

Dionysus visibly sighed in relief.

"The gem is here," Nemesis declared.

Dionysus signaled one of his mainaids to take over for him as bartender. "Then, let's find it," he suggested.

Taking off his apron, Dionysus escorted both Nemesis and Cheiron to the other side of the bar. Together, the three of them began to canvas the area, searching for the gem.

CHAPTER TWENTY-SIX

HECATE WAS AWARE THAT NEMESIS WAS MAKING AN ASS OF herself. Whenever she got an idea in her head, it was very difficult for Nemesis to be convinced that she was wrong. Throughout the journey to Oblivion, Hecate had been calculating the likelihood of Dionysus being the culprit, and she had come up with the probability of less than 25%. He would have wanted the gem, that much was obvious, but he never would have resorted to such drastic actions, especially when he was Nemesis' top suspect, a factor which he would have been aware of. He was also aware that Nemesis could track the gem, since she had been able to find it, even in the middle of the human world. This suggested that the trail back to Oblivion was a red herring, sent to cast suspicion toward him as the guilty party. In truth, though, Dionysus would never have been so sloppy. Oblivion would have been the most obvious place for him to take the gem and, therefore, it would have been the last place he would have taken it. No, he would have taken it as far from Oblivion as possible until the search had calmed down or he had been able to disrupt the tracking device, then he would have utilized the gem's abilities.

It was unlikely that Dionysus knew anything about the gem's location. Hecate had tried to convince Nemesis of that on the way to the bar but, as she had suspected, the goddess had been unreceptive. She had never been much of a gumshoe.

That, of course, still left the mystery of the very obvious trail that was leading the two of them back to Oblivion. Could someone have mimicked the trail? The responsible party would have known that Nemesis would have suspected Dionysus first, so it had to be someone who would have been present during the initial encounter. Looking around the bar, there was no lack of suspects. Sitting at a table, not far away, there was Ares. Ares' lust for blood and power had been unequaled, and many of his actions to achieve those things had been nothing short of diabolical. No one had ever accused him of being incredibly intelligent, though. Ares had always been the "punch first, ask questions later" type. He also wouldn't have bothered with hiring flunkies to attack Hephaestus. He would have been loath to have another carry out an act that he, himself, would have felt more suited for. All those factors eliminated him as a suspect.

Cupid sat in a corner, smoking his cigar, keeping to himself, as his pattern seemed to be. This scheme was well within his skill set. The thought of having others drawn to him, even without the dispersal of pheromones, also might have been attractive. Still, Hecate was hesitant to suspect him. Ever since the loss of his mother, Cupid seemed to have matured immensely. He still held the persona of a playboy, wearing fashionable suits, smoking his cigars, and always wearing his charming, impish grin. All of that was there to mask a contemplative darkness, which he held, just beneath the surface. Hecate knew it was there, and this scheme seemed beneath him. He had other things to worry about. While the gem would have been tempting, Hecate was doubtful that he would have found it worth the effort.

Hecate quickly eliminated the members from the foreign pantheons who were present, such as Thor, Shiva, and Osiris. They wouldn't have known enough about the gem to pursue it. Even if they had, they would never have been able to find Hephaestus' kiln. She may have been hasty in doing so, but Hecate didn't suspect any of them.

She watched the interaction at the bar with caution. When Nemesis leaped over the bar, Hecate had considered getting involved. She didn't know which side to support though. When Cheiron became engaged, she knew things were taken care of. Moments later, the three of them emerged from behind the bar and began to investigate the room. Hecate was satisfied that one of them, likely Cheiron, had gotten Nemesis to see the error in her idea. She breathed an inner sigh of relief and officially eliminated Dionysus as a suspect.

"If you could all pull yourself away from the show behind the bar," a musical voice from the stage commanded her attention "I'd like the honor of presenting this evening's entertainment."

Every eye in the establishment turned to the stage, where a gorgeous Naiad stood, holding the mic. "He's been here many times and, hopefully, he'll be here many more," she gushed. "He's the producer of more platinum albums than Midas has gold. The owner of Panflute records, this satyr has managed to remain current and relevant in an ever changing world, mastering enough instruments to fill an orchestra. Now, the only problem he can't seem to conquer is fleas. Ladies, gentlemen, and assorted others, it's my extreme honor to present Pan, the master musician."

The crowd erupted in savage applause, as Pan took the stage with an acoustic guitar, smiling and waving generously. Hecate took a seat at a vacant table, deciding to allow Nemesis and Dionysus to command the investigation, at least through the first song.

"How are you guys doing tonight?" Pan asked, as he placed a stool in front of the microphone, lowered the stand, and sat down. "You may have noticed that I'm here without a band tonight. That's nothing against my fellow musicians, don't get me wrong: I'd be nothing without them. Well...nothing, that is, besides a brilliant musician, amazing artist, and a better lover than Tommy Lee. It's true, I have references."

He paused for a moment, while the crowd laughed at his joke.

"Tonight, I wanted to try out some new material," he continued his dialogue, casually strumming the guitar as he did so. "As a lot of you know, when I have new songs, I try them out on my guitar first, usually for you guys. That way, you get to hear the full evolution of the song."

More applause, this time less thunderous.

"So, this is a little slice of melancholy that I came up with a while ago," Pan concluded his monologue as he began to strum the opening chords of the song. "It's about having life on the tip of your tongue, but never being able to quite get it figured out."

As he played the intro, Hecate watched his technique closely. The precision with which he plucked and strummed the strings was beyond inspired, it was divine. Having seen Pan perform many times before, Hecate had grown accustomed to this stimulation. Tonight was something new, though. He was going to break new ground here, she knew it.

There's a cold inside my head, I can
feel it like a pulsing, bleeding,
mass of nothing, without meaning
I don't think you understand
but maybe you will tomorrow

There's no feeling in my hand, it's still
there, I think, I think I see it
I'll lie and say I think I feel it
I don't think I understand
but maybe I will tomorrow

Hecate breathed in the music, never wanting it to stop. This song was the only sound that she ever wanted to hear, and Pan's voice was the only one that she wanted to listen to. He was singing creation into being, and new worlds were being born from his lips.

> *I'll party with the people here, but they don't seem to see me*
> *vacant nods, half-hearted scowls, and special brownies all*
>   *around*
> *I've never been a wall-flower; never blended in too well*
> *Morpheus has left me here, 'cause he says I'm not too bright*
> *Welcome to the lie*

The song flowed through the environment like a flood of warm nectar, nourishing and intoxicating. Once it entered the ears, it flowed through the body, bringing joy and hope for the future to any who heard it. As Hecate listened, in awe of the artistic license and poetic verse of the song, she began to wonder why she had never noticed how handsome Pan was before. She had seen him play before many times, but something about the way that he was currently holding the guitar and casually strumming made him seem like the sexiest thing in the entire world. Why had she never noticed that before?

> *There's a lie inside my head, I can*
> *feeling it growing, feeding, moaning*
> *In my eyes, I think it's showing*
> *and I finally understand*
> *but I'll fake it 'till tomorrow*

Looking around her, Hecate could see that the song was having a similar effect on everyone listening. There not an eye in the entire room, save for Nemesis and company, that wasn't focused intently on Pan, drinking in his music like a sun-parched nomad who'd finally found water. Listening to the music, Hecate began to feel as though she'd uncovered the secrets of an ancient civilization, lost in time and space, forgotten until she had found the proof, hidden within the bar graph. It whispered truth to her, only to her, and she felt like the anointed apostle, individually selected to carry the words of power to all of creation.

Why was this music making her feel like this?

More precisely, why did it appear to be having the same effect on every one of her fellow listeners?

I'll party with the people here, but they don't seem to see me
empty eyes and weak handshakes and lots of cold beer all
*   around*
hiding, will you see the truth? If I die, will you need proof
Thanatos gave up on me, says I'm not worth the time
welcome to the lie

After the reprisal of the verse, Pan launched into a musical riff, composed of chords that, it seemed, had formerly been undiscovered. Hecate tried her best to pull herself out of the trance that the music seemingly had put her in. Pan was a good musician, one of the best in history. She knew he was. Could this just be an amazing song? There seemed to be something supernatural about it and the way that it was making her feel, but was there really a magical element to it? She could be attacking windmills, thanks to the item that she and Nemesis were searching for. After all, this was Pan! He had been a trickster, yes, but now he was the CEO of a record company! What need would he have for the gem? Hecate bit her lip and tried to remain focused and grounded. There was something about this song.

Deep inside, I feel a scream, as I reach out for the light
Welcome to the lie

As the song ended, there was a pregnant pause that hovered over the audience for a brief moment, as every present party digested what they had just heard. Pan's face merged from a tense smirk to a full-faced grin as the crowd erupted in cheers, louder than even before.

Hesitantly, Hecate put her own hands together as she studied the surrounding faces. The mystified looks that every one of the listeners seemed to bare, coupled with the intense draw that she, herself, felt was enough to warrant further investigation. Jumping up from her seat, Hecate turned to where Nemesis and the others were still searching. She needed their opinion.

CHAPTER TWENTY-SEVEN

IT WOULD HAVE MADE MORE SENSE FOR THE THREE OF THEM TO split up to cover more of the environment in less time, but Nemesis would hear nothing of that. She trusted neither Dionysus nor Cheiron to surrender the gem should either of them find it before her. While Cheiron seemed to be slightly taken aback by this, Dionysus had stopped him before he could say anything untoward. He had agreed to the arrangement, and the three of them had begun to canvas the bar as a group.

Dionysus heard Pan's song while he was searching, and he almost paused to listen to its completion. The song was beautiful. He could feel it reaching into him, drawing him into its spell, as the chords that Pan played hypnotized him. Dionysus attempted to remain focused on the search, since that was what needed to be done, but the song kept finding a way to creep into his mind. Its haunting melody and composition mocked all the music which had been composed before it for even attempting to suggest that they were in any way similar. This was music. This was real.

For a moment, Dionysus considered that perhaps Pan was

holding the gem, but he quickly dismissed the thought. After all, this wasn't the first of the satyr's songs that had made him feel this way.

Somewhere, in the back of her mind, Nemesis heard the music. It really wasn't anything to pay attention to. The music was nice to listen to, and she was pleased by what she heard, but she needed to have priorities. The gem was the priority. The song sure was pretty though.

"Found it," Cheiron called out from under the table of three scantily-clad fey from Avalon who seemed to have misunderstood Cheiron's searching for flirtation.

"Not yet, you haven't," one of the fey giggled.

"Keep searching," another sighed, seductively, "you're sure to find it soon."

"Or, if you don't," the third pouted, cutely, "feel free to just stay under there as long as you want."

"Ladies," Dionysus smiled widely as he brushed up to the table, taking their attention away from Cheiron long enough for Nemesis to assist him in climbing out from under the table. "I hope that you're enjoying this evening."

The fey closest to him laid her head against his chest, smiling up at him with indigo eyes. "We are having a wonderful time, lover," she cooed lavishly through scarlet lips. "Won't you join us?"

Dionysus laughed as chills danced up and down his spine. "I truly wish that I could, darling," he smiled at the fey as he gently moved her hand away. "Sadly, though, a bartender's job is never over."

As the hand moved past his waist, the fey made a grab for his crotch, and Dionysus had to pivot his hips to spurn her advances.

"Isn't it also the job of a bartender to keep his patrons happy?" the seductive voice from another fey pleaded, as she stood from her seat and advanced on him, her green minidress clinging to her like a second skin, its plunging neckline and daring hem challenging the boundaries of propriety. "Perhaps, you should consider serving your customers something of a more...intimate nature."

Dionysus locked eyes with Nemesis, and she moved quickly to intercept him, pulling both he and Cheiron away from the table quickly. Dionysus had considered banning the fey from Oblivion for a time, but he had chosen against it. They were overtly sexual creatures, yes, but that didn't automatically mean that they were evil. The fact that, once they chose a lover, that lover never returned did raise some questions, though. Dionysus was not afraid of losing them as customers. Looking back, he saw that they had practically forgotten his existence the moment he had walked from the table.

The three of them walked into a more secluded corner as Pan's song came to a close. Opening his hand, he revealed what he had found: it was a dark, dull lump of black composition. Maybe it was coal, maybe it was something else. The only thing that Dionysus knew for sure that it wasn't the Gem of Illecebra. Apparently, Nemesis' location spell didn't know that, though, since her eyebrows raised curiously when she saw it and then frowned with confusion.

"That is not the Gem of Illecebra," she groaned.

"So, then, we continue searching, yes?" Dionysus asked.

"That would be useless," Nemesis sighed. "The spell was leading us to this stone. Someone has found a way to mimic the spell."

Pan's song ended, and the audience applauded loudly.

"I apologize for the injustice that I brought to your bar," Nemesis said in a heavy voice, turning to Dionysus. "I hope that you can forgive my naive accusation."

Dionysus shrugged: "Hey, no harm done. It's not a bar if a fight doesn't break out once in a while. I typically prefer that the violence be directed away from me but, hey, I'll take what I can get."

Cheiron tossed the coal in his hand, shaking his head, disappointed. "You guys really had me going," he sighed. "For a moment, I really thought the Gem of Illecebra existed."

"Dude, it does," Dionysus insisted. "I swear, I saw it earlier. Do you think Nemesis would become involved in any sort of practical joke?"

Cheiron shook his head as he considered the thought.

"Guys, I think we have a problem," the timid voice of Hecate greeted the group, as she joined them, slightly out of breath. "Pan might be holding the gem."

"You've got to be fucking kidding me," Cheiron laughed as he pulled out his pack of cigarettes and lit one up.

Dionysus picked up the black lump and tossed it to Hecate. "We already found the source of the trail," he grumbled. "Someone figured out how to mimic the spell and lead you here."

Hecate caught the stone as it was tossed to her and examined it briefly. "This isn't the gem," she quickly asserted, dropping it to the ground. "I think Pan might be the actual one with the gem. I was listening to the new song that he was playing, and I started to realize how drawn to it I was. I became more suspicious when—"

Dionysus held his hand up in order to stop her speech. "Pan's a really good musician," he said. "If your only proof for him holding the gem is that the song hit a specific chord with you, I think you might need to reevaluate your investigation. Pan is in rare form tonight! Personally, I love when he plays solo shows with an acoustic guitar. It just feels more intimate and real."

"I disagree," Cheiron offered in rebuttal. "While Pan's solo act is good, no one can argue that, I think he needs a backing band, in order to give his music that full, fleshed out sound. Like, when he gets Alenya, that dryad he tours with, to back him up on bongo."

"That's still acoustic, though," Dionysus defended his position.

"Sometimes, I prefer him with an entire band too!"

"And that's fine! All I'm saying is that he's more intimate, with stronger definition, when he's playing solo. Sure, if you want to cheapen his act by adding more instruments, that's your prerogative. All I'm saying is that you're completely wrong."

Hecate and Nemesis locked eyes as they listen to the exchange between the two involved parties. Cheiron was known to be a gruff, unbending, goat of a male, it was true. Dionysus also had strong, diligent opinions, yes, but the two of them were supposedly best friends. They seemed to be arguing over who understood Pan's music better, an argument which was subjective and pointless. As Pan's music continued to fill Oblivion, the tension within the bar grew, not only between Dionysus and Cheiron, but in the very atmosphere.

Before the argument got too intense, Nemesis lay her hand on Dionysus' shoulder, jerking him back to reality. Hecate did the same to Cheiron, and the two of them looked at each other with shock. The anger, which only a second ago had consumed them, quickly abated, and they embraced one another, as brothers should.

"All right," Dionysus nodded. "I'm willing to admit that something might be going on."

"Yes," Cheiron agreed. "Let's go talk to the satyr."

As Cheiron turned to advance on the stage, he collided with a massive chest, positioned directly behind him.

"You spilled my beer," the booming voice of Ares chided him.

"I could argue that you spilled your beer on me," Cheiron attempted logic on the god of war. "After all, you were standing directly behind me, in a very illogical position."

"I could argue that I'm going to kick your ass," Ares roared back.

Balling his fist, he took a swing at Cheiron, who easily dodged. Rotating his hips, the centaur thrust his elbow into Ares' gut, knocking the wind from him. Ares tumbled sideways, toppling into the table of fey, who began to seduce him almost immediately. Ares shrugged them off, stood, and glared at Cheiron savagely.

"Oh, good grief," Dionysus rolled his eyes.

"I didn't do anything!" Cheiron defended himself.

"We don't have time for this," Hecate grumbled.

As Ares prepared to strike again, Hecate quickly manufactured a spell to pacify him. Casting it out, she stopped him in his tracks as he charged, and he collapsed to the ground.

"That should hold him for a little while," Hecate informed the group. "Let's go talk to Pan quickly, before he wakes up."

The four sets of eyes returned their focus to the stage. To their surprise, Pan was nowhere to be found.

CHAPTER TWENTY-EIGHT

On Atlantis, they would either have had presses tight enough to press unicorn horn or they must have known something about centaur blood that Hephaestus did not. The Gem of Illecebra had obviously been modified. It was far too perfect to have just fallen like that. Hephaestus had never seen a unicorn horn before, since the majority of them had disappeared when Atlantis sank, and the others had been so rare that he had never had the chance to view one in real life. Apollo claimed to have seen two during his ventures exploring the world. He spoke very little on it, simply saying that it was like no experience that he had ever had. Considering everything that Apollo had seen, that meant quite a bit.

There were also only a few centaurs left, but Hephaestus knew them. He had once brought Cynothides, an educated and civilized centaur from Macedonia, to his kiln for aid with an experiment that he had been conducting, involving pylons and negative space. At that time, he had asked for a sample of Cynothides' blood, since he liked to have a sample from every known species. Cynothides had been skeptical at first, as any member of a rare species ought to be, but he had finally consented. Up until now, Hephaestus had never had a use for it.

Cynothides had died many years ago. He had been a good friend to Hephaestus, and he was dearly missed. As Hephaestus brought the small sample from his storage, a tear came to his eye. Using this wasn't like using a random blood sample, it was like losing a comrade. The sample wasn't technically irreplaceable, since there were still a few centaurs left, but the relationship was something that Hephaestus would never recover.

He brought the blood to a boil. Diamond was a poor substitute for unicorn horn, but it was the best that he was going to get. He dropped the precious stone into the boiling mixture, then stepped back to observe.

Atlantian technology was far beyond anything that Hephaestus could ever hope to have. While Hephaestus was the master of the kiln, his own abilities had been dwarfed by the alchemists on the lost continent. Rather than resent them, as his fellow Olympians likely would have, he chose to study their techniques. Using one of his drones, he gripped the diamond, repeatedly lifting and dipping the stone in the blood, until it was completely coated in the blood. Once it had its coat, he removed the diamond, transporting it to a press. If the diamond were permitted to cool, it would become unbreakable. Therefore, he placed the stone in a separate oven, simply to maintain the heat.

"My dear Cynothides," he sighed to himself. "You may have just saved the world."

Quickly gathering himself, Hephaestus moved to see how easily he could destroy the rock.

CHAPTER TWENTY-NINE

A LONG, LONG TIME AGO...

PAN SAT ACROSS THE DESK FROM AN EXCITED TALENT AGENT, clutching a sacred demo tape as though both it and his 401K were directly linked. This was a regular ritual for him, it had been ever since he had signed his first artist. Once he had struck gold with those kids from England, everyone wanted him to listen to their music, hoping that he could pull some strings somewhere and get it done. Obviously, he could. He was Pan. That Jewish guy with the guitar who couldn't hold a tune? Pan had been the one to get him started. That woman with the blonde hair, blinding teeth, and big breasts? Pan had been the one to get her away from soul and into country. Yes, he could spot talent like an archer firing on a target. That didn't mean he could create something from nothing.

"I'm telling you, mac," the agent used an already-dated term of affection to try and form a familiarity with him "these guys, and I don't say this often, but these guys are like Led Zeppelin on acid, man. Look, I don't get this excited about acts all that often, you know? You and me, we see hundreds, thousands of acts, every day, right? After a while, it all starts to sound the same, am I right? It's like, come on, find originality, kid! Denial ain't just a river in Egypt, and talent is something that you've been denied. But, every once in a while, something gold comes across my desk, and I'm like—"

Fighting the urge to jump across the stage and strangle this guy, Pan began to analyze him. His John Lennon glasses, the Burt Reynolds mustache, and the hair which reminded Pan of Janice Joplin (why do the good die young?) all completed the persona of a guy who was trying to stay relevant, but didn't know what to relate to. Pan couldn't exactly fault the guy. Everyone was trying to make something happen.

Pan didn't need to stay relevant. Being a music mogul pretty much meant that he decided what was relevant, and people would blindly go along with it, because no one would disagree with him. Of course, they wouldn't know that they were agreeing with him, and they would never admit to it. In fact, many of them would claim that they disagreed with him, simply as a matter of pride. After all, he was the establishment, so fuck the police, and all that California bullshit. Pan absolutely loved those types of people, the people who openly hated what he represented, while blindly following the music that he promoted. It was incredibly satisfying.

"So," Pan interrupted the agent whose name didn't really matter that much, "what do you think your group could bring to the market that no other band can?"

The agent paused mid-sentence, forgetting to close his mouth. Pan stopped himself from smiling with delight. This was another wonderful perk of his job: when he could cut a representative off, in the middle of a rehearsed and choreographed monologue, he felt satisfied in a good day's work. He knew that it was rude to do so, but he couldn't resist. He could practically quote the pitches now. Every band was either "the next..." or "a new spin on something, something." The thing that they all had in common was "you've really just got to hear this."

To his credit, the agent actually recovered from the interruption fairly quickly. "These guys," he continued "are going to shred the charts. They're not just something new, they could be a reinvention of a tired technique. The things they can do with a mixing board are breathtaking. If given the chance, these kids could bring rock'n'roll to the next stage of evolution. I don't want to sound too ambitious, but Stones are going to stop rolling, and Beetles will get stepped on. That's just going to happen. It's a foregone conclusion."

Pan nodded. It wasn't uncommon for an agent to put their band in such a lofty position. Pan already knew that this band likely wasn't the resurrection of Jim Morrison. The agent probably should have just said "you have to hear this," since the more he praised the band, the less excited about them Pan was feeling. It was not as if he was overly excited about them to begin with, but at least he had held some hope that he'd be hearing something new; now, he was just expecting a band that was trying to sound like the same musicians who were hogging the airwaves right now.

"All right, I'm intrigued," Pan lied (the agent had tried so hard; he deserved a little bit of hope). "Let's hear what you've brought me."

"You won't be sorry, sir," the agent leaped out of his seat as though it had suddenly ignited in flame, inserting his sacred cow into the stereo and pressing play. "This is Rubik's Cube."

After a couple seconds of silence, the music sprang to life with a soft keyboard entry. 4/4 timing, just as Pan had been expecting. It was a standard time signature, but there was plenty that a musician could do with that. That wasn't an automatic dismissal.

The drums and bass followed, adding texture and body to the song. The bass was basically just following the keyboard, and that drove Pan a little nuts. So many people dismissed the bass as a support instrument with very few using it to its full capacity. The bass was such a wonderful instrument, capable of so damn much! In most bands, though, the bass is relegated to discount guitar status. That annoyed Pan even more than the 4/4 timing.

Then, the guitar started. Pan sighed generously. There was the progression: C-G-A minor-F. Always. Always the fucking progression.

It was catchy.

It was poppy.

Pan hated it.

He had noticed it several hundred years ago, when he had first tried to give up his impish ways and began studying music. It had stuck out like a sore middle finger now. He couldn't stop hearing the progression. It haunted him like Lady Macbeth's spot: "Out, out, damn chords!" So many songs, so much repetition.

There was, of course, something else about the progression that he hated. People loved it.

It would sell.

Pan hated that it would sell.

CHAPTER THIRTY

ENTERING THE OFFICES OF PANFLUTE RECORDS FELT ODDLY surreal. Hecate looked around the foyer with a contemplative frown, examining the arena. From the outside, the building had looked pretty much like every other office building that was trying to look unique. From the ground, there seemed to be five stories (there was likely a basement as well, but that couldn't be determined). On the door, there had been an ornate water fountain with a bronze statue of a satyr sat, playing its flute. The name, Panflute, could be seen displayed in big, cartoon letters across the building. When Hecate had entered, she hadn't known what to expect. Now that she saw it, she realized that the post-modern décor, matched with the soft white tones, was exactly what she had been anticipating. Hecate admired the warm, disarming tones that emanated from the walls, and the bronze statue of a syrinx which stood in the center of the lobby. The reception desk was on the other side of the lobby, and a sweet, dimpled, blonde, young lady with bright blue eyes sat behind it, smiling widely. Out of the entire environment, her smile was the only thing that made Hecate the least bit uncomfortable.

Nemesis had a different impression of the foyer and the adjacent lobby. It was a fairly open area, uncluttered, with plenty of room for movement, with the statue being the only large obstruction. There were four exits, including the one that they had just stepped through, although two of them were marked as bathrooms, and one of them was on the far side of the room behind the reception area, and it was likely locked. On the other side of the desk, there was an elevator with the numbers 1 – 5 listed on a panel above it. She noticed the comfortably-padded leather chairs in one corner, of which there were five, where two well-dressed men were seated. They were unarmed, engaged in conversation. One of the men looked up at them as they entered, but his attention quickly returned to his conversation. Nemesis didn't perceive a threat.

On the other side of the room, there was a flat, round table. Around it, two men and a woman all sat, laughing and enjoying their time together. They seemed to be in an especially casual meeting, but happy to be in each-others company. Papers were being pushed around, documents were being signed, but all with smiles and laughter. None of them seemed to be armed, and none of them were prepared for a fight. Nemesis dismissed them as a threat. Maybe that was a little hasty, but Nemesis needed to make a quick summation.

As Hecate had, Nemesis found the receptionist's smile to be a bit unnerving.

The two goddesses exchanged concerned looks. The environment was perfect and serene, with soft, jazz music floating through the air, and everything, from the statue to the plants around the room to the tones that the room was painted in, transmitted an air of peace. Nemesis didn't like it. In her experience, anytime the area seemed like it was transmitting an artificial calm, something was being hidden.

Hecate felt a similar unease, but for different reasons. There was something magical going on. Something that she didn't trust.

"Welcome to Panflute Records," the receptionist greeted them warmly. "We may have built this city on rock 'n' roll, but it's modern music that keeps it going. Is there anything that I can help you with?"

Once again, Hecate and Nemesis locked eyes. With a curt nod, Hecate signaled for Nemesis to take the lead. She needed a moment to figure out the magical source and the nature of the spell.

"We'd like to have a conversation with Pan," Nemesis declared strongly as she approached the desk confidently.

"His legal name is Phineus Grim," Hecate muttered, loud enough for Nemesis to hear.

"Oh, right," Nemesis coughed. "Phineas Grim. We'd like to speak with Mr. Grim."

The receptionist nodded, barely acknowledging the fact that Nemesis had called her boss by the wrong name. "Mr. Grim is a very important, very busy man," she informed Nemesis. "Would you like to make an appointment?"

"I would," Nemesis said, stepping to the desk and posturing strongly. "I would like that appointment to be in the next 15 minutes, if you don't mind. Call up to him, and let him know that both Nemesis and Hecate would like an audience. He'll know what it's about."

"Well, that was subtle," Hecate mentally groaned. *"I guess we're not going with the element of surprise."*

"We never had the element of surprise," Nemesis replied, as Hecate realized that the two of them were still psychically connected. *"If he has the gem, he'll have been expecting us. If he doesn't, he'll be interested in seeing us anyway."*

The receptionist's smile never wavered, making her seem more and more fake with every moment of its unyielding gleam. "As I said, Mr. Grim is a very busy individual, even when a hot, two-woman, postmodern, hippie duo shows up. If you have an appointment, I'll be happy to let him know that you've arrived."

"Postmodern?" Hecate complained, examining her ensemble. *"Why would she just jump to that conclusion? This is a classic look! It never goes out of style."*

"Isn't that the idea behind postmodern?" Nemesis asked.

"No, postmodern is a fashion statement," Hecate replied. *"It's a*

very specific form of...you know, it doesn't matter. We just need to get to Pan."

"I told them that, sir, but they kept insisting," the receptionist continued her conversation with "Mr. Grim." "I don't know the name of their group. There's two of them: one of them looks like a hippie, and the other one scares me."

"We're not a musical group," Hecate started to explain, but Nemesis signaled for her to hold her tongue. She quickly realized that it might be advantageous if Pan thought that they were a music band. He might be more willing to meet with them.

The receptionist pulled the phone away from her face and looked to Nemesis with a bright smile and cold eyes. "What did you say your name was?" she asked in a tone, filled with faux cheer.

Nemesis' face broke into an uncommon sneer. "My name is Nemesis," she declared with a chilling tone. "Tell him only that."

The receptionist did as she was told and, after hearing the response, the smile finally faded from her face. "Mr. Grim is sending someone down for you," she said seriously as she replaced the receiver. "It'll only be a moment. Feel free to make yourself comfortable."

Nemesis turned to Hecate and was greeted with a satisfied smile. They had gotten Pan's attention.

"There's magic in the air," Hecate muttered in hushed tones as she stepped closer to Nemesis.

Nemesis instinctively did a quick canvas of the area. "Is it the gem?" she asked in the same low voice.

Hecate resisted the urge to shake her head, keeping everything about their conversation as private as possible. "I'm not Hephaestus' device," she replied. "I can't tell you exactly where the magic is coming from. If I had to guess, though, I would say no, it's not strong enough. I mean, Pan obviously has a way of masking the gem's signature, since he undoubtedly had it at Oblivion, yet he was able to make you think it was coming from something else. It's possible that the gem is here, and we're just not aware of it. This magic is likely something else, though."

Nemesis nodded. "We should go sit down," she said, scanning the room again.

"Where?" Hecate asked, as she turned around to view the room. What she saw made her uncomfortable. The room was emptying quickly, with the two men already standing up from their table and moving toward the front door. The group of three who had been gleefully talking when they had first entered were now hurriedly packing their briefcases.

"Oh my," Hecate breathed and turned to look at the receptionist. She was halfway to the exit. Turning, she flashed her fake smile at the goddesses.

"Good luck," she said in a cheerful voice. "Just remember, very few acts even make it past the lobby."

She giggled as she turned her back, her blonde curls bouncing as she did so. Nemesis wanted to punch her in her perpetually smiling face, knocking a few of her pearly white teeth out so that her smile wouldn't be quite so annoyingly cute any longer. Nemesis was aware that something was coming, but she wasn't sure of the medium.

"So," Hecate began to ponder, as she walked to the vacated table and sat down to await whatever fate had in store, "you don't think I look like a postmodern hippie, do you?"

Nemesis was taken aback by the question, since she was having trouble relating it to the current situation. She considered Hecate for a moment, with her free flowing blonde hair, sparkling blue eyes, and full lips. Her body was that of a dancer's, with strong hips and fluid movement. Nemesis shrugged.

"You do seem to have a bit of flower child locked within you," she admitted. "Is that such a bad thing? The hippie movement was notoriously pro-Earth. With your powers being tied to the natural world, I would think that you would welcome the association."

"It's not as if I object to it," Hecate explained as she eased into one of the chairs delicately. "The hippies stand for love, peace, and planetary preservation. I just don't like being marginalized. My powers are tied to Gaia, in that she and I are one. I move only because she gives me permission. Many of the hippies wear their support of the Earth as though it is a fashion statement: they praise Gaia because it's what their associates do. Many of them don't even know what it is they're supporting. They hear of a cause and support it blindly, because they believe it's what they ought to do. I'm not offended by the association or the practice, really. I guess I'm just wary of being lumped with the group."

"I think you're over-analyzing things," Nemesis critiqued. "After all, they're only words. People are going to say them. What they mean is up to you."

"I suppose," Hecate sighed.

The elevator dinged.

"I'm not, however, exaggerating the amount of magic on the other side of that door," she muttered as she stood from her seat, taking her position next to Nemesis. "We're about to have company."

Nemesis nodded and pulled her sword from her scabbard as the elevator doors slid open.

The creatures who emerged were unlike any magical creatures that Hecate had ever seen. They didn't look like beasts at all, they looked like regular men. As the door opened, five of them exited the elevator: each of them wore a long mullet, mostly held back by bandanas. They wore torn-up jeans, sleeveless shirts, many with visible tattoos, and a couple of them had leather jackets. They each looked like clones of each other, with the biggest differences being their hair color, their choice in tattoos, and the hole locations in their jeans. The only reason that Hecate could tell that they weren't fashionably damaged humans was the magical aura that hovered around each of them like a gas cloud.

Quickly, Hephaestus' description of his attackers popped into her head. These beasts seemed similar to the ones who had attacked him based on his description. Instinctively, Hecate placed a magical barrier around herself as she dissected their magic.

Nemesis didn't see the magic, of course. She only saw five, angry hulks, glaring at her as though she had just drunk all of their beer. As they advanced into the lobby like a singular force, she pulled out her sword and prepared for combat.

The five attackers identified Nemesis as the threat immediately, advancing on her like a mob. As she sank into a defensive stance, five fists struck at her simultaneously. Dancing artfully, Nemesis was able to deflect three strikes, while absorbing the impact of a fourth, and blocking the fifth. She was bringing her sword to the ready in order to perform a strike of her own, when the next series of five strikes came at her.

There was something odd about the way that these creatures were composed. Hecate quickly attempted to decipher how the magic worked, and she found that it was a very rudimentary design with a confusing symmetry. They seemed to have the same root, like multiple machines powered by a single unit. The only variation in their composition was in the subtle textures. Hecate was impressed by how simple the design was, while still embracing a specific elegance. While each spell was unique, they were the same in many ways. The spells moved and flowed, as if they were—

Musical notes.

Nemesis found it more and more difficult to find a place to strike. The five forces continued to pound into her, tireless and relentless in their fervor. Taking a swing at one of the combatants would mean leaving herself open to another, while blocking or dodging a strike meant sacrificing an attack of her own. Nemesis was used to fighting multiple combatants, and she knew the moves to use in order to gain the upper hand. This, however, wasn't like fighting a gang, it was like fighting multiple versions of the same fighter. With frustration, Nemesis swung her sword desperately, hoping to find a blade's home somewhere. The blade sank into one of the creatures' chests, ripping it open as though it were a quivering mass of gelatin. Nemesis felt two fists slam into her, one connecting with her shoulder and one with her ribs, as she pulled the sword free from her victim's body.

Another fist slammed into her jaw, as she watched with shock. The object of her attack simply continued to come at her, his wound gushing a strange shade of blood, as though he were undamaged.

She could see that Nemesis needed her, but Hecate determined that uncovering the spell's design was probably more important. Her mind returned to the first time that she had coupled with Nemesis, during the fight against Prospero with the corrupted potamoi. That combat would have been infinitely more difficult had she not been able to unravel the spell that revolved around the victims. Everything in her wanted to reach out and help her sister right now. If she were to do that, though, she would reveal herself as a threat, and the creatures would begin to attack her as well. That would compromise her—

Fuck it.

Hecate came out of her investigative trance for a moment in order to fire a spell at one of the creatures attacking Nemesis. It struck the beast's back, burning a hole between their shoulder blades. The monster barely paused. Even with the burning remains of a leather vest on his shoulders, it simply turned its glare to Hecate. She maintained her composure and readied another fire spell to hurl into the oncoming storm that was advancing on her.

Nemesis took note of Hecate's assistance. As the stricken man's back turned toward her, she took two more punches to the ribs while she plunged her sword deeply into his back. She dragged the sword down his spinal column, blood and viscera spilling out of the wound like a waterfall crawling down a mountain. The man continued to advance on Hecate, even as Nemesis twisted her sword, puncturing organs and slicing tendons. No pain registered in his posture, no sound emitted from his mouth, and there no pause in his mechanical stride. This was not a man.

By the time Hecate's second spell engulfed the man's body in fire, Nemesis had grown extremely weary of having four sets of fists pounding into her body. She couldn't help but be fascinated by the spectacle, though. Even with his body engulfed in flame, blood pouring down his back, innards spilling out of him like undercooked spaghetti, he continued to advance.

One punch to the kidney sent pain reverberating through her back and brought her head back into the fight. Swinging her sword widely, she managed to send a splay of blood into the face of another adversary. He wasn't bothered. He didn't even pause. These guys were starting to become really annoying.

Hecate felt nothing as she watched the beast before her melting away in flames. Typically when she was combating a creature, she would feel a sting of pain when the creature died, even if that creature was threatening her life. All life was sacred, and each living thing was connected through the vibrations in their cellular makeup. There was never any joy in the killing for her; it was simply a survival strategy. However, with these monstrosities, there was no feeling of grief or regret at having to take a life. These creatures were not alive, they were magical constructs. She was too busy deciphering them to feel anything.

The creature continued lumbering toward her, even as the flames cooked the flesh from its body. Hecate frowned at it meditatively, her protective field negating the threat from the heat. Instinctively, she took a couple steps back, and the creature continued to lumber: strong, relentless, monotonous. If these creature actually were composed of music, it was likely the most redundant and predictable 80's power anthem ever, just pounding forward for far too long through a collection of strained vocals and—

A light suddenly sprang to life within Hecate's head, and she quickly considered the thought. These monsters each had a common root, she had already discovered that. She began to deconstruct the elements of magic that held them together and, as she had suspected, what little variation each of these spells had was all within a common area, like notes located on the same fret of a guitar. A chill of fascination, almost respect, floated down Hecate's spine as she realized that these weren't just magical creatures.

"They're power chords!" Hecate called out loudly, attempting to get Nemesis' attention.

Nemesis was slightly preoccupied, fending off attacks and trying to sneak one of her own whenever she could. She heard Hecate in the back of her mind and tried to push the distraction out. In her time of listening to music, she had never delved that deeply into the theory. She had heard the term "power chord" before. All she knew was that it was a cheap, but effective, way to play a guitar. Examining the creatures who were currently attempting to kill her, it was difficult to comprehend how they could be musical notes.

If Pan, however, was behind the attacks, it was logical to think that his magic would be musically based. He would have deciphered a way to give body to chords somehow. It helped to explain why these creatures were so relentless and oblivious to pain: they were not real people. They had more in common with the Jewish golem...or, more specifically, a symphony of golems. Searching her brain while defending herself, Nemesis tried to recall how best to combat those creatures.

Hecate was doing the same, but from a different angle. The power chord who she had set to flame had finally stopped pounding on her magical barrier, as he had practically melted into nothing. Quickly, Hecate had repeated the technique with a second creature, attempting to give Nemesis a bit of relief. This had proven less than effective. While the beast had burst into flame, its attention had never deviated from Nemesis, meaning that the goddess was now battling three hulking beasts and one burning spire. Sighing in frustration, Hecate decided that physical combat was likely not the best way to defeat these beasts.

A power chord was possibly the most rudimentary guitar technique. It consisted, almost completely, of two fingers, sliding up and down the neck of the instrument. While Hecate's magic was based in the natural world, it wasn't difficult to identify the attributes of another type. Many of the properties were similar, as though they were distant cousins. She allowed her barrier to come down, so that she would be able to see the monsters' design more precisely. As she examined their structures, an idea came to her.

Nemesis was getting beaten. No matter how often she struck one of these men, they registered no pain and they continued to pummel her. She knew that Hecate had been trying to aid her by setting the second man on fire, but the result had only complicated things further. Now, she was constantly attempting to place one of the power chords between herself and the flaming pyre. Her back was constantly being beaten on, as she defended her front from the fire and the tirelessly-attacking buffer. As much as she hated to admit it, Nemesis wasn't sure how much more of this she would be able to withstand.

Suddenly, just as she thought that she could stand no more, the power chord between her and the flaming beast froze, dead in its tracks. Nemesis seized the opportunity as soon as it presented itself, driving her sword deeply into its body, slicing it open as savagely as she could. To her surprise, the creature neither resisted or retaliated. It simply collapsed to the ground.

Spinning quickly, Nemesis saw that one of the power chords who had been attacking her rear was similarly frozen. She repeated the technique, and the creature fell. Dealing with the third was just as easy. Nemesis turned again to face the burning inferno and, to her relief, she saw that it was simply standing there, slowly melting. Sighing with relief, she turned to see the delicate, smiling features of Hecate approaching her.

"What," she gasped "did you do?"

"Well," Hecate explained, as she casually strolled up to the final remaining creature, now clothed in flame, "once I figured out what they were, dealing with them wasn't difficult."

Hecate formed a ball of air in her hand and fired it at the power chord. It fell to the ground, and the fire slowly extinguished, leaving a burnt impression on the lobby carpet.

"A power chord consists of two notes in its most basic form, and they're all on the major scale," she continued her dissertation. "After I identified their cellular structure, all I needed to do was move one of their elements slightly, thus making it a minor chord. They got all confused, and...well, you know the rest."

Nemesis marveled at the nonchalance with which Hecate explained her formula. As Hecate prepared a healing spell to use on her wounds, she tried to consider all the factors that Hecate would have needed to consider in order to postulate the appropriate action. She was relieved, of course, that Hecate was able to do that so quickly and with a level head, since Nemesis would likely not have been able to deal with the five creatures alone. Even more than that, though, she was relieved that Hecate was on her side.

"You're quite scary sometimes," Nemesis laughed as Hecate's soothing powers calmed her wounds. "I hope you know that."

"I do," Hecate giggled.

After the healing salve had been applied, Hecate and Nemesis moved toward the elevator. The door opened and they both entered. Pan needed to be dealt with, since attacking them with Power Chords had been rude.

CHAPTER THIRTY-ONE

A LONG, LONG TIME AGO...

THE ROOM SMELLED LIKE FUNGUS, MOLD, AND WET SOCKS. Psychedelic pictures hung from the wall, behind streams of beads, with tie-died rags littering the floor. As Pan looked around the area, he saw Buddhist, Taoist, and Islamic symbols, spray-painted in various places by people who had very little idea of what those symbols meant. Many of the ideas represented were conflicting, but that could be ignored or forgiven, since most of the people who were in that room were either high, drunk, or both. From what Pan could surmise, the location had originally been designed to be a place of spiritual enlightenment. That purpose had long since been lost, thanks to drug-use, apathy, and hedonistic orgies. Now, the only things that found enlightenment there were the flies who made their home in the stagnation and the flees who hitchhiked into the temple on the occupants.

Someone somewhere was playing guitar. He was playing chaotically, which either meant that he was on drugs or that he didn't know how to play very well. Pan sighed as he advanced to the den. Thinking back over the length of his career, he wondered how he had come to that point. He had interviewed, signed, produced, and toured with some of the most influential artists in all of history, not just modern times. How was it, then, that he now found himself trudging through an opium den, searching for meaning? It had seemed like a good idea when he had come. Many of the most successful musicians had been addicted to a damaging substance. If he hadn't explored this avenue of the industry, he would have been selling himself short. That is what he told himself, as he walked into the back room where the chemicals and the disordered music resided.

Inside the backroom, a man was lying on pillows, his silk robe open, with nothing but untamed hair and a guitar to hide his genitals. Across his chest, clinging to him as though he was a musical prophet, was a woman clothed in only beads and whose wild blonde hair was sprawled. Behind his head, supporting his crown between her thighs, another naked woman sat. She held a cluster of grapes that she was feeding to the man. Each time she bent forward to feed the man, her breasts fell into his face, obscuring his vision. Each time she pulled them away, a smug, satisfied smirk was on his lips. That expression caused Pan to wonder about the man's authenticity. His chin was enhanced behind three days of stubble, his eyes hidden behind rose-shaded glasses. A smoking glass pipe hung loosely from his mouth, and it was obvious that he was inebriated or very practiced at pretending as though he was. His name was Charles McKinney, but he liked it when his flock called him Sunchord. According to many whom Pan had talked to, his music was wildly transgressive and "unlike anything that they had ever heard." So far, Pan was unimpressed.

"Welcome to the haven, little dude," he droned in such a well-practiced "stoner" voice that Pan was almost convinced he was faking it. "You're the music guy, right?"

Pan nodded. "I am that," he confirmed. "It's a pleasure to meet you, Sunchord. I have heard a lot about you and your music."

Sunchord took a deep drag from his pipe, then exhaled a pungent cloud of toxins. Pan coughed instinctively, and Sunchord looked up at him with pity. Taking the pipe from his mouth, he emptied the bowl and quickly refilled it with fresh ingredients. It wasn't just mari-juana, Pan could smell something additional in the mix. That would have made him uncomfortable if he wasn't absolutely sure that the additive was oregano.

Sunchord snapped his fingers and motioned to one of the girls. She stood in a leisurely way, allowing her tangled, brown hair to fall around her like a makeshift robe. As he watched the liberated bounce of her breasts and the uninhibited flow of her skin, Pan almost admired her lack of self-consciousness. The only reason that she felt this way, of course, was because she was stoned. She was so apathetic and disconnected from reality that she no longer cared how she was perceived. This was not a state which Pan envied. Escaping one's reality for a time was one thing. The wanton dismissal of everything that makes one human was another thing completely.

Pan quickly became aware that Sunchord was watching him closely. The woman came to Sunchord, and he handed her the freshly loaded pipe. "Take this to our guest," he instructed her. "Light it for him, and make him feel welcome."

The woman accepted the pipe, bowing slightly as though she were taking instruction from a king. She turned to Pan with clouds in her eyes and a dead smile on her lips. As she approached him, her body swayed with a rhythm that no one else could hear. Pan met her eyes and felt the beginnings of a contact high. There was no disillu-sion, no remnants of a reality lost, and no personality in a box screaming to be let out. There was simply serenity. It was fleeting and it was false, but it was there.

The woman came to him and placed the pipe between his lips, lighting the bowl as she did so. Pan puffed on the substance (yup, marijuana and oregano), letting the toxins into his system. As the woman intertwined her body around his, tangling her fingers in his hair, Pan strained to feel the effects. He found the high eventually, but it was unimpressive. He had sampled Ambrosia with the gods, after all. He hated being an elitist, but that kind of did put everything else into perspective.

Sunchord was apparently pleased with what he saw in Pan's eyes as he guided him and the adoring woman to the pillows. Pan lowered himself to the pillows, and the woman never lost contact with him, wrapping herself around him even tighter. As Pan lay back, she stroked his chest, laying her naked body against him. Pan could smell the beads of sweat on her skin, along with the lingering drugs on her breath and the oils in her hair. Surprisingly, both her armpits and pelvis were shaven, something that Pan thought to be frowned upon in this culture of free thought and independence. It didn't matter to him either way. It was just a curiosity.

When she began nuzzling his neck and nibbling his earlobe, Pan felt sparks of electricity dancing down his spine. Breathing into the pipe again, Pan allowed the drug to relax his mind as much as he could. This was ridiculous, and it was a lie, but it was something that he would have to accept for the moment.

"So," Sunchord drawled from where he sat, as he repeatedly slapped the inside of his elbow, while holding a needle in the opposing hand. "You want to hear my music, don't you, Mr. Record Executive?"

Pan nodded. "That's why I'm here, yes," he confirmed.

"I have to warn you," Sunchord replied, inserting the needle into a vein and shooting up with whatever the hell had been in there, "my music cannot be contained by the restraints of your music industry. I sing what the universe tells me to sing, and that cannot be defined."

He picked up his guitar, sat up and straightened his back, and began to play. Pan listened to the song that the universe was singing to him. It was chaotic and unstructured, maddeningly random. Pan realized that the song would likely make more sense if he were high.

Since he was mostly sober, the music was just predictable and boring.

As the woman wrapped around him, allowing the music to transport her into another world, slipping her hand to his crotch and fondling his cock, Pan wished that the universe would be slightly more creative.

CHAPTER THIRTY-TWO

She had always hated elevators. Nemesis had never been comfortable with the enclosed spaces, especially ones that were moving at a rapid speed. She was not claustrophobic, since that would have been illogical and pointless. She just did not like places that denied her a quick and easy exit.

Examining Hecate's stance, Nemesis noted that she was calm and resolved, as though nothing out of the ordinary were going on. That didn't make her more comfortable, but it did help to calm her nerves in regards to the situation. Pan would not have sent his attack dogs to kill or maim them if he had been willing to have a reasonable conversation about what should be done with the gem. With the level of tech that Nemesis had seen in the lobby, he had undoubtedly observed the combat, and he would have witnessed the final result. There would, undoubtedly, be several more obstacles to face before the confrontation with Pan.

"So," Hecate contemplated as she stared at the array of buttons inside the elevator, "which floor do you think Pan is on? We have several choices, but I think that we can safely eliminate the basement as an option."

Looking over her shoulder, Nemesis saw that there were six floors, not including the basement. She frowned in concentration. "It would make sense that his office would be near the top floor, wouldn't it?" she asked. "I think that we should begin at the top level and work our way down."

Hecate shrugged. "That seems like a logical plan."

She pressed the top button and the elevator began to ascend.

"Can you imagine if we'd had the technology of today back in Rome?" Hecate asked as she felt the vibrations of movement through the wall of the cell. "It would have made the developments that we made so much easier and more substantial."

"It would have," Nemesis nodded. "It also would have made us lazy and complacent, content in allowing technology to do the work which, traditionally, would have been done by hand. With the rise of tech, the need for intelligence and innovation lessens."

Hecate shrugged. "I'm not disagreeing with you," she sighed "but that's a flaw in humanity that was true in Rome as much as it is today: why work for something when someone or something else can do it and give you the credit? All I was suggesting is that the aqueducts would have been easier to construct and the roads would have been paved sooner."

"That's true," Nemesis consented. "If you think about it, though, the level of technology in our constructive tools would be equalized by our weaponry tech. Do you remember the ridiculous wars that we fought simply for dominance? Augustus went up and down the Thames, killed every man, woman, and child within a mile of either bank, and called it winning. Can you imagine the damage that would have been inflicted, if he'd been given semi-automatic assault weapons and combat vehicles?"

"I guess I was limiting my scope to industrial and agricultural tools," Hecate replied. "It may have been short-sighted, but I think I—"

Hecate was interrupted by the sudden lurch of the elevator and an unexpected stop. With a contemplative frown, she looked up to examine the floor reader. There was no clear reading as to which floor they were on. She sighed.

"That was rude," Hecate complained.

"I doubt the elevator cares much for our social nuances," Nemesis replied as she joined Hecate in examining the mechanism.

"It had one job to do," Hecate continued, shaking her head tiredly, "just get us to the correct floor. How hard is that?"

A soft wheeze emitted from an air vent near the back of the elevator. When Nemesis looked toward the sound, she saw a slight fluctuation in the environment, as if the air flow were reversed. A new odor, very subtle and very chemical, entered the environment.

"If I mention that I think we're being poisoned," Nemesis asked with a perked eyebrow "will you spare me the lecture on how oxygen is disappointing us?"

"Absolutely not," Hecate said, her eyes lifting to the vent. "I'll table that discourse for later."

Nemesis felt the air around her head change in density. She fought the panic that crept into the back of her mind as she analyzed the situation quickly. Looking to Hecate, she noticed the goddess staring back at her. She nodded curtly.

"I figured we wouldn't want to be breathing in the toxins, so I supplied us both with an air filtering spell," she explained. "I'm sorry I didn't alert you beforehand. The assumption was that you'd be okay with it."

Nemesis nodded, feeling strange doing so, with the altered state of the air around her. "The assumption was not made in error," she confirmed. "I was only briefly surprised."

Nemesis was able to subdue her level of panic, which was helped by the bubble of fresh air currently surrounding her head. She began to scan the area for an alternate way to get out of the elevator. Her eyes landed on the outline of a door in the roof of the lift.

Unsheathing her sword, she pointed it toward the portal, "I think we can get out through that."

Hecate followed the sword's point to the door, nodding in confirmation.

Scanning the area quickly, Nemesis noticed several ways that she could reach the door to the exterior. Bracing her foot against the side of the chamber, she vaulted herself toward the roof. Driving the hilt of her sword into the door, she felt it come loose. Since the door would have been planned for an emergency escape, it didn't make sense that it would be locked. As she landed gracefully, she looked to the door, then around her, as she took note of the gaseous cloud that was filling the elevator.

"I almost feel guilty," Hecate interrupted her thoughts, "at not being more inconvenienced by these gases. Pan must have put a lot of thought and effort into constructing such a destructive defense. We've circumvented it with little or no effort whatsoever."

Nemesis looked at her with a cynical eye.

"Oh, I'm not saying that I'd prefer the poison," Hecate quickly defended her comment. "I just feel bad for the little guy."

Nemesis shook her head tiredly. "You should probably refrain from calling him 'little guy' when we confront him," she sighed. "He'll likely still try to kill us but if we avoid condescending terms, maybe he'll do it with a better attitude."

"Anyway," she continued, pointing to the now-open door. "Shall we exit?"

Hecate motioned, "After you."

Nemesis wasted no time, climbing up the side and through the escape door in a single movement. As she pulled her lower body through the opening, she felt the change in air around her face again, and she was relieved to realize that she no longer needed an oxygen bubble to protect her from the toxins. She looked up the empty elevator shaft. Through the complex network of cables and wires, she saw the next floor above her. Frowning with concentration, she bent her knees, sinking into a crouch. She could make that jump easily enough. The trick would be getting through the obstructive doorway.

As she considered her options, Hecate floated through the door, herself encapsulated in a ball of air. Landing gracefully, she bent to close the door, trapping the toxic fumes inside. As Hecate stood again, she joined Nemesis in staring up at the next floor.

"I guess it would be selfish of me to think you could use another one of those bubbles to float me up to that next floor, wouldn't it?" Nemesis asked, half in jest.

Hecate shook her head slowly, her eyes never deviating from the objective above them. "I know it seems as though my magic is a bottomless urn of goodies," she replied "but I do have my limitations. My magic is tied to Gaia, like I explained before. If we were outdoors, I might be able to handle that but, inside this artificial construct, my powers have been waning since we entered. I feel like, if I were to use much more of it, I would risk being deadweight during the next conflict."

Nemesis lay a comforting hand on Hecate's shoulder. "Climb onto my back," she instructed her partner. "I can make the jump easily under my own weight. I don't see why your weight should add much complication."

Hecate nodded, sighing. As she climbed onto Nemesis' back, locking her slender legs around her waist, Nemesis considered that this was the first time that she had seen the goddess show weakness. Her actions were always sharp and quick, with a resolve that defied questions. The woman clinging to her back right now appeared weak and impressionable, almost out of place. It was a temporary state-of-mind, though. Hecate was not used to being out of touch with nature. It must feel strange for her, being in this world of silicone. She would surely collect herself in time for the next confrontation. Nemesis trusted her.

Nemesis took hold of the elevator cables and began to pull herself up them. The chords had never meant to be climbed, obviously, and their textures were less than helpful for the ascent. Her shoulders and back throbbed with each hand-over-hand movement. Though she was loath to admit it, the added weight of Hecate was not helping the situation. Hecate was petite and slight, yes, but it was still uncomfortable climbing with anything on her back. Nemesis focused her mental energy on the slick, smooth vines that she was attempting to navigate. She carefully ascended, finding herself level with the next floor in what felt like a couple of hours but was actually only a few minutes. Once they were there, Nemesis felt Hecate squirming, and the elevator door popped open.

"I figured a little bit of magic wouldn't hurt," Hecate's honey-suckle-breath wafted sweetly into her ears.

Nemesis nodded. She swung her body toward the opening. Rocking herself back and forth, she achieved enough momentum, and she was able to launch herself through the door.

Hecate disengaged with her back the moment her feet hit the floor, and she began to smooth down her bunched clothing. As she did so, Nemesis stood and looked about her. The room that they had landed in was black, almost supernaturally so. Looking down to her feet, she could see the floor that she was standing on, but only barely. There were things moving in the area, she could hear them, but she could see nothing in the area. Reaching to her hip, she gripped the handle of her sword for security, as her face furrowed into a suspicious scowl.

"This is really creepy," Hecate whispered, as she stepped up to stand next to her.

Nemesis nodded. "That statement, coming from you," she replied in a hushed tone, "makes it doubly so."

"Oh yeah," Hecate drawled, sarcastically, "because I'm so dark and macabre."

"Hey," Nemesis shrugged "if the shoe fits..."

Before the final word of her sentence was out of her mouth, the room was suddenly filled with blindingly white light. Nemesis was forced to hide her face for a moment as she listened to Hecate yelp with surprise. The air was filled with ridiculously random music, including strange guitars, keyboards, percussion instruments, and some obscure instrumentation that was indefinable.

Nemesis pealed her eyes open and allowed her sight to adjust to the new lighting. She was in an open room, the size of a basketball court. It was relatively empty, aside from the piles of folding chairs that were stacked against the walls, speakers that hung from the ceiling, and a large stage, jutting out of the wall, opposite them. Standing on the stage was, Nemesis assumed, the source of the music. There was a collection of five of the most ridiculously sad-looking individuals that she could ever remember seeing. Each of them held an instrument as though it were the only thing that had ever told them it loved them, as their ten, frightened, eyes stared out into a world that wanted them to suffer.

Standing in front of the stage, shoulders back, arms crossed, stood Pan. He was dressed in an expensive suit with his hair very precisely combed back. He looked nothing like the modest, friendly, figure who had entertained them at Oblivion the previous night. Practically the only similarity was the soulful eyes, dripping with a deep-routed sadness.

"Hey guys," he said, his voice filling with restrained emotion. "We need to talk."

CHAPTER THIRTY-THREE

A NOT SO LONG TIME AGO

Money; it's cold and green and expendable
Money; it's light, it's tight, it's expendable
Money; so dependable, so deductible
I wish I had more money

Money; if it's not there, I'm broke
Money; so don't let me be broke
Money, money, money, money, money doesn't grow on trees
But that's why we've got credit cards, you see

They say money is the root of all evil
So why is it so much fun to have?
'Cause if money is the root of all evil
Wouldn't that make having it bad?
The poor stay poor and the rich get rich on the backs of illegal
*   immigrants*
So, if money is the root of all evil, be bad

Destroyed my marriage (yeah, yeah, yeah, yeah)

Put me in debt (all right, all right, all right, all right)
Just a step in (yeah, yeah, yeah, yeah)
My grand design plan (bring it home now)
I see it now, don't have a cow
My plot unfolds with triumphant sounds
You say money is the root of all evil, you can go to hell
Cause money had brought me success, as you can tell

I hear their jingles: TV and radio
And every time I hear the song, I see the cash flow
Cause two good friends of mine, Visa and Mastercard
Well, they don't like each other much, but they like me a lot
I've got the lowest interest rate in the world, yo
I've got the lowest interest rate
Can you beat it?
I'll just transfer all my balance to discover
That I've got nine months, no interest
Here's my cash back bonus (my cash back bonus)
And my frequent flyer miles are about to kick in
Git my cash back bonus (my cash back bonus)
I get money for spending, so I'm gonna' spend some more
The world is not what it's meant to be
The world is made of money

This little piggy went to market, while this little piggy dot-
    commed
This little piggy said "cash or credit," but this little piggy said
    the cash is gone
Cause this little piggy built a giant statue, and piggies came
    from all around
To see the symbol of prosperity, and it made the little
    piggies bow
Worship the cow, worship the cow, worship the cow
All you little piggies bow down

Apollo stopped the musician, and looked closely at the artist. "Pan," he said "this song is incredible. I feel like you're taking me on a journey through genre, with every stanza being reminiscent of a specific form. It's beautiful. The composition reminds me a lot of David Byrne and the work that he did with—"

Pan's head sank. "It reminds you of something," he sighed. "I spent weeks, mixing genres and timing signatures, throwing in off tempo vocals here, a minor chord there, and it still reminds you of something."

"Well," Apollo's brow furrowed and his eyes darted about nervously, "yeah. Pan, it's not a bad thing. David Byrne is one of my favorite modern composers. The song is fantastic. It really is a work of art."

Pan nodded, placing his guitar back in its case. "Yeah, I know," he sighed. "Thanks for listening."

"There are only so many notes, Pan," Apollo tried to comfort the satyr. "Once you discover new ones, you can create an entire world with them. Until then, we have to stick with arranging the ones we already know."

New notes, Pan thought to himself as he walked away. *There were new notes somewhere.*

CHAPTER THIRTY-FOUR

THE MOMENT THAT HECATE LOOKED AT THEM, SHE BEGAN TO feel for them. The five souls that stood upon the stage, wearing melancholy scowls, were being used. They were not the same as the Power Chords had been. These were real individuals. Something had been changed about them, though. While they were people, something had been changed about them on a cellular level. Hecate could see the strange disassociation, and she knew that it had something to do with magic. It was likely the same sort of magic that had brought the Power Chords to life, but this seemed to be on a deeper level. Something was very strange about these five individuals.

Of the five, there didn't seem to be anything out of the ordinary. There was a tall, thin, pale man holding a five-string guitar, wearing black leather pants and a leather coat that could have fallen out of the Matrix movies. His wrists were littered with scars, only half of which were manufactured, and Hecate could see the pain that the individual had gone through, amplified through the magical spell that coated these individuals like a second skin. On the bass guitar, a petite woman, sporting a catholic schoolgirl's outfit and a neon-red pixie cut, stared into the abyss, as if begging it to stare back into her.

The drummer. A large man with braided hair, ebony skin, and opal eyes, sat behind his set, looking like a Trojan hiding behind his wall. Muscular arms rippled from his massive shoulders like oaken totems, adorned with tribal tattoos, stitching a complex spider web, which bled fluidly into a tank top, stretched to capacity by his broad chest. There was a front man, standing in front of a microphone, appearing as though he hadn't seen the light of the sun in several months. His carefully crafted hair glistened under the lights, thanks to the excessive product. The smeared eyeliner around his eyes betrayed the tears which, undoubtedly, were straining for release. Together, the four individuals painted a sad, miserable, picture. The addition of the keyboardist, however, added a chilling touch.

Fittingly, the individual behind the keyboard was doing the least to manufacture a Gothic facade. Long black hair hung in long, greasy strands around his face, yes, but it was a fairly natural cut and a traditional hair color. He wore black, of course, but there was nothing unique or melodramatic about his clothing choices: it was simply a shirt and pants. His face was not made up, his arms held no visible tattoos, and his nails were cut to a normal length. There was very little about him that would leave an impression, and his inclusion in the group confused Hecate, initially. A look into his eyes, however, sent chills dancing under her skin.

There was the dark. Within this keyboardists gaze lay a vicious hatred, a dark vengeance, a thick and merciless lust for depravity. This creature was not lost, far from it. The keyboardist was not pretending to be hurt, nor were they exaggerating their suffering for dramatic effect. They wanted to inflict pain. They wanted to drink the blood as though it were a tonic. Hecate was impressed by what she saw there. This keyboardist was not a member of the band, he was the band. The stench of black magic and rot wafted off of him, subtle at first, but undeniable once recognized. He was the reason for every manufactured sorrow that this band was feeling. And why wouldn't he continue? Suffering would always sell.

"All music is produced to elicit an emotional response," Pan's voice was saying, tearing through Hecate's meditative analysis of the band. "That's why music is so powerful; you hear a song, and you are immediately flushed with the emotions which were programmed into the tablature by the composer. It's manipulation, but it's very rarely considered as a manipulative technique. After all, who could think that the warm, comfortable feelings provided by Journey's 'Don't Stop Believing' could be used for anything evil? That's why the technique works so well."

Nemesis scowled darkly at the figure, standing pretentiously before her. "That has nothing to do with our reason for being here," she snarled. "Hecate and I have worked very hard to get to this point. Where's the gem, satyr?"

Pan sighed, lowering his head. "Well," he breathed, raising his head once more to return Nemesis' glare with a sneer of his own, "I was going to educate you all with a nice lecture on the subgenre of emo-rock (you know, since all music evokes emotion, calling an entire genre 'emo' is redundant, ridiculous, and oddly powerful). My words, however, would fall on deaf ears. I suppose it would also be useless to feign naivety as to the gem, since you both have kicked some major ass to get here, and those obstacles wouldn't have been there if I didn't have the gem. Yes, I have the gem. No, I don't intend on giving it up. I need it."

As Pan was talking, Hecate watched the band on stage. They appeared to be marionettes, being manipulated and contorted through emotional strands, making them feel what the puppeteer chose to inflict upon them. Hecate instinctively would have accused Pan of being the puppet master but, as she examined the keyboardist closer, she began to consider that he was the one holding the strings. He continued to grow more monstrous the longer she examined him.

"We cannot allow you to do that, Pan," Nemesis continued with her rebuke. "The gem holds great power, too much power for any one individual to hold. It is dangerous, and you would come to that conclusion yourself, if you would stop and consider the ramifications of what you are doing. The only real solution is to destroy the gem. You should give it to us."

"Do you have any idea," Pan argued, fire sparking in his eyes, "how frustrating it is, listening to the same fucking song over and over again? Each musician thinks that they're a gift to the industry, and everyone is going to want to hear their shit but, when you break it down, everyone has already heard their shit before, millions of times! It's all been done! It's all been played! The old Jewish king who said there was nothing new under the sun had no idea how right he was. It applies doubly, though, to music. It's really enough to drive a person insane."

"Pan," Nemesis said, her scowl darkening, with her hand wrapping tighter around her sword's hilt. "None of this has anything to do with the gem. It would be in your best interest to give it to us."

As Hecate watched the scene develop between Nemesis and Pan, she was very aware that the band behind Pan was, seemingly, becoming more active. Looking at the keyboard player, she noticed that his snarl was growing. Hecate continued to analyze the situation, trying to figure out what was going to happen next. Clearly, the band was part of Pan's defense. She simply couldn't figure out how.

"It's even worse when you're an immortal being," Pan continued to rant. "These pithy humans get seven, maybe eight, decades of shitty, retreaded music that they're supposed to embrace and love. We get centuries! Try relating to a millennial when your age is over a millennium. There's literally nothing, no common ground. Stupid pop songs about lost lovers and weekend adventures, idiotic songs about the environment and social issues, trashy songs about street wars and victimized partners...it's all the same shit! I need something new!"

Nemesis sighed, growing weary of the repartee. "Pan," she grumbled through grit teeth, "what does this have to do with—"

"I need the gem!" Pan declared emphatically. "I need it to find something new! The powers of the gem will draw talent to me and, in that talent, I'll be able to find something unique, something original, something...that I haven't heard a million fucking times already!"

That got Hecate's attention. Prying her eyes away from the band, she turned a perplexed eyebrow to Pan. "You did this," she questioned him cautiously, "to benefit your record label? You did this for financial gain?"

"Hecate, look at me," Pan replied, rolling his eyes. "I could give two shits about money, you know that. Have you not been listening? I have plenty of money. What I don't have is music, real music, music that has never been heard before. That's what I need the gem for. It's my last hope that, maybe, I can find something real. After I've found it, you can have the gem, I don't care. I'll give it to you willingly and live with the consequences. Right now, though, I need the gem."

The desperation and longing pried at Hecate's heart. She could see how passionately Pan longed for something, and she could relate to it. She herself had thirsted for knowledge the same way, craving the intimate touch of nature and its secrets. The proposal that Pan had presented was beginning to sound reasonable. Perhaps, if it meant that his passions would be sated, they could allow him to keep the gem for a time, until he found what he was seeking.

"What do you think?" she asked, turning to Nemesis. "Could we—"

"This satyr just tried to kill us!" Nemesis cut her off loudly. "He tried to kill us twice and Hephaestus once!"

"Oh yeah!" Hecate exclaimed, any feeling of compassion suddenly disappearing as she remembered the events.

"I was desperate!" Pan cried. "I wasn't trying to kill Hephaestus, technically, I was just trying to get the gem. The Power Chords—and yes, they're physical manifestations of power chords, good on you for figuring that out—got carried away. I should have just drugged him and stolen the gem, which is actually what I did, anyway. With you guys, I...okay, I actually tried to kill you guys, but you have to understand, I—"

"Did you just ask us to understand why you tried to kill us?" Nemesis asked in a chilling tone.

"Well, see it from my point of view—" Pan continued pleading.

"You just asked us to see our attempted murder," Hecate laughed a bit at the absurdity, "from your perspective."

"You know what: fuck it," Pan threw his hands into the air in frustration, turning to the stage behind him. "I'll let my house band, The Bloody Remnants, argue my point."

All music, no matter how cheap, over-produced, and redundant it is, has an emotional signature. It doesn't matter if it's an annoying ear-worm of a song that makes you smile at first, but later gets stuck in your head, or a beautiful sonata that brings you to tears of passion, simply through the fluid ivory tones of a dancing piano. When one hears music, they naturally expect to feel something, anything. If the song doesn't evoke any emotion at all, it's not a very good song.

No matter how grounded she could have been for the emotional stimulation of music, there was no way that Hecate could have prepared for the impact that flooded over her when the band began to play.

With the first chord played from the guitarist, Hecate felt her knees buckle. She gasped as a storm of negativity pounded past her mental boundaries, tearing her mind to shreds with feelings of loss and abandonment.

Hecate was reminded that this world was not her own. There was a time when she was worshiped, revered, and honored by masses. She was honored and hailed, not only as the goddess of magic, but the guardian of crossroads. Her image had evoked guidance, with her three-pry statues facing all directions, opening the way for travelers. Prayers to her had been prayers of protection, begging her to watch over the journeys of those who walked her paths. She found herself crippled by the feeling of neglect. Tears, which refused to fall, filled her eyes and, as the music enveloped her, she felt the sorrow of abandonment.

As the song continued, the drums began to pound. With the

drums, the emotional attack changed. Hecate felt anger. She had given so much to the people of this world. She had provided guidance and protection to so many! How many of them remembered her now? There were some, yes, but they didn't really believe in her. Their prayers were not prayers of supplication. If anything, they were prayers to an empty icon. They didn't ask her to bless their travels, they asked for an empty image to bless their petty magics. Most of them didn't even understand the harmonic resonance of the universe. They did not see how all of nature connected through the vibrations that flowed in life. They just wanted the shallow, empty image of her to curse their past lovers or provide them with wealth. She was a joke to them. She hated that!

The vocalist began to sing, and it was as if his lyrics were written specifically for her.

The pain and the rage of a world that is gone has filled me.
I feel the sorrow of centuries, and I crave
release.
The pain and the rage of a dying world consumes me.
I feel the pity. I feel the lust. I feel it all, and I crave
release.

Hecate could feel it all. The emotions flooded into her, and she saw how irrelevant she had become. It shattered her. She would never recover what she had wanted. Retrieving the Gem of Illecebra had been a fool's errand. She had wanted to restore power to Olympus, but that was ridiculous. The Olympians would never be what they once were, and most of them were okay with that. What she had meant to contribute to their power would never be appreciated. She had been a fool to ever think that it would.

Nothing I can do.
Nothing I can say.
Nothing I can feel.
Nothing will ever matter.
I have no purpose.
I have nothing.
Release

Even Nemesis, her comrade in arms, knew it. Nemesis knew how useless the gem would be. She was aware of how destructive Hecate was. The only reason that Nemesis was even standing with her now was to make sure that Hecate failed in what she was trying to do. Nemesis was only trying to mitigate damage.

Release

It would be in Hecate's best interest if she just gave this pointless quest up. She wasn't Jason, trying to regain a kingdom. She wasn't Hercules, attempting to restore honor. She was not Odysseus, returning to his love. She was a fragment of a lost world. She was irrelevant.

Release

It would be better for the world if she just gave up this venture.

Release

It would be better for the world if she didn't exist.

Release

No one believed in her anyway. She would not be missed.

Release

The truth of the song resonated in her mind as the pounding bass line filtered through her senses. The sorrow and loss filled her, and she longed to give into it. There was nothing for her in this world. Why would she force the world to host her useless identity any longer? No one would miss her. There was no longer a point to her existence.

As the heart of the music flowed over her, Hecate felt something. Something, someone was touching her shoulder.

"I can't fight this alone," an oddly recognizable voice informed her. "The magic is too powerful. I need your help."

Clawing herself out of the miasma that she was drowning in, Hecate turned a pained face toward the speaker. She saw Nemesis, standing beside her, as though untouched by the emotional impact of the music. She was so much stronger than her. What help could she offer to Nemesis? She was so strong, and Hecate was so useless.

Hecate felt her mouth open, but she had no words. Nothing she said would matter anyway.

Nemesis gripped her by both shoulders with a fevered urgency. "Snap out of it!" she cried. "This is not real! Come back to me, I need you!"

Hearing those words, coming from a figure that she so respected, made something click in her mind. It was the music. It was creating a false reality in her mind. The impact of the music was causing her to feel something that wasn't true; it was a lie. All the sorrow and misery were facsimiles, falsehoods driven into her mind by the music.

"I can't," Hecate pleaded, disbelieving the voice that she heard escaping from her mouth. "I don't know who I am anymore. I can't do—"

The hand flew quickly, before Hecate could react. It smacked her sharply across the face, and her senses were filled with a sharp pain. That pain forced all the other emotions into the background.

"Stop it!" Nemesis demanded forcefully. "You are Hecate, the goddess of magic! Your self-image isn't important right now! We have more important things to worry about!"

Shock from the slap and anger from the resulting pain flared into Hecate's mind. She focused on those two sensations, forcing all the other emotions to the background. The band continued to play, abuse and misery spewing from the instruments like sewage from a drain-pipe, but she resisted submitting to it. Hecate focused on the magical elements that filled the air. Magical flotsam and jetsam floated through the environment so thick that Hecate felt as though she could reach out and grab pieces of them. There had to be a source. Yes, the music was supplying the stimulation, but it was only a conduit. There had to be something that was generating the power.

"I've tried to advance on them," Nemesis was saying "but there is a barrier around them that is preventing me. I know that your magic is in short-supply here, but now might be a time for—"

Hecate held her hand up, signaling for Nemesis to stop talking. She needed to focus. Her magical reserves were waning, yes, but she would need to use them if she and Nemesis were going to survive this onslaught. Isolating the energy was easy and took very little magic. She did that quickly, and the trail that she found lead back to the most natural force: it was the keyboardist. He was the one with the real magic, and he was the one leading the listener to doom and destruction through the song. Hecate focused her dissecting analysis on him, and what she found explained everything, while presenting many other complications. The keyboardist was not a man at all.

"Nemesis," Hecate breathed, drifting out of her analytical state for a moment, "the thing playing the keyboard isn't human. They're a siren."

"Well, that complicates things," Nemesis critiqued, her brow furrowing.

Sirens had not been heard from in a very long time. Hecate remembered when they used to wreak havoc on sailors and travelers, luring them into traps and rocky shores with their enchanting music. Hecate could not remember an instance when their songs had been used to inflict negative emotions, but she could see how their spells could be modified to do so. Before the music had begun to play, she had not been feeling despondent. In fact, she had not been feeling anything, except for urgency and desperation to get the gem back, away from Pan. It was obvious that the song had magical properties. It only made sense that it would be the product of a siren.

"It does not," Hecate replied to Nemesis, her attention never deviating from the diabolical conductor. "It simply puts most of the responsibility on me."

Nemesis turned to her with an arched eyebrow. "Do you have enough magic to combat this creature?"

Hecate took a deep breath. "I'm going to have to," she resolved.

Many adventurers had defeated sirens in the past. Odysseus had done so by tying himself to the ship that he was sailing upon, so that he could not submit to their calls. Orpheus had defeated them by playing his instrument so loudly and so beautifully that it countered the effects of their song. In all the documentation that Hecate had read, she could not recall a single instance in which they had been defeated through physical interaction.

Nemesis stood beside her, weapon in hand, and the music played on, encouraging her to simply give up. The look in Nemesis' eyes was more desperate and pleading than Hecate had ever seen from her. Hecate could not determine whether this was because of the song's effects or if Nemesis was feeling desperately outmatched. She was used to attacking things, head-on, through physical means. She was unable to do so right now, and that must be driving her mad. Reaching into her magical resources, Hecate created a bubble of air around her head. This muted the sound enough for her to be able to focus, but it was also a constant drain on what little magic she had left. It was necessary, though.

Closing her eyes, Hecate could see the magical tapestry that was emanating from the siren's song. The siren was not the one creating the music, directly; rather, it was spreading its influence to the other musicians. Through that interaction, the other band members were able to transmit the siren's song through their instruments and vocals, supporting the idea that they were little more than puppets. Hecate was tempted to feel sympathy for them, but there was no time for that. Sympathy is much more authentic when one isn't fighting for their life, anyway.

If she could compromise the transmission of sound, the magical barrier that was holding Nemesis at bay should be compromised. Pooling the remaining magic she had in reserve was almost painful, but Hecate did it. Forming a ball of energy in her palm took all of her concentration, and spreading that energy through her fingers stretched her to her limits. Locating an outlet in the wall, Hecate forced the energy out of her body into the electrical system. This caused a power surge, just as she had hoped. The room was, once again, bathed in darkness, and only the acoustic remnants of the song continued to play.

Even that faded as the band stopped, undoubtedly dazed, to consider what was going on. Nemesis had some idea of what was going on, and she had no doubt that this momentary reprieve would not last long. She could not see clearly, but she knew where the siren had been standing before the power surge. The magical barrier had been created by the music, and now the music was absent. Gripping her sword tightly, Nemesis charged the stage. Planting her foot, Nemesis launched herself into the air, landing directly across from the siren. Even in the darkness, Nemesis could see their expression, one of anger, pain, and rage at having their spell interfered with. They opened their mouth, as though preparing to speak or sing. Nemesis never gave them the chance. With the focused strike, she forced the point of her blade into their mouth and down their throat. Since she had no familiarity with siren biology, it made no sense for her to twist the blade around inside of their innards, but that was what she did. She could feel the soft squish of organs and hear the satisfying tearing as tendons and arteries were severed. The blade dripped with a thick coat of blood as she pulled it free of the siren's now-dilapidated body, and a pungent smell, not unlike sewage, filled the air. As the siren was in the process of collapsing, Nemesis sank the blade into their torso, just for good measure. Their body opened like a Fabergé egg, spilling its macabre candy across the stage.

"Where are we?"

"Did we get the contract?"

"Dude, where did this guitar come from? It's sick!"

Nemesis abandoned the formerly-enchanted humans, assuming that they could figure things out for themselves, and stepped from the stage. She walked to where her comrade had been, and she found Hecate, kneeling and panting, as though exhausted.

"We did it," the goddess breathed. "I...need to get outside. I'm out of magic. We did it."

Nemesis fought the smile that danced in the corners of her cheeks, as she wrapped her arm around Hecate and supported her standing. "We will leave," Nemesis assured her "once Pan has been dealt with. Don't worry about your magic, I think I can handle the satyr."

Hecate placed an arm around her shoulders, and Nemesis carried most of her weight as the two of them walked to the door. Nemesis had a good idea of where Pan was going to be.

CHAPTER THIRTY-FIVE

Nemesis had a good idea of where Pan would be going. Before the band had begun playing the music, she had noticed him eying a small door near the back of the room. That was likely a back door, leading to his office. That would be where he'd be going.

The music from the band hadn't been a kill strike, he had likely only been attempting to slow them down. Thinking back, most of his attacks had not been attempts to kill them. He would have been familiar with their techniques, and he could have thrown more at them than he had. Had he been attempting to kill them, he would have struck with much more savage voracity. Each attack that he had perpetrated must have been either to obtain the gem or to detain them. He was trying to get away.

Along with being a wonderful musician, Pan was a shrewd businessman. Panflute Records had been one of the most successful music labels in history, thanks in no small part to his ingenuity, market analysis, and advertising techniques. The business had made Pan into a very wealthy little satyr, and he probably had an escape plan that Nemesis and Hecate would not have the resources to prevent once it was enacted. This made it imperative that they catch

Pan before he left the property. Once he was gone, both he and the gem would be untraceable.

"Do you realize," Hecate muttered, as she limped weakly along, clinging to Nemesis for support "that the magic properties of the gem have never been confirmed? We're all going nuts about this gem, assuming it has immense power, but we've never seen it used? It could just be a pretty rock."

"The thought has occurred to me," Nemesis confirmed, as she checked the tracking device, and it confirmed her suspicions. The gem's signature was racing quickly toward the roof. Judging from the trajectory and the speed, Pan was using the stairwell. That would make sense. The elevator likely didn't exit that far up.

Nemesis sighed. Pan had a significant head start, which made catching up with him difficult, unless she could find a better option. Nemesis analyzed the area outside the room: a long hallway lined with office and studio doors, concluding with a single window at the far end. Biting her lip, Nemesis came up with an idea.

"Are you strong enough to hold onto my back?" she asked Hecate, looking to the drained goddess seriously.

Hecate's eyes locked on the window and quickly comprehended what Nemesis was planning to do. She nodded: "I can do that," she said. "Let's just get this done quickly."

"Keep your face buried in my back," Nemesis instructed her as she virtually hoisted Hecate to her shoulders, securing her tightly. Once she felt Hecate's nose between her shoulder blades, she took her grappling hook from her belt, and charged the length of the hall at a neck-breaking speed.

As she neared the window, Nemesis lowered her head and launched herself toward the glass. It shattered around her, as her body sailed through the opening. She felt the glass on her face and heard Hecate's muffled screaming as she twisted her body in midair, and threw the grappling hook upward, toward any external obstruction that it could latch onto. Her body fell for a moment, then jerked to a stop as the hook found a hold. Bracing herself for the collision,

Nemesis allowed her shoulder to take most of the impact as she swung into the side of the building. Hecate's grip around her neck tightened, and her legs momentarily lost their grip around her waist, but she remained secured against her back, so Nemesis could not allow herself to focus on that. Instead, Nemesis looked, and saw that the hook was latched to a small balcony, roughly a floor above where they had been. Quickly, she pulled herself upward, using the building as leverage.

Reaching the balcony, Nemesis pulled herself over the railing, collecting the grappling hook as she did so. There was a glass door that opened into an office. Through the door, Nemesis could see the startled face of the office's occupant: a middle-aged man in a business suit with a receding hairline. She paid him no mind, turning her attention to the exterior of the building. There was another ledge, roughly a floor above them. As she prepared to throw the grappling hook toward it, she felt Hecate's hand leave her shoulder momentarily.

"Did you just wave at the man in the office?" she asked, throwing the hook toward the ledge.

"I just wanted him to feel acknowledged," Hecate explained in an innocent voice.

Nemesis shook her head as she began the climb upward again. She really did admire Hecate's genuine spirit but, in this instance, she would have preferred that she remain focused on the task at hand.

There was a helicopter on the roof. Even from three floors down, Nemesis could hear its propellers flapping against the wind. As she climbed onto the top of the building, she saw the machine, roughly thirty feet from where she stood, awaiting takeoff. She also saw Pan, sprinting across the roof toward the vehicle, carrying a briefcase, sporting a sizable bulge in the pocket of his blazer. As her feet hit the roof, Hecate disengaged with her back, and Nemesis unsheathed her sword. She had never used it as a projectile before, but circumstances left her no option. Using all of her strength, she thrust the sword toward the helicopter with as much accuracy as she could manage.

The blade found its home in the fuel line. Black fluid poured from the machine's undercarriage like hemophilia in a war zone, soaking the battle ground in its pungent scent. Pan froze, mere feet from the helicopter, and looked to where Nemesis stood. Fear canvassed his face, shrouded with shock and dismay.

"What are you doing?" he screamed. "You're going to get us all killed!"

Two men stepped from the helicopter, each pointing a gun at Nemesis. She hardly noticed them as she advanced on the satyr. One of the armed men fired on her. Raising her arm casually, the bullet bounced harmlessly off of Nemesis' brazier.

"Don't shoot, you idiot!" Pan shouted, jumping at the gunman urgently. "There's gasoline all over the place!"

The guard looked to Pan with an offended but comprehending glare: "What do you want us to do, Mr. Grim?"

"Stand down," Pan growled, shrugging off his blazer. "I'll handle this bitch myself."

"Don't touch the jacket," he instructed his team, as he marched to meet Nemesis, fear and dismay being eclipsed by rage and determination.

Looking to where her sword was lodged in the helicopter's body, Nemesis tried to calculate a way to get there without interference. Pan noticed her line of sight and altered his advance to prevent it. There were very few elements on the rooftop that she could use for weaponry. Breathing in deeply, Nemesis resigned herself to hand-to-hand combat.

"It did not have to come to this, Pan," she tried to rationalize, as Pan stepped closer. "I've studied your attacks and know that you have not been attempting to kill, only distract us. If we engage, I will not stop until—"

"No, I was trying to kill you," Pan corrected her. "You fucking gods or demi-gods or whatever the hell you are calling yourselves now are just annoyingly difficult to eliminate."

A chill ran through Nemesis' mind as any hint of sympathy that she had held for the satyr evaporated. As he drew closer, he sank into a fighting stance, placing the weight on his back leg. His left arm was positioned defensively, with his right fist by his hip, preparing to strike. Nemesis cocked her head, adopting a stance of her own, placing weight on her front foot, both hands open and ready to strike. She had not realized that Pan was trained in mixed martial arts. Depending on his skill level, that was going to complicate things.

"You Olympians think that you can tell all the rest of us how we are supposed to live out our existence," Pan snarled. "I achieved something, and now you want to take it away from me. Centuries pass, and nothing changes. It's still you egomaniacs dictating existence for us little people, isn't it?"

"I am not an Olympian, Pan," Nemesis retorted, as the two began to circle one another, each posturing, waiting for the first opportunity to strike. "The gem is too powerful for any to have. I would have come after any who held it."

"Don't try to defend yourself," Pan continued his self-justifying rage. "I offered you a reasonable alternative, and you spit it back at me. This is on you."

Nemesis was the first to attack, and that was her mistake. As they circled one another, she saw that his back leg was less protected, and she struck. Pivoting her front foot, she kicked with her back leg, readying her opposite fist for the follow-up strike. Pan anticipated the attack. He pulled his back leg out of the way of the kick, then struck at Nemesis' extended calve with an open hand. His fingers felt like daggers, as they struck between the muscles of Nemesis' upper thigh. Gritting her teeth against the pain, Nemesis swung her leg back, away from the attacker, and used the momentum to swing her fist toward him. Pan avoided the strike easily, dancing back out of reach.

It was a valid technique, using the strikes of an opponent against them. Nemesis would have to adapt her own striking pattern. As she turned to face Pan, pain shooting up and down her leg from where he had struck her, she heard swiftly advancing footsteps over her shoulder. One of the guards was charging her, blindly attempting to protect his boss. As she took a battle stance again, she thrust her elbow backward, landing the blow just below the sternum. The advancing party stopped, gasping for air. Nemesis spun quickly and caught the man as he was sinking to his knees. Effortlessly, she swung the body around, thrusting it in Pan's direction. Pan jumped out of the way, lithely skipping from foot to foot, fists raised as though sparing.

"So, where does a little goat boy go to get the training that you exhibit?" Nemesis asked, adopting an open stance with her left arm held strongly in front of her and her right hand open, held at chest level. Typically, insults were beneath her, but she needed to find a way to take Pan out of his element. Insulting his pride might be a technique that would prove useful.

"Taiwan, Tibet, and Sensai Norfolk in Birmingham, Kentucky," Pan answered casually as he dropped back into a closed, defensive stance. "After my brothers and I got attacked by that damn bridge troll, I figured I would need a way to defend myself."

"You have no brothers," Nemesis replied, failing to catch the reference.

"You're right," Pan scoffed. "I don't have any martial art training either."

Nemesis assumed a defensive stance that mirrored Pan's, and the two began to circle each other, less than three feet from one another. Nemesis stared deeply into the satyr's eyes. There was cold hatred for everything that she represented, likely referring to the ruling principalities of Olympus, which had never respected him enough. Beneath that, Nemesis saw a crippling ennui, combined with a desperate thirst for purpose and a lust for meaning. Contrasting that was a carnivorous determination to recover a purpose, and a powerful hunger for validity. Lastly, clouded by the plethora of other emotions, there was fear. Pan was nervous and insecure. He hid it well, but the truth betrayed him.

Nemesis only hoped that Pan could not see the trepidation in her own eyes.

The two circled each other, neither willing to make the first move. It was uncommon for Nemesis to take as defensive of a stance as she was taking now, but she had needed to modify her martial techniques to compensate for Pan's abilities. She was out of her element. Pan knew that as well as she did. The methodologies to martial art were far different than sword combat. Against her instincts, she felt her eyes drift to where her sword was, a few yards away, lodged in the helicopter's body. She yearned to hold it between her fingers once more.

Pan needed no more excuse to attack. The moment Nemesis' attention deviated from him, he struck, spinning a strong roundhouse kick toward her left rib cage. Nemesis heard the motion and reacted instinctively. Pivoting her hips, Nemesis blocked the strike with her forearm. She then followed through by thrusting her kneecap into Pan's unprotected sternum. Pan absorbed the blow as best he could, recovering his balance and feigning back. As he attempted to straighten his back, Nemesis noticed that he struggled to do so. He was in pain. His scowl darkened as he fought his way through it.

A gun was fired behind her. Nemesis heard the bullet leave the shaft, and she felt the air tracking its trajectory. Spinning slightly, she raised her arm, and the bullet connected with her brazier. It stung, and the pain reflected through her arm. It sparked, and the spilled oil responded around her. Nemesis jumped away from the quickly igniting fire. By doing so, she accidentally dodged Pan's oncoming attack, as he leaped at her with a jumping kick. Instinctively, she punched to where his face should have been. She was almost surprised when she connected.

Pan took the blow on his cheek. Absorbing the blow as best he could, Pan hit the ground and rolled away from Nemesis, springing back to his feet quickly. His clothing was now stained from the spilled oil, and the fire was spreading quickly.

"Do you idiots see why I told you not to shoot?!" Pan screamed angrily back to his bodyguards, as he spat blood out of his injured mouth.

"Pan," Nemesis attempted to rationalize with him again "this is ridiculous. Nothing is worth this amount of damage. Why don't we—"

Nemesis was cut off quickly by the shocked exclamations from the bodyguards. Both she and Pan looked quickly at them, and they saw the briefcase elevating, being drawn away from where Pan had placed it. It looked as though the case was flying on its own, but a quick glance to Hecate told Nemesis everything that she needed to know. Hecate had regained her power.

"You bitch!" Pan screamed, preparing to charge at her. "Give that back!"

As Pan made a move toward Hecate, Nemesis caught him by the collar. "Enough is enough, satyr," she growled.

To her surprise, Pan's body went limp. "I was so close," he sighed, tiredly. "I just wanted to find something new."

"Get your people off the roof," Nemesis replied as calmly as possible as she dragged Pan behind her. She pulled her sword out of the fuel line and dropped Pan to the rooftop once it was in her grip once more. "The fire is spreading quickly, and an explosion would kill them."

"Are you going to kill me?" Pan asked Nemesis in a tired voice.

Nemesis considered the comment for a moment. "Can you give me a convincing reason not to?" she asked.

Pan sighed. "No," he admitted. "I tried to kill you a handful of times; turn-about is fair play."

Nemesis peered at Pan for a moment: a broken, tired, defeated creature. She wondered if he had been that, even before he had taken possession of the gem. "Clear the roof," she instructed him. "Hecate and I will take care of the fire and try to minimize damage, then we will deal with you."

Pan nodded, and Nemesis turned to where Hecate was holding the briefcase. "Can you put the fire out?" she asked. "We need to get the gem to Hephaestus quickly, before it can create any more chaos."

Hecate's grip on the briefcase tightened as her eyes fell. "Yes," she sighed "to that point…"

"Oh, plot twist!" Pan cackled impishly, from where he lay on the roof in a puddle of oil.

Nemesis felt the oxygen being sucked from her lungs, as though she'd been punched in the stomach. She and Hecate had never had the same reasons for hunting the gem. Until now, cooperation had been necessary and useful. That time was over. Now, their goals were at odds with each other. Now, they were more than friends.

They were competitors.

CHAPTER THIRTY-SIX

A LONG, LONG, TIME AGO...

XILFIM WAS GONE. SHE HAD DIED BECAUSE OF WHAT HE HAD done. Iago told himself that it was not his fault, but his memories of her betrayed him. He told himself that he had only done what was necessary, but even that was an exaggeration. There were many other options that he could have taken, and he knew that. She didn't need to die. This gem, while it had given him what he had desired most, had destroyed his life. She had told him that it would. Even to the end, Xilfim had warned him about the gem's power and his lust for it. Once he had lost the gem, it was only natural for him to suspect her of stealing it. It had been the only logical conclusion. His reaction had been justified. The fact that he had been wrong did not change that.

While he had held the gem, from the moment that he had pulled it out of the furnace, it had changed his life. The magi community had begun to respect him. People had sought his approval as if it were gold. They had reached out to him, begging him to consult with them. He had been offered wealth, women, land, power, and anything else that he could have sought after. People just wanted to be near him, to hear him speak, to smell his skin, and feel his touch. Even Cesar Atalis, the highest name of the land, had offered him a seat in his high counsel. Even when his advice was wrong or poorly given, those whom he had given the advice to blamed themselves, either in execution or translation. They would return to him, seeking his forgiveness, desperate for more guidance. He had felt like an Olympian god. He had been an Olympian god.

Then he had lost the gem. After that, everything that he had accomplished, everything that he had gained, had been taken away from him. It hadn't stopped there.

"You did this," the ghost of Xilfim whispered into his ear. *"You did this to yourself. This is your fault. You could have prevented all of this, if only you had stopped. You should never have crafted that gem."*

The ground shook beneath his feet, and he heard the screams of his fellow Atlantians as they ran from the destruction. An ear-shattering crack pierced the air, and Iago looked toward the sky. Vanicia, the volcano just outside of the city where Iago was living (although living was an exaggeration; he spent his nights on the streets, since there was no charity to be found) was rumbling. Within two days, there would be an eruption. Within three days, the city would be buried in ash and lava. Iago knew that. He also knew that it was his fault.

It was illogical to blame himself. Losing the gem could not have been the reason for this destruction. The fact that it seemed to be following him was merely coincidence.

The earthquake had not been his fault. Earthquakes were a natural occurrence.

The hailstorm had not been his fault. Hailstorms happened.

The plague of rats had been a sanitation problem.

The attacking army had been an act of war.

This volcanic eruption was not his fault. Volcanoes erupted.

Iago looked to the black cloud of gas that was pouring out of Vanicia, and he knew that it was a lie. He was destroying Atlantis, little by little, with each move that he made. One way to preserve the state was to throw himself into the volcano. His only other option was to recover the gem.

Xilfim had been right all along. Iago should never have crafted the gem.

This was not his fault.

It was the Gem of Illecebra.

CHAPTER THIRTY-SEVEN

THE FIRE WAS SPREADING. BOTH NEMESIS AND HECATE KNEW that they were on borrowed time. In a few moments the flames would reach the fuselage and, once that occurred, the explosion would be massive.

"Hecate," Nemesis pleaded with her best friend, "we should contain this fire and get the situation under control. Both Pan and the gem need to be dealt with, but that cannot happen if this current situation isn't defused."

Hecate nodded. She stepped toward Nemesis, holding the briefcase tightly. "I think, perhaps," she said, an uncharacteristic chill in her tone, "that you and I should come to a meeting of minds first."

"Hecate," Nemesis sighed, and tried to rationalize with her friend. "Set down the gem. We need to—"

"Do not tell me what we need to do," Hecate cut her off. "I know what should be done, and that's what I intend to do. You want to destroy the gem, but that cannot be done. It's too powerful, too strong. The only things that were capable of destroying it were sunk with Atlantis."

"That's not true," Nemesis retorted. "Hephaestus is working—"

"Please don't interrupt me," Hecate said, holding up her hand, with what remained of the warmth in her eyes fading. "Since the gem can't be destroyed, we should use it to our advantage. This world needs guidance. I know that you remember the time when we were worshiped. I know that you remember when people sought our blessing. This gem could be the key to regaining all of that."

Realization sank into Nemesis' mind as she uncovered Hecate's real motivation. It had been foolish of her to think that the two of them had wanted the same thing. "You want to use the gem to restore power to the Olympians," she breathed.

"I've never hidden that fact," Hecate replied in an even tone. "It's the only logical option. We need to be remembered. These people, they remember us in stories and cartoons, as mockeries of who we once were! With this gem, we can return to the force of power that we once were. We can make people remember us."

"Wow," Pan muttered, as he awkwardly stood to his feet again, his clothing soaked in the oil. "Now, see, that's ambitious. I was just looking for a musical act. That's straight up diabolical."

Nemesis did not have time to consider the ramifications of what Hecate was suggesting. If she had, she would have seen how manipulative the idea was. She also would have seen that the idea would have worked, and it would have gone well, until they lost the gem. They would have lost the gem, ultimately. Everyone lost the gem.

"The gem needs to be destroyed," Nemesis insisted. "It will be destroyed. Having that much power is dangerous; it's too much power for one individual to hold."

"It wouldn't be one person," Hecate retorted. "It would be all of Olympus! We could hold the gem, and we could keep it safe! There's no reason to think that this wouldn't work. You should want this! This would return power to Olympus, and we wouldn't have to live in hiding any longer."

"It wouldn't work that way," Nemesis growled. "You know the power would corrupt. You know that we would lose it. You know that there would be no way to stop it. It's too much power! The gem sank Atlantis!"

"Oh, that's a myth," Hecate replied, rolling her eyes. "Even in our time, we knew that was just a rumor."

"That rumor had some basis in fact, though," Nemesis insisted. "It could never be confirmed, but it could not be dismissed either. The risk is too high. The gem must be destroyed."

"The gem cannot be destroyed!"

"Hephaestus will find a way."

"Well," Hecate cocked an aggressive eyebrow. "It seems we are at an impasse."

"So it would seem," Nemesis answered, adjusting her grip on her sword.

"Oh, this just got interesting," Pan said, smiling. "Is there a chance we could put the fire out first, before you two get into each other?"

Both goddesses answered him with a glare.

"I was just asking," Pan stepped back defensively. He turned to signal his bodyguards. They had left the roof. That was logical. Pan wondered what they would be telling their wives later, when they asked how the workday had gone. He wondered if they would be listing him as a reference on their resume.

Nemesis readied her sword, preparing for an attack. She had seen Hecate in a fight before, and she knew that she had very little defense against magic. Hecate had the advantage. In her mind, Nemesis began to analyze the best way to combat her. She didn't have long to analyze. A burst of wind connected with her chest, thrusting her off of her feet, tossing her backward about five feet. She landed on her back, inches from where flames were lustfully devouring the spilled substance, creeping swiftly toward impending death.

Recovering quickly, Nemesis rose to her left knee. Before standing completely, she looked to the scene. Hecate was advancing on her, walking past where Pan was standing.

"Look, I admire what you're trying to do," Pan said nervously "but if that fire hits the fuselage—"

Hecate casually pushed him back, and Pan fell backward, landing with an audible plop, as he collapsed into a puddle of oil near where the fire was. Hecate was no longer holding the briefcase which contained the gem. She had laid it on the roof where she had been standing. Nemesis saw it. Pan saw it.

"This needs to be done, Nemesis," Hecate declared, raising her hands as if preparing for another attack. "Just because I am the only one who sees it does not make it any less true."

Hecate was roughly four feet from where Nemesis was kneeling. Anticipating the attack, Nemesis propelled her body forward, ducked her head, and rolled. Closing the distance between the two of them, Nemesis drove her elbow into Hecate's torso. Hecate gasped for air and doubled over as Nemesis sprang to her feet again. With a swift leg sweep, Nemesis compromised Hecate's balance, and she collapsed to the ground. Bringing her sword around, Nemesis pointed the tip directly at Hecate's neck, threatening to eliminate the competition.

Before she could strike, a burst of warm force hit her in the chest. It took her off her feet, thrusting her a few inches into the air and several inches back. Nemesis landed in a crouch, ready to strike again. As she examined the scene before her quickly, she saw that Hecate had gotten to her feet again, the fire was dangerously close to the helicopter, and Pan had sneaked past Hecate to recover the brief-case. He was now racing toward the door in order to exit the roof.

"Pan!" she cried, finding that the volume strained her vocal chords.

Hecate quickly looked to where Pan was running, and she twisted her fingers through the air. Pan's exit was quickly halted as he collided with an invisible barrier. He fell to the roof again and, when he attempted to stand and continue with his escape, he found that he was blocked on all sides.

"Seriously?" he cried. "You fucking mime-ed me?"

Nemesis took advantage of the distraction. She jumped quickly to Hecate's exposed back, wrapped her arm around Hecate's neck, and pulled her body close to her own.

"I cannot defuse this situation alone," she breathed into Hecate's ear. "The fire will reach the fuselage, and the explosion will hurt many people, ourselves being not the least of them. You need to minimize the destruction."

Hecate nodded, and Nemesis released her cautiously. She expected Hecate to turn and attack her immediately but, instead, Hecate turned to the fire. It was dangerously close to the helicopter, seconds from igniting. Hecate thrust her palm toward the helicopter, placing a barrier between the vehicle and the flames. The fire crackled angrily, as it strove to break through. Intertwining her fingers, Hecate cracked her knuckles, then danced her fingers through the air. Nemesis watched with amazement as the flames were swept together, becoming a frantic pyre. As the pillar of flames reached higher into the sky, the sparks died down. The fire consumed itself until it dissipated completely.

It was an amazing feat, but Nemesis could not allow herself to be impressed right now. She could see that Hecate was winded. Using that to her advantage, Nemesis leaped at Hecate once again, seizing her, and sticking the tip of her sword against Hecate's back.

"Turn and face me," she snarled. "Let us finish this with honor."

Hecate spun cautiously to look Nemesis in the face. Nemesis saw defeat in the goddess' eyes, as she lifted the tip of her sword to the akin beneath Hecate's chin. She thought of everything that she and Hecate had achieved together. They had been friends. They had been sisters. If there was anyone who she could have said that she cared for, it was Hecate. Still, the gem was too dangerous. Some things were more important than companionship. It was a shame that it had to end this way.

CHAPTER THIRTY-EIGHT

She had overstepped her bounds. If she had taken a moment to assess the situation, she might have realized that.

Hecate stared into the unflinching daggers that were Nemesis' eyes, and she felt the cold steel of her blade beneath her chin. She was going to die. This was a choice that she had made. It had been a hasty choice and, truthfully, a ridiculous one. As Hecate thought back over her plot, she should have realized how foolhardy it had been. Now, it was too late.

Her instinct was to blame the gem. It was some supernatural influence that was driving her mad. It had been out of her control, the gem had been making her act out of character. In truth, though, it was her fault. The actions had been her own and, whether there was a gem or not, she had to accept responsibility for them. She was not an alcoholic, blaming the liquor for their infidelity. She was no druggie, blaming everything but the drugs for the state of their existence. Yes, the gem held power, but so did she. She had chosen to attack Nemesis. She had decided to be aggressive instead of rational.

Of course, she had also taken her attention off of Nemesis in order to put out the fire. That had been the choice that had gotten her killed. Ironic, since it was probably the only good decision that she had made since the fight had begun.

There was nothing that could be done. Hecate closed her eyes, resigning herself to her fate.

It was almost a relief: she wouldn't need to fight any longer.

All of this, because of a gem. All of this, for the allusion of power.

The tip of the sword pressed against her skin, pushing it to the breaking point. Hecate felt it, in her mind, pushing through her mandible, into her skull. She imagined the pain would be intense, but brief, and she felt an approximation of the pain in her imagination. To her surprise, the reality never culminated. To her shock, the steel left her throat.

Opening her eyes, Hecate saw that Nemesis had dropped her sword. She had sunk to the ground, her head hung.

"I cannot do it," Nemesis sighed. "Kill me if you must, but I will not kill you."

Hecate sank down next to Nemesis, tears filling her eyes. She wrapped an arm over her shoulders. "I could never hurt you," she sobbed.

"I still insist that we destroy the gem," Nemesis choked, finding that a strange salty fluid was escaping from her eyes.

"Oh, just shut up and enjoy the moment," Hecate laughed.

The gem would need to be destroyed. Hecate was beginning to accept that. No matter how enchanting the idea of a restored Olympus was to her, it would cost too much. Maybe Hephaestus really did have a way to destroy the gem. If he did, that was probably the best option. If he did not, Hecate and Nemesis would find another way. The Gem of Illecebra could not be allowed to exist any longer.

"Guys, that's touching," Pan's voice broke the air. "Seriously, I'm tearing up here. Could you maybe let me out of this box, so we could all hug it out together? I'm sorry I tried to kill you all those times. Can we just, I don't know, start over?"

Nemesis and Hecate looked at each other, then at Pan. The briefcase lay at his feet, inside the invisible box. There were still things to deal with.

CHAPTER THIRTY-NINE

THERE HAD BEEN NO POINT IN PUNISHING PAN. NEMESIS HAD considered killing him, since he had been within the realm of justice, but Hecate had been sympathetic. He had been desperate, which did not justify his actions, but it was understandable. He knew that what he had done was unjustifiable. The fact that he had failed so close to being successful would be punishment enough.

Even so, neither goddess was particularly interested in seeing his next show at Oblivion. As soon as they were done at Hephaestus' kiln, Nemesis intended to inform Dionysus of Pan's actions. She doubted that it would make much of a difference, but he deserved to know. Pan was still going to be welcome on their stage but, after what had just happened, Hecate doubted that he would be playing a live show for quite some time.

"This should work," Hephaestus said, as he cradled the gem in his hands next to the boiling fire. "I tested the melting process on centaur blood, and the blood should compromise the integrity of the gem, which will make it destructible. There are a lot of variables which I had to account for, though, since unicorn horn is such a rarity."

"Have you grown an attachment to the gem?" Nemesis asked him, cautiously.

Hephaestus examined the gem in his hands, then shrugged. "No, to me, it's just a rock," he answered casually. "It's a very rare, unrepeatable, priceless rock, yes, but a rock no less."

"If you are having second thoughts about the gem's destructive nature," Hecate interjected, "one of us could toss the gem into the kiln instead."

"Watch this," Hephaestus laughed. With a flick of his wrist, he casually tossed the gem into the boil.

Both Hecate and Nemesis joined him at the edge of the kiln to watch the process. The burning liquids consumed the gem, dragging it into its depths, boiling it, eating the gem from the outside in.

"It's a shame," Hecate sighed. "It was such a beautiful gem, and it could have been used for such great things. Power always corrupts, though. It's such a pity that the gem couldn't be trusted."

Nemesis said nothing. She watched as the fluids spun and covered the gem. She watched until it disappeared from sight.

A smile danced in the corners of her lips. The obsession was gone.

FIN

Dear reader,

We hope you enjoyed reading *Obsession*. Please take a moment to leave a review, even if it's a short one. Your opinion is important to us.

Discover more books by Jonny Capps at https://www.nextchapter.pub/authors/jonny-capps

Want to know when one of our books is free or discounted? Join the newsletter at http://eepurl.com/bqqB3H

Best regards,

Jonny Capps and the Next Chapter Team

ACKNOWLEDGMENTS

Lots and lots of people. First, Miika Hannila and my family at Next Chapter for the amazing opportunities that they've supplied me with. Sarah Kniss, Nate Hartz, and Danielle Mazorowsi for their support, the amazing encouragement, and all the d20s. Josh Margush, my brother and my best friend. Stephanie Margush, my favorite swing-dancing pixie. My brothers and sisters, all of whom make me proud to call them siblings. My parents, who taught me more than any education could. Cat Voleur, my thief in the night, my treasure, and my favorite nightmare. Mike Kahook, Ghalib Ali, Damon & Sarah Gregg, and the rest of the crew from Smoker's ETC. Finally, to Harlow. You know who you are, and you know what you did. Hopefully, it's been a year and a half by now.

If   I   missed   anybody,   sorry.   Insert   your   name   here:
_____

Jonathan "Jonny" Capps

Favorite streamers: ElisabeteTV, Markiplier, Corpse Husband, That_Dahlia, AgirlMegan, Jacksepticeye, Baykoi, FrickinJenn, Day_Sky, Theradbrad, Caddicarus, Gothic, Alanah Pearce, Critical Role. You are all spectacular people, and I appreciate each of you. Thank you for the many hours of entertainment.

Lightning Source UK Ltd.
Milton Keynes UK
UKHW012145270521
384511UK00001B/92